FIGHT
+
Flight

Also by Jules Machias

Both Can Be True

FIGHT + Flight

Jules Machias

Quill Tree Books
An Imprint of HarperCollinsPublishers

Quill Tree Books is an imprint of HarperCollins Publishers.

Fight + Flight
Copyright © 2022 by Jules Machias

ISBN 978-0-06-305394-6

Typography by David DeWitt
22 23 24 25 26   PC/LSCH   10 9 8 7 6 5 4 3 2 1
❖
First Edition

To Matt and Max,
Mom and Pops,
and to my
fellow zebras
and anxious beings

PART I

Avery

Dirt Bikes + Disappointment

Sarah

Flowers + Fear

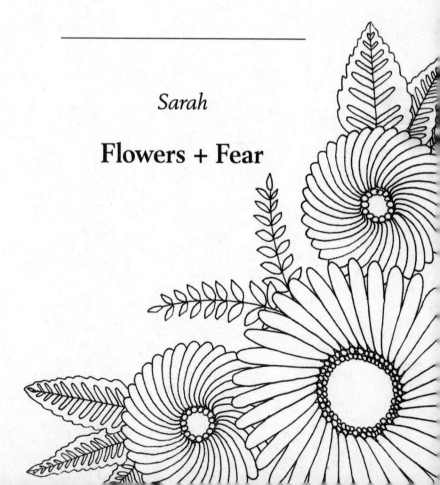

1

Avery

Today's the day: I finally get to use the arm bike at physical therapy, and I'm going to celebrate the milestone by asking my crush to hang out this weekend.

This is assuming I survive the next hour with my physical therapist, Naila. She's a merciless taskmaster who specializes in post-surgery physical therapy for people with joint disorders like I have. Naila is genuinely amused by tears. It's right there in rule number seven on the poster over her table at the PT office: *Don't bother crying. It only encourages me.*

I'm proud to say that when she took my arm sling off the day after my shoulder surgery last week, no salt water leaked out of my eyes—even though I hit an eight out of ten on the pain scale and made a sound like a stepped-on duck.

I take off my studio headphones and drape them around my neck. "Did you know PT stands for pain and torture?" I ask Tuney, who's driving me to therapy today since Mom has an early work meeting. The truck windows are down to let in the warm May air.

"I hear it has to hurt if you want it to heal." She pulls into a parking spot. "You're fidgety as a chipmunk this morning. You get into Mom's coffee?"

I tug at the three black hoops in my right ear. "Nope." Maybe a little. "Just ready to get this over with." I blorp gracelessly out of Tuney's pickup truck onto the parking lot and covertly fix the wedgie situation. Yesterday, when I did my boring thirty minutes of at-home shoulder exercises, I skipped the half-pound weight Naila told me to use and went with a one-pound weight, just to make sure I'd be ready for the arm bike today.

Naila is going to be amazed at my progress. I might complain about her to my best friend, Mason, but really . . . it would feel great to impress her. I get the idea it takes a lot. And I'm pretty sure she would *not* be impressed if she found out that the real reason I needed shoulder surgery was because I wiped out on a dirt bike I wasn't supposed to be riding, instead of because I fell off the monkey bars, which is what I told everyone except Mason. Mason is the only person who won't judge me for doing a risky dirt-bike maneuver despite having developed a joint disorder that makes wipeouts a thousand times worse.

I pause at the heavy glass door, mentally gearing up. Then I grip the metal handle with my left hand and pull.

A hiss of pain leaks through my gritted teeth. *Sidestep*, I think at it. The word that's gotten me through the carnival of "ow" my life has become in the past year, and especially the last eight days since my surgery. *Sidestep.*

The pain in my shoulder and sternum is a jagged bolt of lightning. But I am slippery as a seal, swimming around it. A snake using it as a pushing-off place to slither on by, away. Away.

I get the door open three inches. Four. I scoot my right foot forward, aaaand—

Phew. I've got my hot-pink Croc jammed between the door and the frame.

I take a moment to breathe, then shift my weight off my right knee and pull the door handle again, letting my anger at my ridiculously malfunctioning body fuel me. Right after my thirteenth birthday last summer, I was diagnosed with hEDS—Ehlers-Danlos syndrome, hypermobile type. Lifelong. No cure. I've always been rubber-band flexible, but when puberty hit, I went from super-bendy to breakable in the blink of an eye. After my third elbow dislocation in a three-week period, Mom took me to a specialist. I flunked the Beighton Score test, which measures how extra-bendy your joints are, plus I met a bunch of other criteria that seem totally random to me—like having bumps on my heels and stretchy skin and a weird shape to the roof of my mouth. All of it added up to this fabulous diagnosis.

The door suddenly opens wide and I'm thrown off balance.

"Oops!" Tuney catches my left elbow. "Sorry, squirt. Looked like you were struggling."

I scowl and duck under her arm. I do *not* need help. I'm still perfectly capable of doing simple tasks on my own, like opening doors and putting on my shoes. Also picking up all the things I drop now because my right arm is strapped to my body and totally cussing useless. Thanks to hEDS, I didn't just entirely disman-tle my right shoulder in the dirt-bike wipeout. I also dislocated my right sternoclavicular joint, where the sternum and collarbone meet—which means using my left arm, the supposedly "good" one, for anything that takes more effort than awkwardly handling a pencil causes all sorts of pain-flames too.

If I were a different person, I'd find it ironically

funny that my joints now misbehave as much as I do. But mostly it hurts too much to laugh at it.

The cool, lemon-scented air of the PT office washes over me. Naila glances up from her laptop at her torture table by the window. "Morning, Avery." She raises an eyebrow at Tuney. "Mum busy this morning?"

"Yup. This is Tuney. Tuney, Naila."

"It's nice to meet you," Tuney says. "My darling daughter calls you her drill sergeant, but I'm sure you're quite personable."

I wait through Naila's pause that means she's putting it together that I have two moms. She gets it quicker than most people and smiles at Tuney. "You do have a squirrelly one on your hands," she says in her clipped accent. I asked if she was from India when I first met her, because of her warm brown skin and silky black hair, and she said her parents are from England and Pakistan. I got the sense that she was kind of offended at my assumption and I felt bad for making it. But she moved right past it into dealing with my disaster of a shoulder. "I like my patients to have sass, though. It means more when they admit I'm right." She gives me a smirk.

"I have never once admitted you were right," I tell her.

"Oh, you will. Get checked in and then meet me here at the table."

My functional shoulder slumps. "Not at the bike?"

Her attention is on her spreadsheet. "We need to see how the joint's moving before you jump in."

Of course we do.

Tuney gets me checked in, takes my headphones, and walks to the waiting area with her laptop. I breathe a sigh of relief. I've been here four times since the surgery, always with my fitness-buff mom, who's "encouraged" me through every session. I'm stoked that my first go on the arm bike won't be with her breathing down my neck, reminding me to do everything *exactly* as Naila has instructed.

Naila scoots over to another therapist's table and they compare their screens. I use my heel to pull out the footstool under her table. When I step onto it, my right knee pops loudly and pain spikes through my thigh.

Shut up, I think at it. *No one asked you.* I get situated on the table and start undoing some of the Velcro straps holding my arm in its stinkier-by-the-day brace, unlovingly dubbed "Cthulhu" because it looks like a tentacled beast from the deep when it's not on my body. Most people are out of the brace three weeks post-surgery. But thanks to hEDS, my recovery is progressing at the pace of a three-toed sloth. At my checkup yesterday, Dr. Chen said I might be in the brace four or five more weeks. By then this sucker's gonna reek of fried onions rotting in a dumpster in August, and my armpit hair will be long enough to braid.

He really failed to warn me about all this. He was honest enough to say the first week of recovery would suck—I appreciate any grown-up who tells it like it is—but he left out a lot. Like about how pain meds cause difficulty going to the bathroom. And, well, other aspects of going to the bathroom when your dominant arm is fully out of commission. Multiplied by the bathroom problems hEDS causes.

Naila joins me. "How's the shoulder feeling? Sleep okay on it?" She starts undoing the strap I can't get to.

"Yep. The extra pillow you said to use under my elbow helped." Until I woke up with the pillow on the floor and my shoulder on fire at four a.m. Can't win 'em all, as Tuney says, but it was nice of Mom to get up when she heard me whimpering and help me get comfortable again. And even nicer that she didn't bring up the argument we had before bed.

Naila gently pulls Cthulhu away from my body and helps me lie on my back. Being unable to move my right arm is the grossest, most vulnerably weird feeling. Doing stuff like lying down and sitting up on my own, or going to the bathroom, or tying my shoes and brushing my teeth and scooping Tank's poop in the yard, requires a level of effort I only used to expend on stuff I *liked* doing. Like dirt biking and drumming and jumping on my trampoline with Mason. None of which I can do anymore.

Naila waits for me to stop hissing at the pain before she speaks again. "How did the at-home exercises go? Were you able to feel the movement of the supraspinatus muscle?"

Whatever that even is. "Yeah, I worked the heck out of that sucker. In fact, I moved up from a half-pound weight to a one-pound weight," I say proudly.

Naila's fingers prod a tender spot by my armpit that makes me arch my back and grit my teeth. "So I see. Remember how I told you not to go too heavy too soon?"

I unclench my jaw. "A pound is not heavy. I want to get better *faster*." The half-pound weight seemed pointless. Like lifting a feather over and over. Bo-ring.

"Rushing past PT steps is not the path to make that happen. How many reps of the side lifts did you do before you switched?"

"I don't know. Twelve?" Maybe four or five.

She makes the sound that means she's suppressing a sigh. "The point is to do light weight, lots of repetition. Not jump ahead with weights that are too heavy. You'll exhaust the muscle too quickly and lose the benefits of the exercise."

Well. That explains why it started hurting like a cusser at rep seven with one pound.

"You're going to set yourself back again," Naila says.

I make my own sigh-suppressing sound. Four days after surgery, I was sick of wallowing in the metallic stink it seemed like the anesthesia had left stuck to me. I was desperate for a real shower instead of the baby-wipe baths Mom and Tuney had been giving me. So I struggled my way out of Cthulhu, leaving my useless half-bent arm dangling at my side while I awkwardly washed my hair left-handed, failing to sidestep the ridiculous amount of pain I was in. Ten minutes was apparently just enough time to pull at all the internal stitches holding my shoulder in its socket. Which meant I was in fiery muscle-spasm agony the entire night after Mom strapped me back into the brace and gave me a lecture about following Dr. Chen's orders. I couldn't sidestep the pain even with my arm stabilized and the pain meds making my head spin and my ears buzz. At PT the next day, Naila had to start me back at the day-two exercises.

Now, on day eight, I've made it back up to the day-four exercises. Great job, Aves. Really trucking along.

I know this whole mess is my own fault. But what even *is* life if you can't fill it with dirt-bike rides and climbing trees and trampoline backflips? With pogo-sticking all the way around the block and drumming your butt off to punk covers and having belly-flop contests with your bestie at the pool?

hEDS is such a load of crap. Especially considering it's literally affected my ability to crap. It's the disease that never stops giving.

Thank god for meme-lord Mason. He digs into his trove whenever I bomb him with late-night texts about how scared I am that my future's gonna suck. That everything will only get harder, like it does for everyone diagnosed with EDS. Hypermobile type isn't the worst kind to have—there's a kind of EDS that affects your veins that's legit deadly—but it's still no picnic. Some people can't walk or lift their arms or even get out of bed. And it seems like every kid on the EDS Junior Zebras Message Board has digestive system problems, even though the link between hyperflexibility and gut issues is "not fully understood" by science.

Naila picks up her plastic thingy that measures how far a joint can move and holds it to my elbow with one hand while she slowly unbends my arm with her other hand. "Say when."

Pain jets through my elbow and shoulder. It's ridiculous how stiff the joints have become when they've always been so bendy I could lick my own elbow. I focus on my breath coming in my nose, going out my mouth, until the pain becomes too loud to sidestep. "When!"

"Avery, it's not a competition." Naila lays my arm over my stomach. "Remember how I explained it? You have to tell me when it gets uncomfortable, not wait until the point of pain."

"Right." I close my eyes, feeling as floppy and discombobulated as a newborn.

Naila starts the stretching routine and I check my phone with my other hand. Mason has sent a pic of Frodo Baggins making a lemon-sour face with the words *Thought I'd made it to Mordor. Turns out it was just PT.*

Accurate, I reply. The math class I'm missing the first half of to be here is my favorite class. I got switched out of advanced and into mainstream math in January because my grade was tanking after the whole diagnosed-with-an-incurable-disease thing. I couldn't concentrate long enough to make it through problems that required more than three steps, and it seemed like every problem was a six-step mess. I'm still in gifted everything else, but somehow the joint pain made math kinda fall out of my brain.

Which worked to my advantage, because one, my new math class is now covering all the stuff my advanced class covered last year, so I already sort of know how to do it, and two, Mason is in my new math class, and three, so is Sarah. Also Mason's crush, Helen Vargas, and also Jolene Winfrey, which sucks because Jolene's been a jerk to both me and Mason since first grade. But whatever. I don't focus on her.

I focus on Sarah. I really like to look at Sarah and daydream about . . . anything involving Sarah. I constantly imagine stuff we could do together—play *Super Smash Bros.* and go on Pokémon GO hunts and ride bikes.

Well, except not ride bikes, because I tried to ride one-handed after school yesterday to prove to myself I could. But I couldn't steer and brake at the same time and I crashed into a bush, so oops, now my right knee keeps popping and twinging. I'm super lucky I didn't tip onto my injured shoulder. They would've heard me screaming in Alaska.

Sarah and I could do other stuff that doesn't involve moving around, though. Like watch a movie. She's always drawing and writing in that sketchbook she carries everywhere, doing it like she breathes, like she does it to stay alive. And I saw some cute Totoros and soot sprites over her shoulder a few days ago. So I bet she'd be down for *Castle in the Sky* or *Spirited Away* or even *Nausicaä*, even though Mason says *Nausicaä* is white-people weirdness cranked up to eleven. Despite *Nausicaä* being genuine made-in-Japan anime.

But whatever. After these stretches, I'm going to use the arm bike, and then I'll celebrate the milestone by asking Sarah to come over and hang out this Friday. The girl Sarah used to hang around with at school, the one with the long jet-black ponytail, moved away a couple of months ago. Sarah's probably lonely now, so maybe my chances are good. And Tuney already said I could ask her over. I've had the note in my bag for two days, but I haven't worked up the guts to fork it over. It's straightforward: *I saw the Totoros you drew on your math paper. Want to come over and watch a Miyazaki movie with me and Mason this weekend? I have them all. We could watch whichever one you want.* If Mason's there too, things will be less awkward. Mason is interested in lots of random stuff, which makes him a world-class question asker. He'll have Sarah talking up a storm. If it was just me and her, I'd say something dumb or embarrassing right off the bat.

I'm a little worried that Sarah will figure out I have a crush on her and that it will be a problem. She wears a gold cross on a delicate gold necklace, and one Wednesday in March she came to school with ashes on her forehead. So I think she's Catholic or whatever, and maybe her religion is against gayness. I would be surprised if Sarah was prejudiced like that, but also, being best friends with a kid who has a Black mom and a white dad has shown me that a whole lot more people are a whole lot more prejudiced than you might think. When Mason and I get in trouble (which sort of happens a lot, usually thanks to me), Mason gets in *more* trouble. During the last school shooter drill, he was getting that sweaty-nervous look he gets when reality shoves into our landscape of endless shenanigans, so I cracked a bunch of jokes about giraffes to help him laugh his fear away. Unfortunately, I did it while we were curled up against the classroom wall with our books held over our heads—like books even stop bullets—and the principal, Mr. Ritter, was checking the rooms to make sure we were all Taking This Very Seriously. He gave me a lecture for joking. He gave Mason a lunch detention for laughing. *Two Americas*, as Mason's mom says. She's not wrong.

Naila tells me to lie on my left side facing the windows. She puts a half-pound weight in my right hand and tucks a rolled-up towel between my arm and ribs. "Show me what you've got, wild girl." She holds her hand up, palm down, about ten inches above the table.

Finally! Time to impress. I lift the half-pound weight till the back of my hand touches her palm. The weight feels like nothing. Easy-peasy lemon squeezy.

Naila watches me go through reps two and three, the faintest hint of a smirk on her face.

"Don't give me that look," I say.

Her brows shoot up into her bangs and she widens her big brown eyes. "What look?"

"That fake innocent one. It always means something is about to suck."

She smiles and waits, watching my hand rise to her palm and then lower. Over and over.

By rep nine, I can barely lift the half pound. I struggle through rep ten. At rep eleven, despite enormous effort, my hand sinks to the vinyl table, my supraspin-whatever muscle quivering with exhaustion.

Ugh. Stressey-depressey lemon zesty.

But I am *not* going to tell Naila she was right.

Naila plucks the weight from my hand. "Try it without the weight."

Great. Back to day three.

I sigh and launch into the motion. Ten zero-weight reps later, I'm spent.

No arm bike for me today.

The rest of PT, I do everything Naila says, to the letter. But my brain is full of cuss words and guilty anger. If I hadn't talked Mason into taking the dirt bikes to the park without asking, which I am definitely *not* allowed to do, I never would have face-planted on the sharp turn at the back of the trail I was (as usual) going too fast for. I didn't hit the ground that hard—I wiped out that exact same way last spring—but having even looser joints now means the fall was enough to dislocate my too-flexible shoulder and to pop my sternum and collarbone apart. Mason had to help me home while I bit back the pain screeches. Then he had to go back twice to get the two bikes, then he had to clean the dirt out of the foot peg of the bike I wrecked, then he had to help me come up with a lie about falling off the monkey bars. I'm not supposed to be on those either because my joints dislocate so easily now, but that's way less of a crime than taking the dirt bikes without asking. Just enough that when Mom talked to me about "facing your new reality with this disease," the right amount of guilt showed on my face and my apology had enough sincerity.

Yes, I feel bad about lying. But also . . . my buzzy beautiful dirt bike is *life*. How can I feel guilty about a thing that gives me life? I can't wait till I'm healed enough to get back in the saddle. Maybe with a lesson learned about going easy on the throttle on that one sharp turn.

Well. Even if I don't get to use the arm bike today, even if I'm stuck in a body that breaks instead of bounces, even if I'm freaked out that it's all downhill like the kids on the Zebra Board say it is . . . I've got a bubble of hope in my chest that Sarah will read my note and say, "Sure, that would be awesome. What time should I come over?" I've got Mason rooting and meme-ing for me, forever the most excellent best friend. And I've got Mom and Tuney, who want the best for me and fight to make sure I have it.

I have so many awesome people in my corner. But I'm scared I'll be dependent on my moms forever. It sucks feeling sidelined from everything I love because my body no longer cooperates. I'm always in pain and I feel like I can't control anything anymore and I'm hecking *mad* about it.

I know asking Sarah to hang out won't magically cure all that suck.

But I'm so ready to take a chance on something going *right* for a change.

2
Sarah

Weds., May 1, 8:03 a.m. I can't believe my group just voted me to present our project.

I'm going to freeze up. I'm <u>so bad</u> at talking. Especially when people are looking at me. Or when they're not looking at me. When people are in the same room as me.

We're group four, so we're last. Which means I have twenty minutes to freak out.

I know why they voted me to do it. None of them want to and I was so focused on finishing drawing the birds for our poster that everything else went away. That's the reason I draw, the reason I started this journal: because it makes everything else go away. But if I go away too, and I come back and what I was running from is worse . . . what then?

Last week Mom and Dad found out about my fear problem. I was trying to download an app on the phone they gave me after Aunt Camila died and my cousin/best friend Luci moved away two months ago. "So you can stay in touch with Luci," Mom said when she gave it to me. I only use it to text Luci and to take photos of plants and flowers I want to draw. But last week was an extra-bad fear week, so I looked for an app to help me. I tried to download a free one called "Handle Your Panic," but it said "Waiting for parent permission."

Which meant when Dad got home from flying kites with my little sister, Ruthie, Mom and Dad came downstairs to my room and asked why I wanted that app.

I didn't want to admit I have a problem. I'm the "easy kid," as Mom says. My big brother, James, is always in trouble at school. Ruthie is super clumsy and gets hurt a lot. My parents don't need any more kid-related stress.

But the panic that started when Aunt Camila died has been getting worse, and I'm exhausted from trying to hide it. So I told my parents that since she died and Uncle David took Luci and her brothers to live in Arizona, I've been having panic attacks.

Like a lot of them every day. Heart-pounding, palm-sweating, can't-think-straight fear.

Mom hugged me and said what she always says: "Give it to God. He can help you."

Dad said that when I'm scared, I should focus on a goal instead of on what I'm afraid of. He said, "You don't need an app for praying. The prayers you write and illustrate are beautiful. Have you drawn a prayer asking God to help you through your fear?"

I shook my head. I only pray for other people, not for myself. But I told Dad I would try it. And I did, later that night, even though it felt weird to ask God to vanish my panic.

But panic is still happening. So maybe I prayed wrong, or maybe God was just like, "Nope, have fun with that!"

Now that I've told my parents I need help and they didn't help me, now that I've tried to pray it away, it's worse. My heart's drumming hard right now, because I have to go to the front of the room and explain the birds of New Zealand like I paid attention when Mia and Yasmine and

Carson wrote down facts. I just wanted to draw forever, to sink into art and not be in this science class I have a D in because I'm bad at math and science.

This class was easier when Luci was in it with me. When she was here, I had a C.

Five minutes left till I have to present.

I'll try what Dad said. Focus on a goal.

But I don't know what my goal is right now. My big life goal, as long as I can remember, has been "Help others." It makes me feel like I have meaning and purpose. Even if I'm only helping in a small way. Mostly I do that by praying for them.

Dad would probably say this is a chance to help others in an active way. I'm helping my group by taking on a difficult role.

But it feels massive and terrifying and my heart's going so fast and I'm pretty sure this is only a chance for me to look dumb and get another bad grade.

Okay, this isn't helping.

What if . . . well, what if I pretend to be Avery while I'm up there?

Avery wouldn't panic. Avery is good at jokes and talking

and confidence. And math and probably science. Avery burps loudly and belts out "Hamster on a Piano" and gets excited about random stuff like binder clips and Hot Pockets and aglets. Avery is everything I wish I could be.

Except I don't wish I had whatever disease she has that she and that super-short kid Mason talk about. And I don't wish my arm was in a sling.

But everything else. Avery has short strawberry-blonde hair (is her hair what strawberry blonde is? Maybe she's what people call a redhead) and I wish I could have short hair instead of getting my head yanked all over by Mom's French braiding every morning. Avery has lots of sass and lots of ear piercings and wears big chonky head-phones around her neck at all times. Avery is best friends with Mason and they're always cracking each other up and getting yelled at by Mr. Trevino and they laugh and say "Okay" and keep doing what they're doing. Like getting in trouble is no big deal.

If I pretend I'm Avery, I won't panic. I'll

8:33 a.m. What. a. NIGHTMARE.

I froze. I straight-read the poster, which, oops, Mrs. Roy said we shouldn't do. And when she asked why so many New Zealand birds are

22

flightless, my plan to pretend to be Avery flew out of my head and I froze.

I knew the answer to her question. For once. They have fewer land predators than other places, so they don't need the safety of the sky. But all I could see were those faces staring at me, waiting, and nothing came out. Mia got up and gave me a shove toward my desk with this <u>look</u> on her face, like "Ugh, you're such a disappointment, such a <u>mouse</u>," and finished the presentation, and now my face is on fire and my hand's too shaky to draw so I'm writing, but my mind is a mess and the burn won't go away. I really didn't need another bad grade in this class.

I'm going to feel those eyes for so long.

I want to feel FREE for just one day

23

3

Avery

After PT, Tuney offers a hand to help me up into the truck seat.

I grip the pull-up handle. "I'm not helpless."

"It wouldn't kill you to accept an assist now and then."

"I can take care of myself."

Tuney holds her palms up. "You do you, kid." She walks around to the driver's side.

My stomach dips. Mom had to help me into the truck to come here. She usually plows through my insistence that I can do things myself and does them for me, the same way she answers for me when doctors ask me questions. Tuney . . . well, Tuney says failing is how you learn. One day last summer when me and

Mason were bouncing off the walls after we drank a couple Bangs from the dollar store, she sent us outside with a box of smoke bombs and a lighter and told us not to come in unless someone was bleeding or on fire.

Needless to say, I prefer her parenting style to Mom's.

I grit my teeth, lift my foot to the truck floor, and try to pull myself up into the seat as I step up. Fire shoots through my chest and I whimper. It's *so much harder* to get into this dang truck than it is to sit in the front seat of Mom's sedan.

With a burst of painful effort, I yank myself up and get one butt cheek on the seat. My right leg shoots out for balance and whacks the bottom of the open door—*sidestep*—then I manage to tip my center of gravity into the truck cab.

Tuney sets her laptop case on the seat between us. She looks down at my sweating face and raises an eyebrow.

I blow the hair out of my eyes. With a barely suppressed grunt, I get myself upright. I twist awkwardly to close the truck door, then struggle to pull out the seat belt and clip it in left-handed without jostling my right arm. It's ridiculous how exhausted my whole right side is after doing basically nothing. After *not* using the arm bike.

"Would you like some h—"

"*No.*" I hate how testy pain makes me, but oh my god, *don't* talk to me when I'm trying to hide how much something hurts.

I finally get the dang belt clicked over Cthulhu. Tuney hands me my headphones, then backs out of the spot. I take a deep breath to get my heart under control. I'm so scared the whole rest of my life is going to be accomplishments like "getting into a truck" and "peeing without help" instead of fulfilling my dream to become a robotics engineer who invents adorable AI assistants that do boring chores like washing dishes and folding laundry and cleaning the bathroom.

I pump some 150-beats-per-minute hardstyle into my ears to clear the therapy disappointment out of my head. I take the note for Sarah out of my backpack and read it for the hundredth time, then tuck it into Cthulhu so it's ready to go. I'm not sure if I'm fully gay, because I've had crushes shoot off in every direction like fireworks. So far that includes a genderfluid white kid named Ash (before I realized they were taken), a student teacher from Panama when I was in fifth grade (even though he was eleven years older than me and engaged), Mason for half a hot second (till I realized it would be dumb to risk our friendship), Finn *and* Rey from *Star Wars* at the same time (way older than me and famous so my chances are nil), plus I've spent too many minutes daydreaming about Tris, the stunning sixteen-year-old with the light brown skin and sparkling eyes who I met on the beach when we went to South Carolina last summer.

I guess I'm pansexual, which Tuney says means "attracted to any gender." I haven't met a gender yet that makes me like, *Nope, not my cuppa tea.*

But I have met Sarah. And *yowza*, forget all that other noise—this girl is the *one*.

I take the note back out of Cthulhu. I don't want it to stink when I give it to her.

I take off my headphones when we pull into the school parking lot, just in time to hear Tuney say, "Don't forget, you owe Mom an apology when you get home."

"I haven't forgotten." I drum a rapid rhythm on my knee. Tuney says Mom and I butt heads so much because we're so alike: red hair, headstrong, built with a deep need to be physically active for at least like ten hours a day.

She's probably right. But I'm still mad that Mom made me feel so helpless and dependent last night when she was helping me into the zebra-striped nightshirt she'd bought for me. I was in so much pain from having my arm out of its sling and I was all freaked out from reading on the Zebra Board about how people with hEDS are at risk of internal decapitation, where your neck joints can get so out of whack that the weight of your skull crushes your spine. Mom was shifting my arm in ways that made me want to scream. I felt so vulnerable and useless and scared my body will fall apart so much that I'll depend on her and Tuney for the whole rest of my life. I didn't even *want* to wear the zebra shirt, because zebra stripes remind me I have this disease in the first place.

After my diagnosis, Mom explained why people with EDS call themselves "zebras." There's an expression taught to medical students: "If you hear hoofbeats behind you, don't turn around expecting a zebra—it's probably a horse." So when doctors see common symptoms, like digestive problems or joint pain, they think you have a common problem, like too much stress or not enough vitamin D or whatever. They don't expect you to have some weird, rare diagnosis that explains all the odd problems you've had your whole life that have always been dismissed as unrelated.

But sometimes the hoofbeats really are zebras.

Whatever. I just feel guilty that Mom buys zebra-themed clothes and accessories when I don't want them. And it didn't help that I was topless while we were arguing. Even though she's my mom, it's still weird, now that I have these new . . . *features*. Everything is weird weird *weird*. A 24-7 carnival of what-the-heck-even-am-I. Not a kid anymore. A teenager, but with none of the freedoms I thought that would give me. Stuck in this busticated body that generates armpit stank like nobody's business.

Tuney parks and we get out. It's hella easier than getting in, even with the wedgie. My wheeled backpack thumps over the cracks in the parking lot as we walk.

In the office, Principal Ritter is standing by the security officer's desk. He's a tall skinny bald white dude and Officer Clark is a short stocky Black lady with braids in a tight bun, but despite their different appearances, they have the exact same expression. They're focused on one of her two monitors, showing what looks like a security-camera image of the empty gym.

Principal Ritter clears his throat. Officer Clark tilts her monitor so I can't see it. Ritter gives me a stern look. "Oversleep today?"

"She had physical therapy, sir." Tuney pronounces *sir* like it's an insult. I love her for it.

"Avery, get to class quickly," he says. "Mrs. Hart, here's the late-sign-in sheet." He nudges it across the counter toward Tuney and glances at the monitor again. Officer Clark is frowning at the screen, her eyes tracking something across it. She looks . . . worried.

Strange. She can break up a cafeteria fight with no expression other than boredom or annoyance. I have to pass the gym on my way to my locker. Is a villainous dodgeball going to spring out and knock me off my feet?

Tuney signs me in and kisses the top of my head. "Have a good day, squirt."

"Don't call me that in public."

"Okay, squirt."

"You're the *worst*."

"Love you too." She flips my bangs out of my eyes. "See you at dinner. Goose entrails tonight, your fave." She goes out the door we came in and I head for the door to the main hallway, which has a push bar. If only the door at PT did too.

"Go *directly* to class, Avery," Principal Ritter says as I use my butt to push the door open. "No dallying in the hallway."

"I don't *dally*. It's not easy to do stuff fast with one arm, you know."

He sucks his breath in, mad that I have a point. He's pinched and pale like he's tired and tense at the same time. The same way Mom looks when I've gotten too snippy. He leans down to say something to Officer

30

Clark, but he keeps his eyes on me as I go through the door.

It's a mystery to me why some kids like that hyper-controlling weirdo.

4
Sarah

Weds., May 1, 9:58 a.m. Math class. Avery's not here.

I shouldn't be disappointed. I should do my worksheet, because I have a C- in math and another bad grade will tip me into a D and Mom will lose her noodle. But I don't understand it. As usual.

Sunday after church while I was doing homework, I overheard Mom and Dad talking about a plan for this summer to help me get caught up in math and science before high school starts. I heard words like "private tutor" and "camp" and "behind her peers," and then I went downstairs because I was afraid my heart would pound itself to pieces.

I could ask Mason if Avery is home sick because of

her disease. I think they share a brain. Sometimes it hurts to look at them because it makes me miss Luci so much. We called each other funny names like they do. Luci is "Chonky Kong" and I'm "Banana Sunshine." We used to talk without words like they do. A raised shoulder. A wrinkled nose. A "shoosh" motion. Words were for overnights, when we'd go to bed at 9:15 and talk in the dark for hours. Not having to look at each other meant we could say all the stuff we didn't talk about in the daylight. She could tell me about Mateo and Diego getting into more trouble at high school as their mom got sicker. I could tell her about the silly plots of the storybooks I write with Ruthie, even though I should've grown out of writing kids' stories by now.

Luci never laughed at me. Ever.

Avery and Mason laugh at each other all the time. But not in a mean way.

I wonder how it feels to be laughed at in a not-mean way.

Mason is shaking his legs, drumming on his desk the way Avery does. He's crumpled the corner of his worksheet. He's looking at Mr. Trevino like he's worried he's about to get in trouble. I wish I could help him.

Dear God, Please help Mason feel calm.

10:02 a.m. Turns out he was fidgety because he'd forgotten a pencil. I handed him one and he smiled like a sunrise and all his fear went away.

It felt good. But it also made me jealous. All it took was a <u>pencil</u>, and he was fine again.

I wish I could resolve my fear so easily.

Avery's here now. She came in a minute ago and handed Mr. Trevino a pink late slip. She's sitting behind me.

Mom's been hinting that I should find a new friend, and she's right. I've been daydreaming about being Avery's friend. I imagine us like vines growing toward one another. But I'm afraid to be Avery's friend because . . . well, reasons.

She has a disease and I don't know what it is or if it will make her die like Aunt Camila died.

She's bold. I'm a mouse. I doubt she'd even <u>want</u> to be my friend.

If we become friends and she comes to my house, Mom might take one look at her short hair and nose ring and all her ear piercings and say, "I meant someone from Bible Study. Not someone like <u>that</u>."

Mom wants me to find a friend just like Luci. Luci, Mom likes. Because Luci can sit still through two hours of church. Luci does what she's told. Luci eats food she doesn't like so she won't hurt anyone's feelings. Luci kept my kite-flying dad company at the park long after I got bored and went looking for plants to draw. Luci helped Mom and me with the kids Mom babysits. Luci, like me, feels driven to help other people, in big and small ways.

Avery's sort of . . . not like that. I get the idea she gives her mom and dad trouble. She's probably what Mom would call "a hell-raising spitfire." Like my brother, James.

The girls in my Bible Study group are hell-raising spit-fires, though. Mom thinks that because they're church kids from church families, they're . . . I don't know, better. Nicer. Instead of how they really are, which is cliquish and sarcastic and sometimes plain mean. Like last night when Jenna Lutz and Mariah Welch kept snickering when it was my turn to read from the Bible. Doing it behind their hands so Mrs. Marshall couldn't figure out where it was coming from.

I just sent Luci a pic of this drawing. Guess I should stop drawing with every single pen I own and attempt this confusing worksheet.

Math is the Worstest

5

Avery

I peeked in the gym on the way to math. It was empty and smelled like socks and sweat.

In math class, I hand Mr. Trevino my tardy slip and slide into my desk behind Sarah. Her golden-blonde French braid is so pretty I get a little dizzy over it. The lighter hair around her face is so neatly woven into the darker hair at the back of her head. I love how her shoulders hitch up the tiniest bit when she sniffles. She must have allergies. She sniffles a lot.

It's not scary to give a girl a note. At all. It won't feel like I'm putting myself on the line. I won't be devastated if she says no. I won't want to crawl into a hole and pretend I haven't spent weeks daydreaming about having a real conversation with her. One that doesn't involve integers or X/Y graphs or absolute value. I will just give her the note, and she'll say yes or she'll say no. Life will go on either way. My arm will still be wrapped in Cthulhu, shaky with PT exhaustion. My neck and knee and sternum will hurt. I'll have a mom called Mom and a mom called Tuney and a best friend whose mom isn't exactly wild about me these days. I'll have to watch instead of participating in concert band and I'll still be scared my life is downhill from here.

But I'll feel one way about all that if Sarah smiles and nods, and a different way if she furrows her straight, thin eyebrows and shakes her head.

The smallest action can shift our whole perception of reality.

Ugh. This is way scarier than a sharp turn on a dirt bike.

This isn't gonna turn out like that did, though.

Mason has noticed me holding the note and getting all squirmy. He mouths *Just do it* and gives me a thumbs-up.

Okay. Okay. I'm gonna do it.

Here I goooooo—

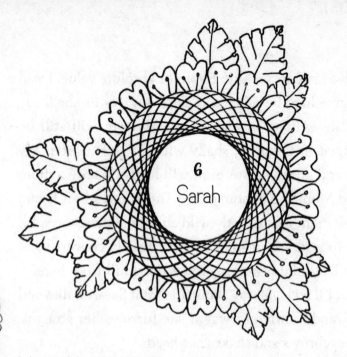

6
Sarah

Weds., May 1, 10:15 a.m. Avery just gave me a note! Avery wants me to COME TO HER HOUSE ON FRIDAY oh my gosh.

I can't think. I've already panicked twice today and my brain's worn out.

I bombed it when I tried Dad's goal-focusing tactic. And when I pretended to be Avery. What can I do, what can I . . . okay, Luci was scared about getting her tonsils out last year. Aunt Camila said to get into calm logic-mind and out of scared-mind, Luci should focus on the positive. She said making lists can help.

So . . . I'll make a calm, logical pros-and-cons list about going to Avery's house.

PROS

I need a friend who doesn't live in Arizona.

Avery would be a cool friend. She's what James would call BOSS. If he called an eighth-grade girl "boss," which he wouldn't, because he's seventeen and mega-BOSS.

Maybe I could learn from Avery how to not be a mouse. Avery is fearless.

Avery is good at math. Maybe she could help me.

I could be helpful to her, with doors and carrying her bag. That would make me feel useful and good.

CONS

People you care about can die. Or move away. Like Aunt Camila died and Luci moved.

They understood me. Avery might not.

Avery has a disease and might die. What if she becomes my friend and she dies?

What if her mom dies and her dad moves her away?

What if losing someone else makes the panic even <u>worse</u>?

What if the rest of my life is nothing but panic? What if I'll never be able to go to college or get a job or get married or <u>anything</u> because all I do is panic? What if I become one of those people who can't leave their house because they're too scared to do anything ever at all?

That's way more cons than pros. And I lost my logic and my heart's going too fast.

So, so, I'll tell Avery I'll ask my parents, but I won't actually ask. I'll just say they said no. That's safer. I won't lose anybody because I won't have anybody.

Like now. I have nobody.

What if it's like this for the rest of my life???

7

Avery

The double beep over the PA scares the bajonkers out of me before I realize it's only the active-shooter-drill alarm. "This again?" I grumble to Mason. "It's only been like a month."

"Don't look at me," he says, facing the front. "I'm not getting in trouble for laughing at you this time."

"It's not my fault you bust a gut when I'm funny." I fold my worksheet and stuff it in Cthulhu. If we're gonna hide behind the bookshelves for ten minutes pretending we're just *soooo* scared, at least I can get caught up.

A heavy slam in the hallway rattles the windows. Sarah whips around to look at me, her blue eyes huge. "What was—"

BANG!

—It's so loud I feel it through the floor. Everyone freezes.

A girl in another classroom starts screaming. Mr. Trevino stands up from his desk with a confused look.

"This is a drill, right?" Mason asks.

The PA crackles to life with Principal Ritter's voice: "Attention, students and staff. Shooters are in the building. Move to your lockdown loca—"

Bwooop, bwooop, bwooop!

I lock eyes with Mason. The fire alarm has never gone off during a shooter drill before.

A loud *pop-pop-pop* sounds in the hallway over the blaring fire alarm.

Oh god.

This is not a drill.

"Hide!" Mr. Trevino shouts as he dashes toward the door.

Pandemonium. Sarah bolts for the gap under Mr. Trevino's desk. Mason slams into me on his way to who knows where and fire shoots through my shoulder. I gasp and grab him so I don't fall. Another sharp bang sounds in the hallway as Mr. Trevino locks the door. More screams. I try to yank Mason toward Mr. Trevino's desk, but my right knee pops and pain shoots through my thigh with such sudden ferocity that I'm certain I've been shot—

"Let me *go*!" Mason struggles to escape my one-handed grip.

I haven't—I haven't been shot. I just lost my shoe and did something terrible to my knee. I refocus on Mason. "We can fit under Mr. Trevino's desk with Sarah!"

"There's not room!"

"There is! Come *on*!" I can barely hear myself think over the pain and the *bwooop, bwooop, bwooop!*

Another loud *pop-pop-pop* startles me. I lose my grip on Mason. He tears toward the projector stand, but Jolene is huddled behind it and shoulders him away. I scurry over to Mr. Trevino's desk and hide beneath it with Sarah, motioning frantically at Mason to join us.

He doesn't see me. His wide eyes dart around. But every hiding place is taken. Tears roll down his face.

"Mason!" I hiss. "Over here!" My voice is swallowed by the earsplitting fire drill, impossible to sidestep in any way.

More screaming. This time from the classroom next to ours. I can't help it: I'm crying and shaking too, fear eating me alive. We're going to get shot. We're really, actually going to get shot at school. I'm going to die with my arm strapped to my side. It's happening so *fast*.

"Hey," a quiet voice says. "It's okay."

I catch my breath and focus on Sarah, three inches from my face. "This is *not* okay!"

"We're hidden. We've done all we can. We just have to wait."

"To *die*?" I smear tears out of my eyes. Mason is crying under a desk. Everyone else has found a hiding spot, but there he is, exposed, and it's all my fault. My lost hot-pink Croc points at him like an arrow. He's the first kid the shooters will see when they bust open our door. "They're gonna shoot Mason!" *Bwooop, bwooop, bwooop!* Screaming. *Pop-pop-pop.*

"They won't." Sarah's calm.

"How do you know?" I'm crying so hard I'm practically drooling, my *fight* instinct gone totally out of me. *Bwooop, bwooop, bwooop!* "I have to call him so he'll come over here!" I grab at my pocket, but I've left my phone at my desk.

"Here." Sarah hands me hers. *Bwooop, bwooop, bwooop!* On her screen is a message to a contact labeled "Family." *There's a shooter at school. If I don't make it out, I love you all.*

"Ohmygod, I didn't—" The last thing I said to Tuney was *You're the worst.* "I have to call Tuney. And Mom. I have to tell Mom I'm sorry, I have to—Tuney said it's goose-guts night, I need to eat dinner with my family—"

"Text Mason first." Sarah nods at him. His phone is sticking out of his back pocket.

"I'll call him." *Bwooop, bwooop, bwooop!*

"Text. If the shooters make it in and his ringer's loud, it'll draw attention to him."

Oh god, she's right.

With shaking hands, I type his number. It's the only one I have memorized. *There's room for you under Mr. Trevino's desk*, I write.

Bwooop, bwooop, bwooop!

The door handle rattles like someone's trying to get in. Mason's sobs are so loud I can hear him over the alarm, over the slams and screaming from other rooms. His voice is loud, eerie. Like he's caught in a trap and ready to chew off his leg to escape. Helen Vargas, his crush, peeks out at him from behind a shelf across the room.

The door rattles again. There's a heavy pounding like it's being hit with something.

My eyes dart to the edges of the room. Everyone is either staring at the door or staring at Mason. Like they're waiting for him to get shot and they can't look away. In the corner, Mr. Trevino looks out from behind the heavy wood supply closet door. *Bwooop, bwooop, bwooop!*

He's the grown-up. *He* should be pulling Mason to

safety. But he's just gripping the door. His face has gone a sickly yellow under his thinning blond hair. *Bwooop, bwooop, bwooop!*

Mason chokes out another sob with the word "No" buried deep inside it.

I start to bolt toward him. But my T-shirt is stuck on something. I grunt and turn around.

Sarah's gripping my shirt. "Don't. There's no point in both of you dying."

"I have to get him!"

She yanks me back under the desk with surprising strength. I struggle to get away from her, to get to Mason, but her grip is tight and the knee and shoulder pain is as loud as the fire alarm. "Look at me," she says. "Look at my eyes."

She won't let go of me. I stare into her eyes, blue pools of stillness in her pale, calm face. A wisp of blonde hair has slipped out of her French braid and is caught in her eyelashes. It moves when she blinks. "Take a deep breath," she says.

"But Mason—"

"I know. You stay. I can move faster." She darts out, grabs Mason by the shoulder, and drags him to our hiding spot with the same strength she used to pull me back.

He howls as Jolene and Helen watch. He grasps at

chair legs, trying to scramble back to where he was. Sarah wrestles him into the cramped area under the desk with us.

It's impossible to find a position that doesn't hurt my shoulder or knee. The tight space smells of Cthulhu's stink and my sweaty sock and pee. Because . . .

Oh no. Mason's jeans are wet.

I wrap my good arm around him. He buries his face in my shoulder and cries, his cold hands gripping my left bicep like a vise.

"Thank you," I tell Sarah.

She sniffles a little and nods.

The three of us huddle there for years and years. Listening to the screams and the blaring fire alarm. Flinching at the *pops*. At the slams and bangs and the sounds of our classmates in various stages of meltdown. Peeking out at the terrified faces. Even Jolene has gone as pale as her bleached-blonde ponytail.

I take my headphones off my neck and awkwardly try to put them on Mason one-handed, hoping he'll be less terrified if the sounds are muffled. He ducks away from my hand but doesn't let go of his grip on my arm.

"What's goose-guts night?" Sarah asks me quietly.

"Code for lasagna." I grip my headphones and stare at the door. Hoping it won't rattle.

This is what Principal Ritter and Officer Clark were

looking at on the monitor. They saw something in the gym. And I was stupid enough to look in there.

I'm lucky I didn't get shot on the way to math.

A huge *bang* outside rattles the classroom windows. Sarah and Mason and I all startle. My ears ring.

It takes a moment to realize the fire alarm has stopped. I feel weirdly calm in the silence, like my brain has shorted out and there's no more fuel left in me to feel fear with.

The sound of kids crying makes its way in. And then Mr. Ritter's voice over the PA:

"This concludes the drill. I hope you've taken it seriously this time, and that you've learned from the experience. Please resume classroom activities."

8
Sarah

Weds., May 1, 10:25 a.m. I don't understand.

I wasn't scared. I'm not scared now. The one time I <u>should</u> have been terrified, I was calm. Like Dad-flying-a-kite calm. My heart barely even raced.

God. I'm so, so glad Luci wasn't here for that. It would've been the last thing she needed after watching her mom die.

Part of me wants to text her about it. But what would I say? I almost just died?

I didn't, though. It only seemed like it would happen.

But it was fake. Just sounds.

The teacher from across the hall, I don't know her name, came in as soon as the drill was over to talk to Mr. Trevino. She must not have a class this bell. She was trying to keep her voice down but she kept getting louder and Mr. Trevino kept saying "Shh." I don't know if he was saying it to her or himself or us. To Jolene, who proclaimed about six times that she knew it was a drill all along. Clearly lying.

Mr. Trevino apologized to us. He said we don't deserve what they just did. He's given us the rest of the class period to get ourselves together. To text our families that we're not going to die. That we're fine.

No one in this room is fine. Not him. Not the other teacher. Not Jolene or Mason or Avery or any of us. I feel calm, but not . . . not fine.

I don't understand why I didn't panic. My instinct is always to fly, not stay and fight.

I didn't fight, exactly.

But I didn't try to fly away in my mind. I didn't scurry away from my fear like a mouse.

Avery seems like a <u>fight</u> person.

But she wanted to fly.

I'm going to be untangling this for a long time.

Avery and Mason are sharing Mason's desk next to me. Jammed in so tightly they look like one person with two heads. Avery gave him the hoodie she keeps in her backpack. It's around his waist, hiding the small wet patch on his jeans. Her left arm is around his back, her hand on his upper arm. Holding him close, like she's still trying to keep him safe. They're like a Spirograph design looping in on itself.

I wish I could squeeze into that seat too. Mason looks stunned. Avery looks furious. But they have each other.

Why didn't I panic???

9

Avery

Everyone is their own flavor of mess at lunch. I'm a furious mess whose knee hurts like hell and whose guts are weird after I wasted ten minutes of my lunch break in the bathroom. I've sent only one-word answers to the texts from Mom and Tuney: *Are you okay?* (No, but I say yes.) *Was it terrible?* (Yes, but I say no.) *We can't believe what we're reading on Facebook. Do you want us to come pick you up?* (Yes, but I say no.) Mason's a silent mess. Bree is a can't-stop-crying mess and Dariellis is a stomachache mess. The cafeteria herd is thinner than usual, but the noise level is not lower. The two hundred kids in here are all kinds of mess: too loud (Jolene) or too quiet (Helen) or pretending too hard that we weren't terrified an hour ago that we were gonna die (everyone who didn't get picked up by their furious parents).

The lunch monitor is not a mess, because she gets here at eleven, according to Dariellis, and missed the circus of trauma. She's walking around with a sympathetic look that's ticking me *right* the heck off. I'm so mad I can't even eat. And I am not a girl who skips a meal, especially when it's a peanut butter and Nutella sandwich made by Tuney instead of Mom—meaning it's heavy on the Nutella—plus ghost pepper nachos and the last three Thin Mints.

Mason picks at his sandwich. Bree keeps wiping her pale face with the heel of her hand. A streak of mascara by her left eye curves up like a failed cat-eye. I'm tempted to pull a Tuney and lick my thumb and wipe it away, but my functional hand is still shaky. I'd probably jab her in the eyeball by mistake.

I put a Thin Mint in front of Mason, hoping to entice him to eat. He picks it up and sets it back down, then continues building Stonehenge with torn-up bits of crust. I texted him after the drill that he should go to the nurse for new pants. But he said he'd be too embarrassed to tell her he peed himself, plus nothing would fit him because he's such a shortie. I answered that too-big pants are better than pee-soaked pants. He wrote, *It's really not that much.*

I put the other two Thin Mints in front of Bree and Dariellis by their cafeteria tacos. "Did you hear about the guy whose left arm and leg got chopped off?" I ask.

No one looks at me. Dariellis has her phone five inches from her face with the brightness turned up. It shines a bluish light on her dark brown skin, making her look ghostly and tired. Bree is frowning at a social studies packet like she's mad at Mesopotamia. Neither of them are eating their tacos. Mason keeps licking his lips like he's drained and in need of a meme dump.

"He's all right now," I say. "Get it?"

No one laughs.

My Thin Mints and bad jokes are useless against this degree of oof. Last period, my social studies teacher, Mr. Clayton, was trying to walk us through his "Creative + Strategic Problem-Solving Model," but it was a big honking flop because how can you be creative or strategic when your brain is still churning out I'm-gonna-die feels? When kids keep getting called to the office because their parents are here to get them? We're all in a weird recovery mode. Reliving this morning over and over.

I half regret turning down Mom's offer to come get me. But I hate looking weak.

I can't freaking *believe* I cried in front of Sarah. Who was totally calm, and who never answered my note because the freaking *principal* decided to pretend *dudes* with *guns* were gonna *kill* us and this is one more huge thing I have no control over and I hate what it's done to my friends and I *hate* what it's doing to my mind and I *hate*—

"That poor sandwich, though," Dariellis says.

I look down. Chocolate has smooshed out of my crusts under my fist. "Oh, for frog's sake." I lick Nutella off my hand. "Are you guys as mad as me? Because what the nugget futt."

"I'm mad," Bree echoes dully. "Like somebody kicked my cat."

"You don't look it. You look hopeless. Like the opposite of yourself." She's way upbeat. Sometimes obnoxiously so. We get into arguments because she's always pointing out the rosy side of life and I'm always pointing out the real side of it.

"Well, I *am*," she sniffs. "Just because I don't look ready to bust into the office and yell at Mr. Ritter doesn't mean I'm not angry."

"Busting into his office is exactly what we should do," I say. "Don't you guys want revenge on them for punking us like that?" I hold up my ghost pepper nachos. "What if I smashed these and scattered them all over Mr. Ritter's office? Getting ghost pepper any-where near your eyes or nose is no joke." I once rubbed my eye while eating these chips and was weepy for two hours. "Bree, you could sneak the crumbs in when you're reading the morning announcements tomorrow."

Bree doesn't even bother to roll her eyes.

"Just let it go." Mason pulls my hoodie from under his butt. "I want to forget it happened. And for everyone else to forget it too."

"But it *did* happen. They scared the ever-loving crap out of us to prove a point!" In the most humiliating way possible. Making us sob and pee and hurl. Which Dariellis apparently did as soon as third period was over.

"I'm never not taking a shooter drill seriously again," Bree says. "If they wanted to scare us straight after you and Mason were cracking up at the last drill, it worked."

A stab of guilt hits and I tug at my earrings. "At what freaking cost? We're all going to have nightmares for months. What they did was *so* not okay!"

"We know," Dariellis says. "You don't have to keep saying it."

"Then we should make a punk-them-back plan!"

"Avery, *don't*," Mason says quietly. He might've inherited his mom's russet-brown skin and long, thick eyelashes, but he didn't get her talent of ending a conversation with a firm tone. "There's enough ticked-off parents. Just let them deal with it."

"You of all people should want revenge," I tell him.

"Why, because I—" He glances at Bree and Dariellis. "Melted down? That just makes me want to forget this. Like I *said*." He scoots away on the bench. "So can we talk about something else? Or just *not talk*?" He angrily bites his crustless ham sandwich, then looks like he regrets putting it in his mouth.

I stifle a grunt of frustration. If he doesn't want to get revenge for himself . . . well, I'll get revenge for him. For *all* of us. For Bree and Dariellis and Sarah and me.

I don't know what form it'll take. But that drill is the reason my knee is worse than it was. The reason I just had to waste ten miserable minutes in the bathroom with a bad case of the bubbleguts. The reason my friends are falling apart, and enraged parents are showing up, and my crush didn't answer my note. I feel like I'm going to burst into tears again.

The drill made me feel more out of control than I've ever felt in my life. And that's saying something. Especially lately.

I'm gonna make Mr. Ritter *pay*.

10
Sarah

Weds., May 1, 2:16 p.m. English. My classes have been a wash. The teachers too shaken to teach. The kids too unfocused to learn. A third of the desks in this room are empty. Every teacher has apologized and said we didn't deserve what happened. In art, Mrs. Gianno put out the bins of markers and said to draw whatever we wanted, then left us to it while she typed furiously on her laptop. I spent that class and all of French drafting animal mashups for Ruthie while I tried to think of some way to help everyone so they don't feel so upset. But I don't know how I could.

I'd text Luci to ask her advice if I wasn't worried it would upset her to hear about the drill. Sometimes it feels like I traded a best friend for a phone. A little rectangle of glass and metal that I can't hug or laugh with. I

can't even use it to find a stop-your-panic app without my parents finding out and telling me I just need to pray my fear away.

Luci might suggest . . . hmm. Probably making lists of things that help me feel better, to help me think of a way to help everyone else feel better.

Sounds
trains at night
birds in the morning
piano keys brushing
  together in the soft
  parts of a song
the wind before
  a storm

Sights
Ruthie's grin
Green growing
ANYTHING
Grant Lake on a
  calm blue day
when trees
  and clouds fit
  together like
  puzzle pieces

smells
fresh-cut grass
books
creek mud

tastes
Aunt Camila's
  tamales
The crumbly inside
of a jawbreaker
The last chips
  in the bag

feelings

Being with
Chonky Kong
Exploring a creek
Sun on my neck
Holding a sharp
pencil over a blank
sheet of paper

words

nincompoopery
defenestration
dingleberry
whippersnapper

I wish I had Dad's calm, constant faith. He's always so certain everything happens for God's reasons, even if we don't understand. When Mom gets flustered, which happens a lot because of James, Dad wraps his arms around her and gives her a back-cracking hug. He's skinny like me and James, and James is taller than him now, but during those hugs, Dad seems ten feet tall and made of soft fuzzy bunny + big strong bear.

The tension drains out of Mom when he hugs her like that. Her shoulders are stiff at first, and then she puts her head on his shoulder and sighs. It always gives me a warm, safe feeling.

Mason is two seats over. He looks as spent as I feel. He's doodling circles on his paper. Avoiding looking at Helen, who keeps glancing at him.

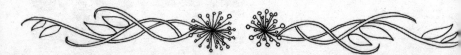

I can't stop thinking of the drill. Mason sobbing. Avery freaking out. I remember in vivid detail the way time slowed and the bangs and blasts came at a steady rate. Like . . .

Like they were timed, on purpose. To scare us just when we'd start to think it was over.

I can't believe they <u>did</u> that to us. Why would anyone <u>do</u> that? What's <u>wrong</u> with them? We are <u>kids</u>!

Fern Hatfield just bolted for the door. She's going to—

Oh no, she's in the hall getting sick. Like Aunt Camila at the end when she couldn't keep anything down.

She's not going to die. It's illogical to fear when someone gets that kind of sick that they'll die. I shouldn't be scared.

Mason went out to help Fern. I should go too. But her sounds are breaking loose everything I didn't feel during the drill. I feel it now. Cold, poisoned feeling deep in my lungs. My skin is burning. My belly is smashed empty-flat and too full all at once and there's something wrong with my heart like there was something wrong with Aunt Camila's and God please make this stop, please please PLEASE <u>PLEASE</u>

3:17 p.m. With James, driving home. It's weird how I can be so certain my heart is messed up when I'm panicking, and so certain it's fine when I'm not panicking.

I'm glad James picked me up so I didn't have to ride the rolling germ box that is the school bus. I almost cried when I saw him behind the wheel of Mom's car in the pickup line. I thought for a few minutes this morning that I'd never see him again. Seeing him suddenly made me realize how much I love the flawed beautiful mess of him.

He knows about the drill. I have no idea how. It's been three years since Principal Ritter kicked him out of the district, and he still knows everything that happens here. Maybe because his ex-boyfriend goes to Maple Creek High and they still talk. A lot. So much that his new boyfriend, who goes to St. Joseph's with him, is not okay with it.

When I got into the car, James asked if I was terrified during the drill.

"No," I told him. "I don't know why."

"You didn't panic?"

"Not till later." Not until Fern . . . did the thing.

James said some people are good in emergencies and fall apart later. And some people fall apart during the emergency but then they're fine later.

I guess I'm that first type. I keep it together when Ruthie falls down the steps or breaks a finger or trips and cuts her knee open. Then later I get scared thinking of how it could've been worse.

James just asked if I'm mad. He said he'd be mad. He

said he <u>is</u> mad, for me. He said he wants to give Principal Ritter a piece of his mind.

He already did that when he was an eighth grader at Maple Creek Middle. The piece of his mind he gave Mr. Ritter had lots of profanity in it. Plus there was the car egging and the tire flattening and the house TP-ing. If Dad hadn't been the voice of reason, Mom might've shipped James to the boonies with no return address. Lucky for him he only got kicked out of the district and sent by Mom and Dad to Catholic school to "straighten" him out. It's kind of funny that two months into his first year there, he told them he's gay.

I'm looking at Avery's note again. Her handwriting is messy. When we pass up our homework in math, I always look at her sloppy paper and realize I did some of the problems wrong. But then it's too late to change my neat, wrong answers into her messy, correct ones.

It was oddly reassuring today to see Avery so afraid. Like . . . I feel less intimidated by her now.

I just asked James if he's ever relieved when people turn out to not be perfect. He's gone broody, scowling as he grips Mom's fuzzy pink steering-wheel cover.

"It depends," he said. "On the person. On what I hope we could be."

I hoped this morning that Avery and I could be friends. Now I just hope I make it to graduation without being shot.

11

Avery

If Mom opens my lunch box and finds everything uneaten, she'll worry. And she'll worry more if she finds my smashed sandwich, which I was too distracted to throw away at school. So when I get home, even though my guts are still messed up, I eat my sandwich and chips. Tank, our pit bull, helps me out with the crusts. When I'm done, I trudge up the steps. I miss running up them on all fours. I never bothered to grow out of that habit, but surgery put an end to it for me.

I usually look at memes in my room for an hour after school since there's no moms around to tell me to do something productive. But when I curl up in my chair by the window and search "active shooter memes," none of it is funny. It just scares me all over again. If there ever *is* a shooter at school, it'll be a kid who's gone through the drills and knows how we'll react.

Mom texts asking if I want her to come home early from work. I tell her I'm fine, even though I'm having one of those rare moments when I want to curl up on her lap and bawl my eyes out while she hugs me. Mom is an ace hugger.

I look at news stories about shooter drills for a while. It makes me feel even worse, because ours wasn't that bad compared to ones where they used actors covered in fake blood. Or shot teachers with pellet guns. All they did to us was try to scare us with sounds. I can't even bang my frustrations out on Galien. My drum kit broods in the corner. Wondering why I've ignored him for the past two weeks.

"I'm sorry," I tell him. "It's not you. It's me. We'll be together again soon." I hope.

The rainbow alien sticker on the kick drum remains expressionless.

I move to my bed and sit with my legs under me in a W shape, my knees sticking out ahead of me and my feet pointed outward behind me. I'm not supposed to sit like this because it "causes stress" on my hip and knee joints, but it stretches my thighs and makes them feel better, so whatever. I FaceTime Mason and crack my knuckles while I wait for him to answer.

When he finally does just before I'm ready to give up, he's sitting in his desk chair, hugging his knees. "Sup," he says with none of his usual bounce.

"Were you just sitting at your desk ignoring your phone?"

He shrugs.

"Are you okay? I've been worried about you all day."

"Because I peed myself in front of the entire freaking class? Including Helen, who thinks I'm disgusting? Including Jolene, who's going to make my life miserable about it?" His Gandalf poster looms behind him in his cluttered room.

"I don't think anyone noticed. Like you said, it wasn't that much. And you had my hoodie."

"I stank all freaking day." He unfolds from his curled-up position and I see that he's changed clothes. "Aren't you not supposed to sit like that?"

"I couldn't smell you at lunch," I tell him. "I really think—"

"Because taco day overpowered me. Trust, the pee funk was *there*."

"I'm sorry," I say. "Tank says hi." I turn the phone down to show him Tank, sleeping on the floor by my bed.

"It doesn't matter," Mason says. "I only have to face everyone for a few more weeks."

"Four." I've been counting down the days till summer break. "Then two months of freedom till the whole new world of Maple Creek High. Where everyone will definitely have forgotten, 'cause we'll all be stressed about being freshmen." Especially Mason and me, since we have summer birthdays and are among the youngest kids in our grade.

"I'm not going to Maple Creek High," Mason says flatly.

I laugh. "What, you're just opting out? Cool. Me too."

"My mom said this is the last straw." He glances over his shoulder at his closed bedroom door. "They're putting me in private school next year."

"What?!" No!

"Yeah." His voice and face are grim. "She wanted to take me out right away. Like today. But Dad said we should wait since it's so close to the end of the year."

My right arm twitches uselessly in Cthulhu. "What the futt? They can't just—"

"Well, they are. Mom already hated Maple Creek 'cause of my IEP. And the getting-in-trouble."

"But . . ." Mason is supposed to get extra support per his Individualized Education Plan, but he doesn't usually get it because our school doesn't have enough counselors and occupational therapists and stuff to help all the kids with ADHD. "So she was looking for an excuse? And this is it?"

"I don't know. It's all . . ." Mason dips his chin to his chest and rubs his hand over his short hair. "It's all messed up. Today was so messed up." His voice is muffled.

"So let's *do* something! You gotta be mad too, right? You were stuck out in the—"

"I'd rather not relive it, thanks."

I slump. "I'm sorry. I'm not trying to make you. I know it really sucked for you." I grit my teeth in frustration. "There has to be some way to get your mom to change her mind."

"You know how she is once she decides something."

"But like . . . you're just gonna accept it? You're not even going to argue?"

"Aves, I don't know." He slouches back in his desk chair. "It's all just . . . ugh. One giant ugly ugh." He folds his arms on his desk and rests his forehead on them, giving me a view of the close-cropped hair on the top of his head. "Today sucked so much." His voice is muffled.

"Yes. It did. That's why we need to get—"

"What?" Mason sits up and looks over his shoulder. I can hear his mom calling his name. "I gotta go," he says, and hangs up.

"Garrrugh!" I fling my phone at my chair. But I suck at left-handed throwing and miss. My phone case leaves a mark on the wall and Tank jerks awake. "Shut up!" I yell at the wall. "Shut up shut up shut up!" Then I fake-laugh so I won't start crying.

An hour later, I'm staring at a worksheet about the Byzantine Empire with zero comprehension, rubbing Tank's head with my foot and sulking over having to watch Carson Navarro struggle through my part on the drum kit in band class today. I knew what he was doing wrong—he was an eighth beat too early on the kick drum, hitting it before the snare—but I was too discombobulated to point it out without snapping at him, plus the off-beat rhythm was giving me shooter-drill vibes. It blows that he got the part I was gonna play in our end-of-year concert, and it blows even more that he's butchering it.

I know it's not his fault I'm a better drummer because I have a home kit to practice on and he only gets to play at school. But *aargh*. Listening to him is the definition of frustration.

By the time Mom gets home from work, my mind feels as breakable as glass. My guts are getting in on the action, twisting up in knots and making all sorts of gurgling noises.

"Sweetheart!" Mom rushes across my room to hug me. "Are you okay?"

"Hi, Mom." My nose is smooshed next to her armpit. I get a strong whiff of her lavender deodorant as her laptop bag falls off her shoulder.

She catches her bag in the crook of her elbow. "Oh, honey." She holds my shoulders and looks into my eyes. Her short red-blonde hair is messy and mascara dust has settled in the faint lines under her eyes. Her entire face is made of concern. "Was it awful?"

"Ow." She's not actually hurting my shoulder. But I'm gonna melt if she keeps looking at me like that, and I don't know if I'll ever be able to rein in the tears.

"Ooh—sorry." She lifts her hand from my right shoulder like it's hot. "I've just been so worried. Tuney too. Are you okay, really?"

"I'm fine. Why wouldn't I be?"

"The parents on the Facebook page say it was horrible. So many of them got texts from their kids saying 'Goodbye' and 'I love you' and—"

"It was just another drill. It wasn't that big a deal."

Mom laughs, but not like she finds the situation funny. "Fake gunshots and explosions? Actors screaming? That's a big deal, honey."

"No, it's *not*. So can I do this worksheet, please?"

She sucks in her breath and steps back, her head

tilted. "You're angry. It's protecting you from your fear."

I try not to roll my eyes. She likes to tell me what I feel like she's inside my head and can read it. "I don't want to talk about it."

"Well." She touches my left arm. "When you're ready, okay?"

"It's literally *fine*." I scrawl a messy answer to a question.

"I love you, baby."

"Love you too, Mom."

She leaves and I fold my legs back into a W shape. At least she didn't hassle me about my PT exercises. I don't have to do them at home on the days I go to the PT office.

When I got diagnosed, Mom learned everything she could about EDS. She got me signed up on Zebra Board. She advocates for me when we visit doctors, bringing up stuff I mean to ask about but forget. She keeps all my medical info in this super-organized file folder system.

I know she does it because she loves me. Because she wants what's best for me.

She just makes me feel so *smothered* sometimes. Before, when we argued over whatever dumb thing, I'd play drums extra loud or go climb the tulip tree in our backyard or jump down the stairs and land hard on every step just to annoy her.

I poke Cthulhu with my pen. It's not nearly as satisfying.

At dinner, my guts are still all rumbly and weird. All I want to do is blorp into the bathroom and watch Tik-Tok on the toilet, but Mom's big on "family dinner," so I gotta pretend to enjoy it. Tuney keeps pausing her fork halfway to her mouth and blinking at me with teary eyes. Every time she does, I look at my barely eaten lasagna. If she cries, I'm gonna cry. "What?" I finally ask. "Why are you so weepy?"

"Because they made you think you were going to die. And I don't like how it feels to hate someone. Even a guy as vile as your principal."

I half shrug my left shoulder. It sends pain through my chest. "I didn't think I was gonna die. The whole thing was super fake and dumb." I stab a chunk of pasta like it did me wrong.

"That's not what we're seeing on the Parents of MCMS Facebook page," Tuney says. "People are saying they spent a minute and a half doing everything they could to terrify you."

My fork stops on its way to my mouth. A minute and a half?

I guess . . . when I think about it, that's probably right. It only *felt* like eternity. Ninety seconds of fake bangs and shouting was all it took to break everyone down.

"Mason's mom is—" My throat tightens. "She said Mason can't go to Maple Creek High next year. That he'll go to private school. Because of this." I shove in lasagna.

Mom looks sympathetic. "I'm sorry, honey. But to be honest, I'm tempted to pull you out too if this is how they plan to run these drills now."

My food doesn't want to go down. I chew and chew, trying to keep my face blank. Tank puts his paw on my thigh, a trick that usually earns him a nibble from my plate.

Tuney and Mom exchange a look. "We've got to do something," Tuney says. "She's a mess. They can't do this to her and the other kids again."

"I'm not a *mess*." I finally manage to swallow. "I'm just mad. When Mr. Ritter came over the PA after, he said he hoped we took it seriously. That we learned a lesson after everyone laughed at the last drill." I grip my fork. *Everyone* was basically me, and Mason because of me. "If all my limbs worked, I'd kick his butt for making it seem like the whole thing was our own fault." Like it was *my* fault in particular.

"Revenge isn't the answer," Mom says with that note of sternness that drives me up the wall. "In this case or any case. You know better."

I clench my jaw. It absolutely *is* the answer in this case. And plenty of others.

Tuney notices the storm on my face. "How about a Netflix night? Aves, how much homework do you have?"

"I did it all in a fit of rage when I got home."

"Okay then," Tuney says. "Why don't you pick what we watch?"

We've been traipsing through old episodes of *Stranger Things*, but I don't want my foul mood to cloud my rabid love for that show. "I don't care. As long as there's blood and gore."

While we're watching the episode of *Locke and Key* where Kinsey drags her fear out of her head, I send Mason a string of texts. Asking if he's okay. Telling him if he wants to talk, I'm here. Asking if he has any ideas about how to get his mom to change her mind, because I can't imagine going to Maple Creek High next year without my best friend by my side. Helping me keep my sanity with his goofiness and his willingness to go along with my zany plans and his endless curiosity about how the world works.

But he's either ignoring me or having family meeting night or his phone's dead. I love *Locke and Key* with a fierceness, but I can't get my head into it tonight. I keep churning through ways I can get back at Ritter the Rat without getting caught. Steal something of his? Trick him into saying something embarrassing during morning announcements? Maybe I could put a custom-made bumper sticker on his Fiat that says *I eat mulch*. Or, more accurate: *I hate kids*.

I sigh. Nothing I come up with is any good. I need Mason for this.

Sleep is impossible. For once, it's not because I'm in too much pain to get comfortable.

Well. Actually it is. But it's my brain that's aflame more than my shoulder, for a fun change of pace. And my knee is trying to get in on the action. It's a steady four out of ten on the pain scale. Right at the border of what I can sidestep.

At 1:38, I sit up in bed and flip my curtain aside. My trampoline sits below me in the backyard, covered in maple seeds. Its springs catch the faint moonlight.

I'd give *anything* to go out there for some bounce therapy. To spring high up into the air and flop on my back into the trampoline's center, maple seeds shooting into the air around me and then fluttering back down as inertia takes over and my bouncing slows.

I get up and go downstairs for a glass of water. Tuney's laptop is on the kitchen table.

I'd be so ticked if my moms snooped in my phone. I should *not* open Tuney's laptop.

I type in her password one-handed, then open Chrome and click the Facebook bookmark.

I don't know my way around this social-for-old-people site. Looks like a newsfeed with posts from people I guess Tuney knows. I poke around until I find a Groups tab. It loads a list of stuff like "Transgender Community of Watson County" and "Dank Memes for Coding Geeks" (okay, Tuney, I bet they're *so* dank) and "In Defense of Pit Bulls." I finally find one called "Parents of Maple Creek Middle School (MCMS)" and click it.

The top post is about the drill. A woman with a sunflower profile photo has written "SUEING MAPLE CREEK MIDDLE Who's with me????" The comments section is a raging debate between people who are furious and people who say drills like today's are necessary because middle schoolers don't take anything seriously, plus a smattering of people telling her she spelled *suing* wrong.

I read through every single comment, slowing down on the few that mention Mr. Ritter. One person said she used to think he was a decent man. Some guy replied that Mr. Ritter obviously did it in the interests of student safety and the lady needs to get off her high horse, then they devolve into a fight about snowflakes and anti-vaxxers. I find another thread debating whether Mr. Ritter needs to address the "public outcry" against the drill. The people who think today was a good idea say no statement from him is needed because the drill speaks for itself. The people who think the drill was a bad idea say it's the school board that needs to address it, not him, since it wasn't his decision alone.

My face burns at the memory of the angry lecture he gave me in front of everyone after that standard-issue drill last month. Even if the terrible realistic drill wasn't his decision alone, I would bet my dirt bike that in the debate about whether to do it or not, he was a strong voice arguing *for* it. He obviously wanted to teach us all—and maybe me especially—a lesson.

The comments start to get repetitive and my eyes glaze as I scan them. At the regular drill, I was only trying to make Mason feel better. Mr. Ritter didn't have to prove that shooter drills are serious business by putting us all through today's hell.

His cruel choice made me feel weak. He made me look weak in front of Sarah. He made me think I was powerless to control what happens to me.

I am *not. Powerless.*

I close the browser and shut the laptop, then tiptoe back to my room. I rearrange the complicated pillow system that causes the least pain, then lie there staring at my dark ceiling. Turning over ideas about how to get back at him. About what I could do that would make him feel as powerless as I felt today.

Now *this* is a problem for the Creative + Strategic Problem-Solving Model.

12
Sarah

Weds., May 1, 7:10 p.m. In my room, supposed to be finishing my homework. But it's warm and golden outside and it's cold and dim down here and I couldn't focus, so I googled "how to stop panic."

There's <u>so</u> much stuff.

I guess I'll make a list of the tips that seem useful. I can look at it later as a reminder.

1. Take three slow, deep breaths.
2. Say aloud: "I'm not dying. This is only fear. It'll pass."
3. Come back to your senses: Find five things you can see, four things you can hear, three things you can touch, two things you can smell, one thing you can taste.
4. Repeat a mantra. (I need to find a Bible verse.)

I like that I can do these with no one knowing. I just did three deep breaths. I wasn't feeling panicky, but I do feel calmer now.

Mom gave me a long hug when James and I got home. It was hard to not cry, but being surrounded by the chaos of the kids she babysits helped me keep a lid on it. She said she's been praying for me since she found my texts an hour after I sent them. Then she asked me to make a snack for Riley and Grayson and to change Layla's diaper so she could clean up the mess Riley made in the bathroom.

All I wanted to do was draw and recover my wits. But it made me feel better to be useful. To pretend it was a normal day. The only difference was that Mom kept giving me the worried looks she usually only gives Ruthie or James.

It helped that we took the kids outside for a little bit. I love May, with its explosion of green and its rain of maple seeds and the bursting white flowers of black locust trees and the sweet honeysuckle scent. Like the earth is sneezing off winter. I always feel hopeful in May. It means summer is coming, and I'll be able to do lots of art and soak up the sun and the heat and the green. Dad loves May too, because spring storms make great wind for kite flying.

When Dad got home from his mechanic job, he gave me one of the bunny + bear hugs he gives

Mom. I again almost cried when he said, "I'm so sorry you went through that, sunshine." But I didn't, because 5:45 at our house is meltdown o'clock, whether that's James getting mad at the Fox News Mom watches or it's a babysitting kid or it's Ruthie or it's Mom getting fed up after a long day taking care of other people's kids. I feel sad that Dad always gets home from work in the middle of that. I don't need to contribute to it.

After the good hug, Dad went to change out of his uniform and then we all sat down to dinner. While we ate, James and Mom started to wind up into an argument, so I tried the "Come back to your senses" tip so I wouldn't get anxious about it. Five things I saw:

1. The faded floral wallpaper all dinged up from me and James and Ruthie and the babysitting kids. Holding the marks of us growing through childhood, learning how to be in the world.

2. The dead bugs trapped in the ceiling light.

3. Our faux-oak table with its dents and scratches and all the layered stories it could tell of our lives.

4. The pinewood hutch that belonged to Grandpa and Grandma Bell before they moved to a trailer park in Florida.

5. My family.

I realized that I felt a lot of love for what I saw, especially my family (even with the arguing). For James with his hurricane moods and Ruthie with the six Band-Aids on her elbow from wiping out on a rock at the creek and my always-calm dad and my mom who loves us so fiercely that it comes out as strictness. I kept thinking of them during the drill, like, I just have to make it home and everything will be fine.

Home's not really <u>fine</u>, though. It hasn't been for the last two months. My house used to feel <u>safe</u> before Aunt Camila died and Luci left. And now, sometimes, it doesn't. I know it can keep me safe from storms and other people and, I don't know, gangs of rabid opossums. But it can't keep me safe from <u>me</u>.

Panic isn't <u>me</u>. Right? But when I'm having it, it <u>feels</u> like me. Every part of my mind becomes fuel for it. It burns through me and uses me all up.

My heart started thump-thumping hard while I wrote that, so I tried the three-deep-breaths tip while I drew.

I had to do eleven breaths instead of three. But it <u>worked</u>. I didn't panic.

It can't be that easy. Can it?

Maybe I wasn't really about to panic. Maybe it was just a small, normal fear. And that's why it worked.

I'll do it again next time. To test it.

Anyway, by the end of dinner, it started to bother me that my parents didn't seem as upset as I (kind of selfishly) wanted them to be. I texted them today to tell them I might die and that I love them. And then we all ate baked potatoes like nothing was different.

It kinda hurt.

James noticed. I should feel grateful that he cares, but as usual, he ran his point into the ground.

James: Why aren't you freaked out? Sarah almost died today.

Mom: She didn't almost die. And don't assume we're not upset. Getting her messages was awful.

James: You don't act like you're upset. Can't you see that's bothering her?

Me: It's fine, James.

Dad (calmly): Even if preparing for a terrible possibility is no fun, if it saves your life when the real thing happens, it's worth it.

James: Oh right, so instead of voting pro-gun Republican whack jobs out of office, twelve-year-olds should be terrorized by fake explosions and gunfire to prep them for when a real shooter shows up?

Me: I'm thirteen. Almost fourteen.

Dad (still calm): Republicans aren't pro-gun whack jobs. Many of us vote the way we do because we believe in the sanctity of human life.

James: But liberals secured the right to vote for women and African Americans, built Social Security, passed the Civil Rights Act, ended segregation, created Medicare—

Mom: Conservatives fight abortion and save the lives of innocent babies and preserve the traditional family unit—

James: You're insinuating gay people can't have families!

. . . and then it was just carnage and yelling and James storming off to his room rage-crying (again) and Dad sighing (again) and Mom covering her face (again) and Ruthie getting silly (again) trying to make someone laugh so we can seem normal.

Do other families work like mine? Luci's kind of did,

with Mateo and Diego being "rabble-rousers" (per Uncle Dave) and "hell-raisers" (per Aunt Camila) and "nightmares to live with" (per Luci). They're not like James—emotional, often too passionate about his beliefs, willing to go totally bananas to settle a score. Mateo and Diego get in trouble for pulling dumb pranks and laughing at their punishment.

But in all the times I had dinner at Luci's, nobody left the table in tears. Their arguing was a loving sort of bickering. Not so large and loud that it broke their togetherness.

I just sent Luci a picture of part of the dinner-argument art (not the stuff about the drill). She still hasn't responded to the progress photo of our baby sunflowers I sent her this morning. I planted the seeds outside my basement window during that warm spell in mid-April, and they're already six inches tall. But next week it's supposed to get really cold.

I know I can get more seeds and start over if they die. But the ones I planted are the ones Luci and I bought at the dollar store right after Aunt Camila got sick. I think of the baby plants as "ours." When I look at them, I feel connected to Luci.

Luci just wrote back! She said, "I'm sorry dinner's still awful. But your art tho! I feel like I'm there too." She asked if I've shown my Spiro drawings to Mrs. Gianno yet.

I wrote, "I will tomorrow." Luci's been after me to show Mrs. Gianno my art.

After living through today, showing her my art

seems like a silly thing to be nervous about. So I <u>will</u> do it tomorrow. I'll take three deep breaths, or maybe eleven, and then do it.

I wonder what dinner at Avery's house is like. If that "Tuney" person she mentioned is a sibling whose soul is too big to fit in their body, like James's. If her mom and dad get that grim look when something goes wrong that they don't know how to fix.

Well. It doesn't matter. Losing Luci and Aunt Camila was bad enough. I get little pieces of Luci when we text, but it's a shadow of what we used to have.

I don't need to get attached to Avery only to fall into endless panic about losing her too.

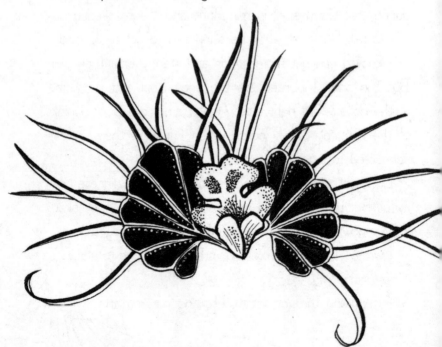

I go back to my aunt's last day
again and again and again,
looping through my senses
in a Spirograph swirl:
Antiseptic smells.
Harsh fluorescent lights.
Aftertaste of turkey sandwich
I ate one bite of
on the way to say goodbye.
Beeps and whooshes.
Cold ICU air, still and restless
at the same time.
Luci—my cousin, my best friend—
muffling choked-up fears
with tear-smeared palms.
Diego's angry eyes.
Mateo's brave, broken smile.
Uncle Dave's grim despair.
And Aunt Camila: Luci's mommy
in the bed gasping, gasping—
"Was it peaceful?" a woman
whispered to Mom at the wake.
"No," Mom said.
Eyes on the closed coffin.
"It was not."

13

Avery

Everything at school on Thursday feels off. Like that time we went on a cruise and there was a big storm and the whole boat tilted a little. Just enough to make me question where the heck my gravity was.

When I walk into math class trying to hide my limp, Sarah's head is down. She doesn't look up as I pass by. I take the opportunity to get a look at what she's drawing. The left page looks like a journal entry, and on the right page is a poem. Around the edges of the poem are Spirograph designs. Really intricate ones, way better than any I did with the old set at Grandma Hart's house. I always got frustrated when the pieces slipped, and then I'd throw them across the room and go do something active.

Sarah's are *amazing*. She must've made the designs earlier, and now she's turning them into symmetrical flowers and leaves and looping them together with vines. I want to stop and really look, but she notices my gawking. She shields the book with her hand so I can't see it.

But not before I catch a glimpse of my name near the bottom of the journal page.

I sit down and take out a packet of Pop Rocks. I dump some in my mouth and tuck the packet under my math book, then drum a one-handed rhythm on my desk to hide the sound of the tiny delicious explosions in my mouth. The ones my brain is matching exactly because *my name* is *in Sarah's journal*.

Mr. Trevino starts class the moment the bell rings. He asks us to take out our books and turn to page 182. Then he clears his throat. "We should talk about yesterday," he says.

There's a collective sense of the room holding its breath. A lengthy silence ensues. I press my lips together, trying to smother the sound of Pop Rocks.

"What happened was cruel and unfair," he finally says. "And I need to apologize. I should have tried to protect you. But instead I . . ." He grips his desk, his knuckles white. "I . . ."

Jolene laughs nervously. I gulp down Pop Rocks and gape at Mr. Trevino. I have never seen a teacher cry.

But he looks like he's about to. Opening and closing his mouth like he doesn't know how to say whatever's in his head.

Teachers do not cry. It's a universal truth.

Right?

"I hid behind a door," he says. "While some of you . . ." He glances at Mason. "Some of you were left feeling exposed and terrified." He clears his throat. "I'm very sorry."

I look at Mason too. He's hyperfocused on scraping a smudge on his desk with his chewed-down thumbnail. A few desks over, Helen is watching him as well.

"If any of you want to talk about what happened, we can do that now," Mr. Trevino says.

"You seriously didn't know it was fake?" I blurt out. A stray Pop Rock snaps.

He shakes his head. "We weren't told ahead of time."

"Aren't you pi—aren't you mad?" I ask.

He nods curtly. "But that's not what I want to talk about. I'm concerned about all of *you*. And I know a lot of your parents are upset as well."

Jolene laughs again, louder this time. "That's an understatement. My mom's *furious*. She called Channel 12 News last night."

"I'm told a story is in the works at several stations," Mr. Trevino says.

"Can we just do math?" Mason asks.

I grip my desk with my free hand. He looks like he wants to be anywhere on earth but here. "Yeah," I say. "Honestly, we appreciate that you want to check on us and stuff, but like . . ." I glance around the room. "It's all any of us have been thinking about for the last twenty-four hours. We want to think about something else for a while. Even if it's math."

Mason gives me a grateful look.

"Is that true?" Mr. Trevino asks, scanning the room.

To my surprise, a lot of kids nod. Jolene just looks sour. Sarah discreetly blows her nose.

Another long pause. "Well. If you decide you want to discuss it at any time, we can. In the meantime, turn to page one twenty-eight."

"You mean one eighty-two," Sarah whispers just before Mason says "One eighty-two" aloud.

"Right," Mr. Trevino says. "Thank you, Mason."

That's the first time he's said that since I moved to this math class in January. But Mason doesn't look glad to hear it. A muscle in his jaw twitches like he's grinding his teeth.

We settle down to the business of polynomials.

Band class is just as frustrating as yesterday. I'm doing Carson's old bell-kit part one-handed. But stretching my left arm out to play hurts my sternum and I can only hit one note at a time anyway and it gets lost in the cacophony. Which sucks and makes me feel useless.

When I started drumming, last school year, I figured out quick that percussion drives the entire band. Whenever I messed up a rhythm, everything fell apart and the other kids would give me the stink eye (even though they never thanked me when I didn't screw up).

With lots of practice at home, though, I started getting it right. It didn't take long to get legit *good* at it. Using each limb in harmony to build a heavy, pounding beat for every other instrument to ride gives me a hefty serving of *heck yes*. It's the same deep thrill I get from driving a dirt bike on a curvy, mud-slick trail. All the skill and experience stored in my brain gets translated into glorious movement and action, like my soul and body are pulsing in time with the rhythm that keeps the universe moving.

Today it's more like my soul is being trampled by angry hippopotami. Carson continues to butcher my percussion part. I pretend I'm not mad about it. Ms. Everett tells me to stick to just three notes on the bell kit. Like that's even remotely as satisfying as pounding a kick drum, the toms, and the snare, then polishing the phrase off with a solid whack to the hi-hat.

At least Carson has the hi-hat down pat. It's like the exclamation point at the end of a sentence. Kind of important.

In Spanish, my last class, I drop my backpack on the floor and squat to get a pencil out of it. My knee pops and fire shoots through my thigh. I fall onto my butt, my good arm flailing for something to grab so I don't tip into Dariellis's desk.

"Dude, are you okay?" she asks.

"Great." I lurch forward and grab my desk. I try to use it to stand up, but when I pull, it scoots toward me instead of providing support.

Dariellis offers her hand. I grit my teeth and ignore it. I manage to tip forward enough that I can stand. But I can't put much weight on my right knee. I sink into my chair, trying to disregard my pounding heart. The drill *sucked*, but at least it was a distraction from the fear that my body's going to fall apart bit by bit until I'm useless, stuck in a bed forever, in pain and unable to help myself or to experience going to the bathroom like a normal human does.

I lurch my desk back into position and pull my folder out of my bag.

After class, Mrs. Cisneros asks me to see her before I leave. I jam my stuff into my bag, hoist it painfully onto my good shoulder, and limp to the front of the room. I could use the backpack's wheels and pull it, but it makes me look and feel weak, and I've had enough of that lately to last a lifetime.

"Are you all right?" she asks. "I saw you tip over when you came in. I'm glad Dariellis was there to offer you a hand."

"I'm fine." And I *didn't* need Dariellis's hand.

She waits a moment, like she's trying to decide if I'm lying. "Your work recently hasn't been up to your usual standards. Would you like to talk about what's bothering you?"

I laugh and point at my sling. "Like this? Or thinking I was about to get shot yesterday?"

She gives me a look of sympathy mixed with exasperation. It reminds me of Mom. "Things were slipping a bit before your surgery."

Ugh. I thought the increasing brain space I've had to devote to managing pain for the last half year had only affected the math part of my mind. I don't want to drop to lower levels of my other classes too. "Nope. Everything's fine. Can I go? I don't want to miss the bus." It's gonna be a chore to get there on time with my knee hurting like this.

"I know you're tough, Avery. I like that about you. But don't be so tough that you don't accept help when you need it."

Is she in league with Tuney and Mom? "I don't need help."

She presses her lips together the same way Mom does when the conversation isn't going how she wants it to. "In that case, I'd like to see a return to your As and Bs before the end of the year. Think you can manage that?"

Okay, now I'm just mad. "Yeah. Can I go?"

She sighs. "Sure."

Of course I miss the freaking bus. It takes forever to limp to my locker and then to the building doors, where I watch the last bus pull away. I bite back a cuss word and push through the heavy door with a grunt. I walk to one of the big concrete balls that prevent terrorists or whatever from driving into the building with a trunk full of bombs. The ball is painted our school colors of red and yellow, which gives it an unfortunate McDonald's vibe. Chewed-up gum is stuck all over one side of it.

Before, I would've hopped up and sat on it, even though we're not supposed to. Today I lean on it and take my phone out to call Tuney and tell her I'll need a ride home when she gets off work.

Movement catches my eye and I look up. Helen is hauling butt toward the pickup line, dragging her big ol' trombone case. She stops at the curb next to a girl with her back to me. The girl is wearing a shirt the same shade of blue as the one Sarah had on in math class today. She turns and—

Gulp. It's Sarah.

I need to know why she never answered my note. Even if she says, *Sorry, I don't want to hang out with you,* at least I'll know the deal.

It takes a moment to drum up my courage to face what might be a rejection. I start walking, doing my best to hide my limp.

I reach Sarah as a few cars pull into the lot. "Hey," I say. "You never answered my note."

She laughs nervously. "Yeah, um, I got distracted."

"By the threat of imminent death?" I ask with a grin that feels fake. "I can't imagine how that was distracting." Maybe if I'm funny, she'll want to hang out.

"It was slightly nerve-racking." She tucks a strand of hair behind her ear and I try not to stare at her delicate wrist. Her eyes follow a maroon sedan. "My ride's here."

"Lucky you. I missed the bus." I waggle my phone. "I was about to call Tuney when I saw you."

"Who's Tuney?"

"My mom. One of my moms." I guess if she's gonna react to that, it's better to get it over with.

But she just nods as the maroon car pulls up to us. "Um . . . where do you live? Maybe we could give you a ride?"

"Oh my gosh, that'd be so great. Otherwise I'm stuck here till four thirty."

"Well. My brother—James, that's him—likes any excuse to drive." She points at the high school kid behind the wheel.

I grin. "Awesome. I live in Sycamore Valley."

"We're in Glensprings. Not too far out of the way, I think." She opens the back door. "James, this is Avery. She missed the bus. Can we give her a ride?"

"Sure!" The kid is thin and pale like Sarah, with a wild cowlick making a chunk of his light brown hair stick up in the back. He has a round face and doesn't look old enough to drive, despite his obvious height—there's barely any space between the top of his head and the car ceiling. He's wearing a private-school uniform.

My mood dips at the sight of it. If Mason really does go to private school next year, he'll have to wear a uniform like that.

But he's *not* gonna go to private school, and I *won't* have to go to Maple Creek High without him. I'm going to figure out how to fix that.

"You can have the front seat," Sarah says. "Do you

need help with your bag?"

"Nope. Thanks, though." We clamber into the car. I haul my backpack in and turn it sideways so it fits in the cramped floor space.

James holds out his hand to shake mine, then notices the sling. "Ooh, bummer 'bout the busted wing. What happened?"

"Fell off my dirt bike." Whoops. I should've stuck to the monkey-bars story. I don't think Sarah would rat me out to my parents, but better safe than sorry.

"Wicked." James makes a you-rock sign. "I mean, like, sorry you got hurt. But you should teach Sarah to ride a dirt bike. She could use some toughening up." He grins at his sister in the rearview mirror. "Eh, Sunshine?"

"I'm plenty tough," Sarah says as I struggle with the seat belt.

Sunshine?! Holy heck, I *love* that. It completely suits her.

James shoves my hand away and clicks my belt in with a quick, fluid motion. "What's your address, dirt-biker babe with the dope piercings?"

"James!" Sarah says. "Avery, I'm sorry. He has no filter."

"Filters are for coffee and fish tanks and car engines," James says. "Not humans."

I can't help laughing. James is forward but likable. I tell him my address.

He tries to peel out of the parking lot. But the wheels just spin in place for a second and then the car moves forward at a normal pace.

Sarah stifles a sigh in the back seat. I fail to hide my grin.

14
Sarah

Thurs., May 2, 3:18 p.m. James and Avery are hitting it off so well I feel like I don't belong in this car. They've been talking about music for five minutes. They both love Alan Walker, NF, and AViVA, none of which I know.

Now they're talking about books. Percy Jackson stuff and the Wings of Fire series. Neither of which I've read.

Now they're talking about movies and TV shows. "Divergent," "The Umbrella Academy," "Stranger Things." All stuff I haven't seen because Mom and Dad say I'm too young. What even are Demodogs and Mind Flayers and nail bats?

Now James is talking about some "Stranger Things" girl named Robin. Who—

Okay, whoa, Avery said is hot.

So Avery is gay? Or bi? James just said, "Dude,

you're gay? Me too!" And Avery said, "I'm as straight as a pink unicorn running up a rainbow," and now they're cracking up.

That note about coming to her house. Was that like . . . did she mean as a <u>date</u>?

Oh my gosh.

Avery is acting like she feels awkward. Like . . . she let something slip?

James has boy friends. Like, friends who are boys. So maybe it wasn't meant as a date.

But—well, then why <u>not</u>?

Oh, right. Because I'm a mousy introverted Spirograph addict with panic attacks and Avery is a dirt-biking tough-chick drummer who's afraid of nothing.

Except getting shot. She was so afraid of that, she cried.

I don't think three deep breaths would've helped her yesterday. I tried it again today, in French class when I thought about Fern getting sick and then again at lunch when I accidentally looked in the bucket where everyone dumps their drinks so they can put the bottles and cartons in the recycling. The breaths worked when I was thinking about Fern. But not when I saw that disgusting liquid mix that looked like . . . okay, I need to think about something else.

I just got my Bible out of my bag and looked for a verse to use for the tip about repeating a mantra. I think the first part of 1 John 4:18 will be good:

"Perfect love casts out all fear." It will remind me to focus on what and who I love instead of on what I'm scared of.

I've been thinking about what I can do to help everyone feel better about the drill, other than praying. Maybe I can make a flyer or poster or something protesting the drill. Or asking Mr. Ritter to never do it again. But I don't know what I would put on it, or how I would distribute it. That might involve talking to people. Which, yikes.

A text just came in from Luci. She must be at lunch. It's her usual response to the daily sunflowers photo, an emoji string of plants and hearts. And she asked if I showed Mrs. Gianno my art.

It felt good to finally answer "Yes!" I told her how Mrs. Gianno asked if I traced my designs from a book, and that I said I did them myself and Mrs. Gianno looked surprised and said they were "quite lovely."

It felt great to hear that. It felt like the day I realized I can make Celtic knots with Spirograph. I love how the tiny puzzles weave in and out of themselves, the way my thoughts do. Luci wrote back. "You were good at art before I moved. And now you're 🌟🔥🌟🔥🌟 !!!"

I told Luci that Mrs. Gianno said I have a good eye for balance. But then she said my art is flat symbols that represent things. Leaves, trees, flowers. She said she could see hints of my style developing, and that if I want to advance, I should try new styles and new subjects. Especially drawing from life. She said that drawings become <u>art</u> when they have an emotional component that shows the viewer why the artist chose the subject they did.

I don't know if I get it, though. I think a drawing is <u>good</u> when it looks like the thing you were trying to draw. So I just smiled and said, "Okay."

She said what every kid <u>loves</u> to hear: "You'll understand it more when you're older."

Which felt insulting. Was she saying my drawings are pretty symbols that lack emotion? What's wrong with pretty designs? Drawing them makes me feel good. Sometimes I'm happy with the result, but that's not the point. The point is to use creativity to feel better.

It doesn't always work great, though. Like how it seems lately that praying doesn't work.

I sent Luci a photo of the Conté pencil and blender Mrs. Gianno gave me. "She said I should give these a try. IDK how to use them tho."

Luci's not answering. I guess her lunch break is over and she's back in class.

I still wish I could talk to her about the drill. But it would stress her out.

We're in Avery's neighborhood now. The houses are, as James just said, "off the <u>hook</u>." We're pulling into the driveway of a house that could fit three of ours into it. Maybe four. Maybe it's a mansion.

So. Avery is rich. And gay. And has two moms.

She and James are exchanging social info so he can send her music. And now they're talking about Principal Ritter. Avery said she hates him.

Aaaaand that's all it takes. James is off on his Ritter Rant.

One more thing they have in common. Maybe Avery would rather be BFFs with my brother than with me. She sure is lit up talking to him.

Oh, interesting—Avery just told James she's going to find a way to make sure a drill like that never happens again.

Hmm. That's kind of like my goal of wanting to help everyone recover from it.

I wonder . . . is there a way we could combine our goals?

15

Avery

Who knew Sarah had a brother who's gay and *cool as heck*??? Wonders will never cease.

As we're finishing dinner, Mom asks how my day was. As usual, I say, "Fine."

"C'mon, kid, give me something to work with," Mom says. "It had to be better than yesterday, right?"

"Low bar." I stab a Brussels sprout.

"How are the other kids handling it?" Mom asks. "How's Mason?"

"Everyone's avoiding thinking about it." Not me, though. I'm going to fix the scared eyes and jumpiness and the weird, shrill laughs from Bree and Dariellis and lots of other kids at lunch. I'm going to fix Mason's silence. I just have to figure out *how*.

Tuney spreads butter on a chunk of French bread. "You look mad," she tells me.

I swallow. "How was *your* day, Mom?" I ask.

"Oh, you know." She spins her fork through her fingers like it's a tiny baton. "Did a little underwater basket weaving, rode a unicorn, saved the world. The usual."

"C'mon, kid, give me something to work with," I say.

"Fine, I finished a spreadsheet I've been working on for two weeks, spent an hour in a meeting that could've been an email, and ate the last croissant in the break room."

"Wow, so work-ey. Much excite."

"You know you can't wait to grow up." She checks her smartwatch, then eats her last bite of rice and gets up to rinse her plate. "Sorry to eat and run, but acro starts in twenty." She kisses the top of my head. "Sure you're okay?"

What am I going to do, say no? "I'm fine, Mom. Go do your weird stretching thing."

"Acro isn't stretching. It's a beautiful art form." She heads upstairs to change into her workout clothes.

I ask Tuney if Mom is the one who lies on the mat or the one who does all the moves. Mom took up acro a few months ago after she got bored with CrossFit. Before that, she went through a Peloton phase, and before that, trail running. It's no mystery where my gotta-move-around nature comes from.

Tuney waits until she's finished chewing, because, as she likes to say, *I am a* lady, *thank you much.* "She does the moves. Putting her old dance skills to use, I guess."

"Mom was a dancer? When?"

"Before we had you, she taught a Zumba class for retirees. And she did modern dance in college for about ten minutes."

I can't help giggling. The image of younger Mom teaching old ladies how to shake their booties to salsa music is too good. "Can I go do my PT?" It'll get me out of clearing the table.

Tuney's already reaching for the laptop she left leaned against a table leg. "Go for it."

I settle in front of the TV for my exercises. I'd much rather go upstairs and drum the part Carson's screwing up, just so I can hear it done *right* and drive out his *wrong* version looping through my head like an earworm from hell. But instead, it's me and this half-pound weight, duking it out yet again.

While I'm on my side, lifting the dumb thing over and over, James sends me an invite to his Discord server. I grin and sit up. We exchange a bunch of *Stranger Things* memes, then he sends a GIF of Lucas flinging a firework at the Mind Flayer with his wrist rocket and says, *This is what Ritter the Rat deserves for scaring the crap out of Sunshine. That godawful drill is NOT helping her panic attacks.*

Sarah has panic attacks? She was so calm when we were under the desk. And every other time. If she's sitting in front of me in class having a freak-out, she's good at hiding it.

Some parents want to sue Ritter, I write. *Or I guess it's the school they want to sue.*

That's not enough, he says. *Ritter deserves worse.*

Way worse. He yelled at me and my BFF in front of everyone after we laughed during the last drill. I was only trying to help Mason stop stressing. I send James a screen grab of a photo of Ritter from the school website and add a GIF of exploding fireworks. *BOOM. Somebody should blast fireworks outside dude's bedroom window at night. Give him a dose of his own medicine!*

For real. Like Sarah's freak-outs needed more fuel. He sends a photo of Sarah pushing a baby in a swing. She's smiling and her hair is glowing from the setting sun behind her. *The girl is honestly too pure for this world.*

Would it be weird to make this photo my phone wallpaper?

Yes. It would. Especially if she saw it.

I'll just download and favorite it so I can find it

whenever I want. *Is the baby your sister? Brother?* I ask James.

One of the kids our mom babysits. Sarah's good with them.

Of course she is. I bet animals instinctively trust her too.

You know . . . James writes. *We could actually make that fireworks idea happen.*

My mind lurches into overdrive. *Seriously?*

I know where Mom hides the car keys at night.

I sit up straight.

If we did this, it would force Ritter the Rat to understand what he put us through. It might even make him apologize, like Mr. Trevino and the other teachers did, and promise that Maple Creek will never run another drill that makes us think we're going to die.

If he does *that* . . . maybe Mason can stay in the Maple Creek district.

Creative + Strategic Problem-Solving win. *Mason's brother has a friend who likes to brag about his secret fireworks stash*, I write, my heart pounding with excitement. *Maybe I can get a couple big mortars off him.* Xavier's friend Brad, a tall white dude with an overbite, is at their house all the time, and he isn't immune to cash bribes. Last fall I convinced him to give me and Mason a lift to an R-rated Halloween horror movie with a twenty-dollar bill Tuney had given me for my lunches for the week. I stashed some protein bars in my bag and ate those for a few days instead of a real lunch. It was so worth it. Even though I got gnarly nightmares from the movie and the protein bars turned out to be fiber bars that caused gas so heinous it could've slayed Satan himself.

James replies: *You get the fireworks, I'll come up with a strategy. Deal?*

My stomach dips. He's the first person to take me seriously when I've talked about revenge. And he has access to a car.

This . . . could happen. I could feel in control of my life for the first time in *months*. It won't fix my messed-up flesh prison, but man, it would feel *so good* to shove Ritter's cruelty back in his face. It'd feel way better than these nugget-futting PT exercises that seem totally useless. *I'm so in*, I write. Mason's coming over tomorrow night, but I should be able to score an invite to his house sometime this weekend, and Brad will likely be there because he's always there on the weekends. *Think we can make it happen next week?* I still want to hang out with Sarah this weekend too. If she wants to, that is. And while I don't plan to get busted for this . . . well, it's probably a majorly bust-able offense. Legally, even.

Yikes. Could I go to jail?

No way. It's just loud sounds. Like the drill was just loud sounds. And Ritter didn't go to jail for unleashing those on us.

Next week totally, James writes.

My heart thumps harder. I've never snuck out at night. I've done other stuff I'm not supposed to, like riding the dirt bikes without asking. But this is some next-level shenanigans.

I grin. It's like high school shenanigans. And hey, I'm almost a high schooler. Might as well get a jump on things. *Excellent*, I respond. *Can't wait!*

LMK what fireworks you manage to snag, he writes. *I'll ask around too.*

I hope he's discreet about "asking around." But I kinda don't care if he's not.

I'm so excited after our conversation that I abandon my boring PT exercises. I limp upstairs to Galien and attempt to pound out a rhythm. The only part I can keep steady without twisting into a position that hurts my shoulder and sternum is the kick drum. But the solid, steady *boom* of it gives me just enough satisfaction that I feel, for a brief few moments, like I might actually make it back to being happy-active *me* again. To doing all the tree climbing and trampoline jumping and dirt biking with Mason that kept me sane before this mess put a hitch in my giddy-up.

The kick-drum rush isn't a whole entire good feeling. It's like 20 percent of a good feeling. But it's more than I've had in a while.

I've missed it.

It takes me until bedtime to realize that if Sarah finds out about what James and I are planning, it'll wreck my chances with her—as a friend or as something more. She doesn't exactly seem the type to enact a revenge plot. If I told her about it, she'd probably look at me with some sweetly heartbreaking mix of pity and disappointment.

So I'll just have to make sure she doesn't find out.

PART II

Avery

Hurt + Hope

Sarah

Symbols + Symptoms

16
Sarah

Thurs., May 2, 5:02 p.m. I only have a minute since Mom needs help with the kids so she can start dinner. Ruthie and I just had the <u>best</u> time. She needed fossils for a science project, so even though the babysitting kids were like "Whee, it's bonkers o'clock!", Mom said I could take Ruthie to the creek.

We spent a whole hour there and it was <u>GREAT</u>. Ruthie got all the fossils she needed and I found lots of creek glass, little colorful pieces worn smooth by the water and sand and rocks. I know our little creek so well, all the bends and twists it takes through our neighborhood. Even so, every time we followed a curve and came to a still pool, I felt that going-exploring feeling I loved so much when I was a kid. I <u>still</u> love it, and I love seeing Ruthie feel it. It fills me up with happiness and hope. I took lots of photos of plants so I can draw them later.

And I took a selfie of me and Ruthie with creek-clay stripes on our faces like we were football players. I sent it to Luci and she sent back a pic of her grinning face with stripes made of unicorn stickers and it was almost like she was there with us.

Maybe me and Ruthie's happiness will leak out of us and get all over James and our parents and they won't argue.

Thurs., 7:10 p.m. No dinner meltdowns! A miracle!

But I'm panicky anyway, because of a new development in my summer plans. Or rather, my parents' summer plan for me. Apparently I'm going to the Roselawn STEM Camp for Girls because I need to "get up to speed" in math and science before high school next year. And it's downtown, and I'll have to ride the city bus there and back. Alone. They paid the down payment on Monday, and with Dad's next paycheck they'll pay the rest.

There are not words for how freaked out I am about this. I did twelve deep breaths. It didn't help. I said "This is temporary" aloud like ten times. Helped a little. Not enough.

Maybe if I make a list. Like a list of my fears, so I can get them out of my head and see if they're all that scary.

I'm so bad at math and science. I'm going to suck at whatever I'm supposed to do at camp.

I have to ride the bus???? Alone??? With grown-ups???

I have to walk through downtown to get there??? Alone??? How will I know where to go?????????? What if someone tries to talk to me?????

Will I have <u>homework</u>? What if it eats all my art time?

If I'm too busy/stressed to do art, and I have to do science and math all day while I'm dealing with panic attacks, I just, how am I going to

7:23 p.m. For future reference: making a list of fears does not help.

My Spirograph addiction is going to reach new heights. Assuming I have time for it, between camp and panicking and helping Mom and having homework. This thorny mess is pushing "help everyone recover from the drill" right out of my head.

I keep looking out my window at the little sunflowers. I'm not going to bother Luci with my problems. After dinner, I found a message from her that said Mateo got detention again and Uncle David is furious.

I just tried "Come back to your senses." Five sights, four sounds, three things I can touch, two smells, one taste. The basement smells like mildew. All I taste is fear.

I could handle this if I was as calm as Dad, or as brave as James or Avery. If I was brave instead of mousy, I could tell Mom and Dad I'd rather help Mom babysit. Or go to an art camp. But I can't imagine telling them that. Mom was so firm about the camp when she explained it as Ruthie and I were loading the dishwasher. Dad nodding behind her as he wiped off the table. Ruthie interrupted with, "No fair! I want to go to a STEM camp!"

Dad said gently, "You don't need it, pumpkin. Sarah does."

It's like the part of my brain that should be able to do math and science is missing. Or maybe the art part is hogging too much space. I look at numbers and variables and the periodic table and equations and diagrams of food chains and my brain goes all swimmy and won't hold on to anything. It's like trying to build a Lego house with Legos made of Play-Doh.

Aaaaaand three deep breaths and some art so I won't panic again.

Okay, I think breathing deep turned the fear down. A little. It didn't end it, but it was something to focus on that isn't certainty that my heart will malfunction under the strain my fear is putting on it. And then I got out of it a bit faster by using the senses tip to focus on the Spirograph art taped to my walls.

I need all the panic to just <u>stop</u>. Like right now. These baby steps aren't enough.

When I went upstairs to sit on the porch and look up into the branches of the oak tree in our front yard and breathe, I noticed the mail had come. I took it out of the mailbox and promptly had a mini freak-out. There was an envelope from Roselawn STEM Camp for Girls with "Schedule Enclosed" on the outside in red.

I thought about trashing it. But then Mom would send me downtown on the bus with no schedule and I'd have to explain to someone at the camp that I didn't have one. So I sent a pic of the envelope to Luci and wrote, "Help, my summer just got eaten by math and science!" Then I put the envelope on the table with the other mail. It weighed a thousand pounds and sucked all the light out of everything.

I shouldn't have bothered Luci.

7:46 p.m. I didn't think it could get more stressful than the STEM camp. But it did.

After I helped Ruthie with her homework at the kitchen table, Mom sat next to me with a look of concern that immediately made me worry.

She started by apologizing for being so busy. She said I'm the kid who gets the least attention because I cause the least problems, but that she wants to change that. To make sure I get what I need too. She hugged me and thanked me for my help with the babysitting kids.

That part felt good.

The next part did not.

She said she's been thinking about what I said about being scared all the time now, and that she wants to help me. That she thought she'd found a way.

For a minute, I felt hopeful. Like maybe she'd say something more than "Pray about it."

I should've known better. She said she's taking me to the hospice with her this weekend to read the Bible to dying people.

I froze. I think she wanted me to say, "Yes, that sounds like it will help me." But I sat there like a statue, failing to breathe three deep breaths or any way at all.

Dad came in from the living room and saw me frozen. He said, "Sunshine? You okay?"

I tried to shake it off. But all I could think was that

it's going to be like watching Aunt Camila die all over again. Smelling chemically sickness smells. Listening to air wheezing in and out of lungs. When I told Mom and Dad about the panic, I didn't tell them it's hyperfocused on sickness and dying. "I'm okay," I said in a croaky voice.

Mom put her hand on my arm and looked at my face. Really <u>looked</u> at me. She said, "It might seem counterintuitive, but going to hospice always makes me feel better. I think it'll do the same for you."

Dad said, "I agree. It's a great opportunity, honey. And afterward, if the weather's good for it, I'll take you to the park and we'll fly the dolphin kite. Okay?"

I just nodded. Mom hugged me again and said "I love you" and then went to watch TV. I came downstairs to my room to freak out all over this journal.

I can't tell Luci I'm terrified of hospice. She literally <u>watched her mom die</u>. She doesn't need to hear me whining about reading to a dying stranger.

But I <u>really</u> need someone to talk to.

8:02 p.m. I just did something risky (brave? stupid?) because . . . I don't know.

Because I need a friend.

I asked Mom if Avery could come for an overnight tomorrow. Even knowing Avery has a disease. Even though we might become friends and I might lose her like I've mostly lost Luci.

I asked anyway.

Mom still had worry on her face when she looked at me. I guess that's why she said yes right away. She didn't even ask what church Avery goes to, which she always asks when any of us wants to have a new friend over.

I immediately regretted asking. Because <u>disease</u>. Because <u>losing people</u>. Because <u>wow</u> I had too much stress already and it suddenly seemed foolish to add this in too. Like it won't be a distraction. Just more freak-out fuel.

But.

Maybe, maybe . . . if I spend Friday night and Saturday morning with Bravery-Avery . . . maybe I'll be up to handling hospice. Maybe I won't have a panic attack in front of a dying person who doesn't deserve to have one of their last sights be a thirteen-year-old losing her mind. Maybe Avery and I can find a way to work together on my hazy, not-yet-formed plan to help everyone recover from the drill. Working on something together could be a good distraction from all this stuff churning in my mind.

I just texted James and asked him for Avery's number. I have to get past this fear that Avery and I will become friends and she'll die of whatever her disease is, or she'll move away. Then I have to get past the fear of asking her if she wants to come over. I have to brace for a yes or a no, both of which have their downsides.

The Conté pencil and blender Mrs. Gianno gave me are on my nightstand. I haven't had time to look up how to use them. What if I'm awful at it? I feel like Mrs. Gianno expects me to create something good with them. I don't have room in my head right now to add in the fear of disappointing her.

Dad told me two years ago, when I was nervous about leaving elementary school and starting seventh grade, that middle school can be tough.

He was not wrong.

I forgot to grow out
of poking under rocks
at the creek
searching for bugs and slugs
and slick-slimy salamanders
sunlight and wonder
always around the next bend
But maybe that's okay
because Avery forgot to grow out
of burping the alphabet
and singing "It's Raining Tacos"
and hiding her enthusiasm for Pop Rocks
So maybe that means
we are the same
in one small way
And you can base a whole
entire
friendship
on that
(I hope)

17

Avery

"Yes!" I shout at my phone when I get Sarah's text. "Yes yes yes!"

Tuney sticks her head into my room, where I'm watching YouTube meme reels and halfheartedly doing the PT exercises I abandoned earlier. "The heck you yelling about, child?"

"Can I spend the night at Sarah's tomorrow night? Please please pretty please?"

"I thought Mason was coming over for pizza and Marvel Trivial Pursuit."

Oops, forgot. "Can we do that Saturday?" I still need to score an invite to Mason's this weekend so I can ask that Brad dude about fireworks.

"Saturday Mom and I have a date and you're going

to Grandma Hart's. Who's Sarah again?" Tuney comes in and sits on my floor. "Fix that, please." She points at my W legs. Tank ambles over and flops down with his giant head in her lap.

I move my legs. "She's a girl in my math class. An artist. I asked if I could have her over to watch a Miyazaki movie, remember?"

"Oh, right. The *cute* one. With the French braid."

My face flushes. "Tuney! I just want to be her friend."

"Sure. The same way you wanted to be *friends* with Tris from the beach."

"This is totally different. Tris was—"

"Gorgeous? Too old for you? I'm just giving you grief, child. Settle down." Tuney lies on her back and pulls Tank closer. "You sure you want to ditch Mason for a girl? He might not be too happy about that."

"He'll understand." He usually does when I change plans at the last minute.

"Then work it out with him. I'll run it by your mom. In the meantime, get Sarah's parents' numbers so we can digitally meet them." She takes out her phone. "What's her last name? I'll see if they're in the MCMS Facebook group."

"Bell." I don't meet Tuney's eyes. I'm pretty sure she doesn't know I snooped her Facebook, but I still feel guilty. I reply to Sarah: *Tuney said yes but has to check* with Mom. *Can I get your parents' numbers? Or one of them? I think my moms wanna make sure y'all aren't cereal killers or anything.*

Serial, Sarah writes.

lol I know, I'm just being silly.

Oh right.

Sometimes I forget my humor doesn't translate over text. I've accidentally offended Mason a couple of times that way. Lucky for me, he's quick to forgive.

"Oof, Tank, you gotta move." Tuney shifts him next to her. "I don't see anyone with the last name 'Bell' in the Facebook group." Tank steps on her chest and she howls. "Tank, off! I need that for boobing with!"

"Pretty sure Tank doesn't care about your lady parts." I write to Sarah: *What time? If my mom says yes?*

Six-thirty.

Man, she's terse. *Should I bring anything? A few Miyazaki Blu-rays?*

We only have a DVD player.

How many times can I put my foot in my mouth in one conversation? All the times. *I'll see what we have. Anything else? Sleeping bag?*

A warm one. My room is the basement right now and the floor is cold.

Right now? Are you getting your house remodeled or something?

Three bedrooms, five people. We take turns. It's my year for the basement.

Ah, got it. I want to ask her a million questions about her life, about her parents, about whether sleeping in a basement is the reason she's always sniffly. But I don't want to seem nosy. I send the crossed-fingers emoji with *I'll let you know what Mom says.*

Then I text Mason and tell him something came up and I can't do pizza night tomorrow but maybe we can hang at his house sometime this weekend. All he says in reply is *K*.

So I guess it's okay.

Mom said yes. I'm over the moon and also worried, because it occurred to me that I have a hard enough time in a cushy bed with this ridiculous sling, so a sleeping bag on carpet is gonna be a real challenge.

I'll make it work.

Friday morning, I'm jittery with excitement. Mom worked out the details with Sarah's mom last night. Tuney's going to bring me to Sarah's after my five o'clock PT appointment. Hopefully I won't be too exhausted from it.

General arts second period is, as usual, a disaster. We're making fake stained glass with colored tissue paper and card stock that we cut holes in with an X-Acto knife last week. I couldn't hold the paper down while I was cutting, so mine looks like it was done by a preschooler. Mrs. Gianno says she's grading me on effort not output right now. But it's still embarrassing to produce something so bad. The whole exercise feels pointless. The class drags. I try to make the time go faster by plotting a way to get that Brad guy to give me some firework mortars, but then I get so excited thinking about revenge that my hands shake and my project looks even worse.

The bell finally rings and I head to math, picking dried glue that looks like dried snot off my sling as I walk. I'm so focused on the glue that I fail to dodge a kid hurrying in the opposite direction. He clips my right shoulder.

I cry out at the shocking pain.

The kid turns and sneers at me. It's Logan Green, one of Jolene's friends. "Barely touched you, drama queen!" he yells as he hurries away.

I step out of the flow of kids and close my eyes, trying to breathe around how bad it hurts. *Sidestep*, I think at it. *Sidestep*.

I gulp air, trying to focus on breathing. But the pain is like fire, and I'm starting to cry.

Mason shows up at my side. "Aves? You okay?"

I can only grunt in response. I open and close my

left fist, my breath quivering in and out of me as I try to get the tears under control.

"You need to go to the nurse?"

I press my lips together and shake my head. A few more deep breaths and the pain comes down from an eight to a seven. "I'm okay," I gasp, but my throat's still tight and it comes out as *Ah-kee*. I try it again and it sounds more normal.

"Gimme your bag," Mason says.

"I don't need you to—"

"Don't be a stubborn butt." He tugs it off my good shoulder.

The pain drops to a six as the weight stops pulling at my left half. A sigh of relief comes out. "Thank you," I say.

"What happened?"

"Logan ran into me." I smear tears away. "I'm glad you came by. Thank you for reals."

"That dude sucks. He flicked an actual freaking booger at me in science the other day." He hauls my bag up and puts it on his unoccupied shoulder. "Now I'm balanced."

We start walking to math class. "I'm sorry about canceling tonight," I say.

"It's cool. I wasn't looking forward to getting out of my house or anything. It's not like my mom's been wound so tight she's basically stopped talking."

"Oof." Mason's mom goes very quiet when she's mad. It's a mystery to me how anyone can do that. When I'm ticked, it measures on the Richter scale. "She's still angry about the drill?"

"You have *no* idea. I think she's said like three words since she told me I'm . . ." He whacks a locker with his fist as we walk. "You know. Out of here."

"I heard some people are gonna sue the school," I say.

Mason's face gets the tight look that means he doesn't want to talk about whatever I said.

"Maybe if they do, it'll make your mom change her mind," I say. "I can't imagine next year without you."

"Why'd you cancel tonight, anyway?"

"Oh. Uh—" Dang. I haven't thought of a good reason. "Well . . ."

"Must be good if you can't even say it," Mason mutters.

"Do you want to hang out tomorrow afternoon instead? At your house?"

"I guess." He's built a mega-cool Minecraft town on his PS3 and we usually dink around in there for an hour making stuff. That's about as long as I can sit still before I gotta get up and pound out a drum rhythm on the TV stand or do a goofy rubber-limbed dance to the Minecraft music to spark his bright, contagious laugh.

We go into the math room as the bell rings. He drops my bag by my desk.

Sarah turns in her seat as Mr. Trevino closes the door. "I'm happy about tonight," she says with a smile. "I'm glad you can come."

My heart leaps. "Yay, me too!" Oops, too much enthusiasm.

Sarah turns around and Mr. Trevino starts taking attendance. I glance at Mason, who's looking at me like he's putting it together. *Tonight?* he mouths, pointing at Sarah.

My face burns. I shrug with my good shoulder and take my phone out. *She invited me over,* I text him. *And, you know, like . . . crushes make people kinda stupid?*

He turns away. But not before I see the disappointment in his eyes.

I'm sorry. You know I've been trying to figure out how she and I can hang for weeks now.

"Avery, put your phone away," Mr. Trevino says.

"Sorry." I tuck my phone into my bag as Jolene snickers.

Mason doesn't look at me the whole class period.

* * *

"Where's Mason?" I ask Bree and Dariellis when I sit next to them at lunch. For the first time ever, he isn't at our table.

"Haven't seen him," Bree answers.

I look all around the cafeteria. No Mason. I take my sandwich out of my bag and rub my aching knee under the table. I hope he's not hiding in the bathroom. He does that sometimes during classes when jerks like Jolene and her crew get to him. When they mock his lack of height and heft, or call him a broken record when he makes weird noises over and over. Or say that his voice sounds auto-tuned because it's high-pitched and kinda squeaky. Or call him "hyperactive adopted boy" because his white dad (who works part-time) makes it to more school functions than his Black mom (who works full-time). It drives him up the wall when they call him that.

I wish everyone could see what I see in him. I wish they could see how intent he is when he gets deep into something, like Minecraft. When he's not interested, his ability to focus goes out the window. He said once it's like his brain is made of water, and the surface of boring stuff, like schoolwork, is coated in oil. His mind just rolls off it, no matter how much he knows he needs to buckle down and get it done. His meds help, but the latest he can take them is lunchtime, because they keep him awake at night if he takes them any later. They wear off right when school lets out. Which means homework is heckin' *hard* for him.

He tries to get around the problem by getting up super early in the morning, taking his meds, and doing his homework on the bus. But he usually runs out of time and winds up with incompletes, which makes him look irresponsible when he's literally doing everything he can. Plus taking his morning meds early means they wear off before his lunchtime dose, so the classes right before and after lunch are extra tough to get through. And just for added fun, his meds kill his appetite 24-7, so food doesn't have much appeal—hence him being one of the shortest and skinniest kids in our grade, waiting anxiously for a puberty he once told me he's worried will never happen for him.

If people could see how hard he works just to break even with Bs and Cs, instead of seeing a hyper little goofball who's always talking or laughing when he shouldn't and failing to get his work done, maybe they'd stop being jerks to him. Maybe they'd stop making crappy racist assumptions that he acts the way he does because he's Black, instead of because he was literally born with a differently ordered brain. Maybe they'd get that he's fidgety and restless and makes strange sounds to let off the pressure from trying so hard to fit in.

I twist to crack my back for the fifth time today. Thinking about Mason is making me feel even worse about bailing on him. I try to joke with Bree and Dariellis, but they're obsessed with some tag trend and pay more attention to their phones than to my attempts to make them laugh. I keep rubbing my shoulder, trying to push the ache out. It hurts way more than it usually does during the school day. And I can't blame it on the weather this time.

I hope Logan didn't knock any internal stitches out. Naila will have a cow this afternoon if she thinks I did something to set myself back again.

It's starting to seem like I'll *never* make it to the arm bike.

Naila has a cow, because I can't do some of the exercises I could do last time. "What did you even *do* to yourself?" she finally asks. "It's like you're determined to go backward."

Her comment stings. "It's not my fault. A guy ran into me in the hallway." Anytime someone says *It's not my fault*, it's usually their fault. But I'm definitely the victim on this one.

She frowns. "Were you looking at your phone while you walked? You *really* need to pay attention to others so you can get out of their way."

"It was *my* way, not his." I'm glad Tuney's here with me instead of Mom, who would be on Naila's side. "And I was picking glue off my sling, for your information."

Naila raises an eyebrow. "Why was there glue—oh, never mind."

"It was important. I was about to see a cute girl and the glue looked like snot."

Naila's crankiness dissolves in a laugh. "All right, I'll get off your case. For now." She gestures to the cold seat. "Go sit. No sense pushing you through exercises that won't help you heal. I'll get you hooked up."

Sweet relief. I head over and sit in the padded office chair. Naila wraps the packs over my chest and shoulder and upper arm while she and Tuney talk about how cold it's supposed to get next week. Naila switches on the machine that pumps frigid water through the packs.

Slowly, as the cold works its magic and calms the angry heat from the PT session and getting run into by a large dude, the pain dissolves and I start to unwind. I usually look at my phone while the icy water does its work, but today I close my eyes and just enjoy it. Wishing I could ask Naila to wrap my knee too, because that pain is creeping up on the shoulder pain, trying to challenge it for first place. But I'm not ready to tell anyone yet that I've screwed up another joint. The last thing I need is *more* PT.

Just before the ten minutes are up, I text Mason. *I'm really sorry. Do you want to hang out tomorrow afternoon? You seemed maybe not too sure.*

Okay, he writes back. *If you're not too busy fangirling over Miss Pretty Blonde Braid.*

Don't call her that, I write. But then I erase it. *How's 1:00?* As soon as it sends, I remember I'll be at Sarah's, and I want to be there as long as possible. *I mean how's 3:00?*

Fine. See you then.

18
Sarah

Fri., May 3, 6:16 p.m. Avery's coming over in fourteen minutes. Approximately.

At lunch today, I finally focused enough to get some thoughts together about how I can help everyone. Every single kid hated the drill, but it seems like each is responding in their own way. We all went through it together, but we reacted individually.

I think that's making everyone feel alone. It's having that effect on me.

So it makes sense to aim my "help others" energy at ending the alone feeling. The one thing we all have in common, whether we reacted with fear or anger or sobbing or whatever, is a strong desire for there to never be a drill like that again.

I did some googling and found info on how bad it is for kids when shooter drills use simulated shooting and violence. If Avery and I work together, we could make a poster to put up at school that has the info I found. And we could put up a blank paper next to it that says, "Sign if you agree there shouldn't be any more realistic drills."

It could maybe give everyone a common focus. Like instead of being stuck in fear and reliving the drill, which I think lots of kids are doing, the poster would get everyone to talk about the future instead. And maybe having a common cause could make everyone feel less alone.

If I can convince Avery to apply her bold, brave brand of energy to this, I think we could come up with something really good. Something that might actually work, and encourage Mr. Ritter to never do a drill like that again.

It's either a great idea or a total long shot. I'm nervous Avery will think it's a long shot.

But I have to do <u>something</u>. When I think about Ruthie going through a drill like that, or about Luci being there for it, I get a lot more mad than I got for myself when I went through it.

Speaking of Ruthie, she wiped out in the driveway after school. She was kneel-riding James's old skateboard and her skirt caught in a wheel and she tipped forward and busted her chin open. So I was on my own for an hour with the babysitting kids while Mom brought her to Urgent

Care, and of course James didn't offer to help. Ruthie came home with two stitches she's very proud of and Mom came home looking tired. Mom took over watching the other two kids while I did my weekend homework with Layla in my lap trying to grab my pencil.

I probably didn't do a very good job on my homework. Especially math. It was hard to focus with so much in my head, plus an eighteen-month-old trying to eat my eraser, plus three-year-old Riley and two-year-old Grayson howling at each other over the Matchbox cars. I don't know how Mom spends all day with those kids without losing her mind. Two hours of them after school leaves me spent.

I cleaned my room after the kids all got picked up. I cleared off the desk, made the bed, and tucked Mom's adult coloring books into my nightstand. I put the Conté pencil in there too, because every time I look at it, I feel like a mouse. I tucked four bottles of hand sanitizer in different places so I can use them if her disease turns out to be contagious. Which I know is irrational, because she wouldn't be at school if she was contagious. But my brain is not exactly feeling rational.

My phone kept buzzing in my pocket during dinner, which was spaghetti and salad because it's always spaghetti and salad on Fridays. James told me most Catholics only do meatless Fridays during

Spiro-ghetti & Salad

Lent. Our family does it year-round.

Sometimes I think Mom is in an imaginary competition with the other moms at church to be some sort of Super-Catholic. Like she's trying to make up for her wild-child past before she met Dad and converted.

I did three-deep-breaths all through dinner because I was nervous the buzzing was Avery texting to say she couldn't come over. Part of me wished it was. Part of me prayed it wasn't. The rest of me hoped it was Luci, who never answered my text about STEM camp. Trying to breathe around the panicky feeling made it hard to eat. "Mom," I kept saying in my mind. "Mom. I need help. I'm scared."

She gave me the concerned look. The one she's been giving me since the drill. But she didn't say anything. She couldn't hear me, because I couldn't say the words.

The texts turned out to be Luci sending a pic of Diego falling into a ditch and then others of him covered in sand and looking mad, then sheepish. "Cast your peepers on this dingbat. He was trying to jump over the ditch and tripped on a cactus right when Mateo took the photo."

"I didn't think I'd miss them so much, but I do!" I wrote back. They felt like brothers. When they all moved, I lost a whole other family. (I almost wrote "whole nother." Why do people say that when no one writes it?)

My little sunflower plants look so small and spindly from down here in my room. I can't wait for them to grow into tall stalks heavy with big, colorful blooms. Sunflowers are hope, and summer, and the hope of summer. Luci's favorite season, and mine too. I want to reach into the future and grab summer with both my fists, yank it toward me, sink my teeth into it and pull it close. Pull it all the way to now.

Or I did until I found out about the STEM camp.

Oh gosh that's the doorbell.

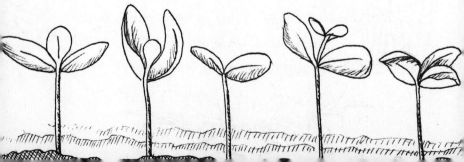

19

Avery

James answers the door and raises his hand for a high five. "What's up, strange thing?"

I put my duffel down and slap my left hand awkwardly against his raised right one. "Hi. Um, this is Tuney." I nod at her behind me. "Tuney, James." I already told him I have two moms and that one of them is trans. He said it was "wicked rad."

James flashes a peace sign at Tuney. "Nice to meet you, ma'am. Come on in." He opens the door wider and she gives him one of her million-watt smiles for calling her *ma'am*.

We step into their small living room, where a girl who looks about nine is on the brown carpet, focused intently on stapling some papers. Her tongue peeks out of her pursed lips. Fox News, which Tuney and Mom hate, is on with the volume low. The house smells like pasta.

The girl looks up. She has a big Batman Band-Aid covering most of her chin. "Are you Sarah's friend?" she asks.

"I hope so," I say. "I mean yes."

"Cool. Sarah needs a new friend. She's lonely now that Luci's gone."

Luci. That must be the dark-haired girl I used to see Sarah with at school.

A tired-looking woman with a long brown braid comes in, drying her hands on a dish towel. She does a double take at me, maybe because of the piercings and the sling, then quickly fakes a smile. "Hi," she says to Tuney. "You must be Mrs. Hart. I'm Chrissy." She drapes the dish towel over her shoulder and holds out her hand. Her pale pink T-shirt has a rose on it.

Tuney shifts my sleeping bag and shakes her hand. "Thanks for having Avery over. She's been talking non-stop about it since yesterday."

Sarah's mom keeps smiling, but not like she quite means it. She's sizing Tuney up—taking in her height, her broad shoulders. Her Adam's apple. She looks down at Tuney's size-eleven flats. "I like your skirt," she says. Like looking at Tuney's skirt was an excuse to check out her feet.

Tuney sets my sleeping bag down. "Thanks. It has pockets." As usual, she demonstrates by sticking her hands in them. She only buys skirts or dresses that have pockets, since, as she says, the fashion industry is run by patriarchal dipwads who leave pockets out of women's clothing so they can sell more purses and handbags. "When should I pick Avery up tomorrow?"

"Sarah and I are headed to volunteer at noon," Sarah's mom says. "How's ten o'clock?"

Shoot. I was hoping we could hang until right before I go to Mason's.

"Ten is fine." Tuney squeezes my good shoulder. "Okay, kiddo?"

"Just curious, what church does your family go to?" Sarah's mom asks.

"Oh, we're not religious," Tuney says.

Sarah's mom's face kinda falls. "That's too bad. St. Mary's is always open to new members if you'd like to join us. We have a youth group too. Sarah goes every Tuesday night." She nods at me. "Avery, maybe you'd like to join sometime?"

"Sure," I say as Sarah comes into the room.

"I'd like to know more about it before—" Tuney starts.

"I'll pick up a brochure for you at mass on Sunday," Sarah's mom interrupts. "Sarah, you can give it to Avery at school." She puts her arm around Sarah, who's wearing a fluffy white hoodie with a sunflower on it.

"You must be Sarah," Tuney says. "Nice to meet you."

"It's nice to meet you too, Mrs. Hart." She lifts her hand. It's shaky and she's way pale.

"Such polite kids." Tuney smiles as they shake hands. "Avery, take a page out of their book, will you?"

"I'm polite!"

"Sure you are. Well, thank you again, Mrs. Bell. Behave, kidlet."

"Like I wouldn't." At least she didn't call me *squirt*.

"Of course. You're an absolute angel at all times." She glances at a framed crayon drawing of an actual angel on the wall, then kisses my forehead. "Call if you need anything."

"Yes, ma'am."

"Pfft," Tuney says. "I bet you call all the nice old ladies 'ma'am.'" She gives me a careful side hug, then goes out the door.

Sarah's mom closes it behind her. "Sarah, you can show Avery your room, then please come back upstairs."

"Okay. Avery, please follow me." Sarah picks up my

duffel and sleeping bag.

"I can take those," I say.

"Oh. Um . . . this is lighter." Sarah sniffles a little and gives me my sleeping bag.

This already feels super awkward.

I follow her down the wooden basement steps, glad she's in front of me. My knee's so janky I have to go one step at a time like a little kid. It doesn't help that the steps are uneven.

When we reach the bottom, I look up, expecting to see her room's door. But there's no door. There's a laundry nook a few feet ahead of us, a doorless doorway to the left that opens on a room with a deep freezer and a bunch of storage bins, and . . . well, we're in Sarah's room, which is the space to our right.

The twin bed is covered with a colorful quilt that looks homemade. The floor isn't carpeted like I imagined; it's gray-painted concrete. There's a small white desk, a desk chair with a blue seat pad, a white bookshelf, and a banged-up white nightstand that has a framed photo of Sarah hugging the girl with the dark ponytail. Evening sunlight makes its way through the cloudy propped-open window near the ceiling, and a lamp with a light gray base lights the rest of the small space. A shelf along the pale yellow cinder-block wall holds clothes and books. A poster of a vibrant green forest scene hangs above the bed, and the rest of the walls are covered in taped-up Spirograph designs like the ones I saw in Sarah's journal.

"So . . . this is it." Sarah looks around the room like she's seeing it for the first time. "Is it the same size as your closet?"

"Just about." Oops, too honest. "Not that there's anything wrong with it," I say hurriedly. "It's . . . cozy. I like the splashes of color that cheer it up." Outside the window, I can see some small plants in a row, like someone planted them there. "What are those?"

"Sunflowers. But they might die in the cold snap next week." Sarah sits on her bed with her hands tucked under her thighs. "Um . . . what do your parents do? Do they have good jobs, since your house is so big?"

"My mom works at a nonprofit that helps homeless people get into affordable housing. Tuney does information systems consulting for giant companies that have lots of money."

"What's information systems?"

"Honestly? No idea. I think it has to do with data networks. She's tried to explain it to me like ten times and I still don't get it. Tuney's wicked smart."

"You're, um, really smart too. Is Tuney your real mom? Um, your biological mom?"

I love this question. It's so fun to mess with people. "Both my moms are my biological parents."

Sarah tilts her head. "But . . ."

I laugh. "Tuney transitioned when I was two. They tried to get me to call her 'Mommy Two' instead of 'Dad' but I couldn't talk that great yet and it turned into 'Tuney.'"

Sarah laughs too. "That's cute, actually." She tucks a wisp of blonde hair behind her ear. "We have to go back upstairs till bedtime. Okay?"

"Sure." I'd rather stay down here and talk to her, but I get the idea she isn't one to argue with her parents. "You made all these designs? They're super good." I point at the walls. "Do you have a giant Spirograph set?"

"Just this." She picks up a plastic bag with Spirograph pieces in it. "It was Dad's when he was a kid. It's missing pieces, but you can still make cool stuff with it if you take time to line up the numbers on the cogs how you want. Oh, and I have this." She rummages in a nightstand drawer and comes out with a small plastic box. She pops it open to reveal a plastic circle and cogs. "It's from the dollar store. I made those with it." She points at the designs above the lamp. They have more wiggly lines than the others.

"That's so cool. Spirograph is like art made of math."

She drops a cog like she's startled. "I never thought of it that way."

"Dude, your flower art is amazing. I could never draw anything so good."

She picks up the cog, blushing. "You could, though. Spirograph makes it easy. You just draw loops around the loops that are already there, and then triangles or hearts for the leaves."

I laugh. "You didn't do *that* with Spirograph." I point at a drawing of cherry blossoms.

"Well—it's just shapes, though. It's not hard."

"For you maybe."

Sarah puts the plastic box back in the nightstand. "We can hang out with Ruthie if you want. Maybe we could play some games?" She glances at my sling, then plucks a bottle of hand sanitizer from the top nightstand drawer. She uses it quickly and puts the bottle back.

That was weird. "Sure, games sound fun." We traipse up the steps, which is easier than going down them on my right knee. Before we reach the top, we can hear James arguing with a man I assume is Sarah's dad. The guy sounds calm and rational, but James is . . . not.

"I told him I'd meet him at seven," James nearly shouts. "I need to leave!"

"And as soon as you've finished your chores, you can

go," the guy says. "As discussed."

"You don't! Understand! Anything!" James yells. "You don't *get* me! I need to be with people who do!"

"Let's see what Ruthie's doing." Sarah leads me down a hallway with family photos in tarnished gold frames on the walls. As the argument rages, Sarah knocks on a door that's open a few inches and then slips inside, motioning me to follow. She closes the door as soon as I'm in. "Hey, Ruthie," Sarah says. "What are you up to?"

Ruthie's on her bed with a marker and the papers she was stapling. "Pretending I live somewhere else," she says without looking up.

"This is Avery," Sarah says. "Remember, I told you she was coming ov—"

"Oh yeah!" Ruthie bounces up and bounds toward the foot of the bed like she's going to jump off into my arms. I take a quick step back.

"Ruthie, no!" Sarah quickly steps between us and catches her. "Avery broke her arm."

"Dislocated shoulder, actually," I say. "Hi, Ruthie."

"Hi, Avery. I broke my arm once. And now I have two stitches." She points at her chin.

"What happened?"

"Skateboard," she says like that explains everything.

"Ah, yes," I say. "They bite if you don't watch out.

What are you working on?"

"Chipstritch versus bumblephant." Ruthie flops out of Sarah's arms onto the bed, grabs the bundle of paper, and hands it over. "Wait!" She snatches it back and does some folding, then re-presents me with it. It's now a book. "Sit. Read." She points at the bed.

"Chipstritch versus . . . oh, bumblephant. I see." The cover has an animal with a chipmunk body and an ostrich head battling a bee with an elephant's head. "Did you draw these? They're great." I sit on her bed with my legs in a W since no one will lecture me for it.

"Sunshine did. She's good at art. I'm good at coming up with animals, and we're both good at writing the stories." The yelling from the kitchen escalates, followed by pounding footsteps and a slamming door.

"Do they always get along so well?" I ask as Sarah says, "Ruthie has a great imagination."

There's an awkward silence. I try not to think about what would happen if Sarah—*Sunshine*, aaaah that's *so cute*—found out what James and I are planning.

"Yes, it's always like that," Ruthie says. "And I *do* have a great imagination." She takes the book back, opens to the first page, and smooths the papers on my lap. "Read."

"Every Midland Match begins with a battle of the

152

bongos," I read aloud. I smile at Ruthie. "I play the bongos, you know."

"No way! Do you have some? Will you teach me?"

"Well, I used to play. And the kettledrum and the bells and the glockenspiel and the drum kit. I have all those except a kettledrum. But I'm on a break till my shoulder's healed."

"Oh. You can't play with one hand?"

"Not so much. I used to think drums would be the easiest instrument to learn. But then I learned drumming is a full-body experience." One I miss so bad my teeth ache with it. I turn to the next page, where the chipstritch and the bumblephant are now wielding Nerf battle-axes. "Once the bongo battle decides who will strike first, the animals take their positions."

Sarah looks embarrassed. "This is kind of silly. You don't have to read it."

I laugh. "Are you kidding? I love this."

"We have to write the ending when we get to it," Ruthie says. "It's not finished."

So that's what we do. Ruthie is a hoot, almost funny enough to make me wish I had a sibling. As the book goes on, other animal hybrids join the battle, which is to determine who gets to be the Almighty Chief Pumpkin Flinger of Destiny, a position that changes hands at each full moon and serves to punish anyone caught stealing chicken nuggets from the local nugget dispensary.

After we write the end of the story (the bumble-phant sucks a row of clementines into his trunk and blasts the chipstritch until the chipstritch topples into a mud puddle), we play Trouble and Uno and Sorry!, then a drawing game that results in some extremely silly pictures. Ruthie shows me other books she and Sarah have made, all of them about animal mashups like penguin-geckos ("Pengeckos!" Ruthie says proudly) and squirrel-rabbits ("Squabbits!") and hummingbird-rats ("Hummerats!"). I forget we're hanging out with a fourth grader until Sarah's mom pops her head in at nine and tells us it's time to get ready for bed.

While we're brushing our teeth, I fake putting toothpaste on my brush because I suck at left-handed brushing and usually get toothpaste on my face. Sarah doesn't need to see that. "Do you always go to bed so early on the weekends?" I ask.

She spits in the sink and rinses her brush. "We get to stay up late on weekends."

This is late? Dang. "What time do you go to bed on weeknights?" I try to screw the cap back on the tooth-paste but drop it between the toilet and sink, crammed together in this tiny box of a room. "Shoot. Sorry."

"Eight forty-five." She retrieves the cap and rinses it. "What time do you go to bed?"

"Nine thirty on weeknights. Whenever I want on weekends."

She nods. "It was like that at Luci's house."

"Luci's that girl you used to hang around with?"

"Yeah. My cousin. She moved."

"You guys seemed close."

"Best friends." Sarah drops the toothpaste back in its cup inside the cabinet and closes the door fast. It slams and she jumps like she's scared herself. "Ready to go downstairs?"

"Sure."

"I'll tell my mom we're headed to bed."

In the living room, Sarah leans down to hug her mom, who's on the couch with Sarah's dad watching a nature show that looks boring and wholesome. "We're going to bed," Sarah says.

"Okay, hon. Phone."

Sarah hands it over.

"Avery, you too, please." Sarah's mom looks at me expectantly.

"Um . . ." I touch my phone in my back left pocket. "I usually keep it with me."

"In our house, kids don't take phones to bed," she says firmly.

"Oh . . . kay?" Weird. I hand it to her, half expecting her to ask for my passcode.

She doesn't. She just tells us to have sweet dreams and to please be upstairs by eight.

On the way back down the steps, me behind Sarah again to hide my limp, I ask why we have to get up so early.

"Mom only makes breakfast once."

"You don't just eat cereal when you roll out of bed?"

Sarah turns to glance up at me. "I guess we're sort of weird."

I stop my careful descent. "I didn't—I mean I wasn't . . ." I look at my feet. "You're not weird."

"I think we are." She pulls in her breath like she's going to sigh, but then doesn't. "You can take the bed. Is it okay if I use your sleeping bag?"

"You don't have to do that."

But she's already unrolling it. She fetches the hand sanitizer in the nightstand and uses it as she sits on the sleeping bag cross-legged. "I'll turn my back while you get changed."

"Actually . . ." I tense. I *hate* asking for help. But I sort of need it. "Would you mind giving me a hand getting Cthulhu off? One of the straps is hard to reach."

"Oh." She looks startled. "Cthulhu?"

I point at my sling. "Named after that freaky monster with the octopus face."

"Okay," Sarah says uncertainly. "Just . . . tell me

what to do?" She sits next to me on the bed slowly, like she's afraid she'll break me.

I undo the straps I can get to, then point around my back. "There's a Velcro one there. Also I'm aware that this thing totally smells funky, but washing it is a whole ordeal and I have to be out of it for a couple hours while it dries, but my arm's not really ready for that so I have to, like, build this super-particular arrangement of pillows and stuff so I don't—"

"Hey." Sarah puts a hand on my good shoulder. "It's okay. Cthulhu doesn't smell."

My skin goes hot. She's so *close*. "He definitely does."

She smiles as she tugs the Velcro apart. "No worse than my stinky basement."

"Your basement's not stinky."

"Yeah, it is."

I giggle. "We're even, then." I shift the loosened sling and suck my breath in at the pain. "Okay. *Now* you can turn your back. And please ignore any sounds I make."

Sarah glances at her sketchbook on the nightstand. "I'll go upstairs to give you some privacy." She picks up the book. "Or—do you need help getting it back on?"

"Just with that one strap. I can do everything else. Um, this usually takes a while. Can you maybe give me a few minutes?" I don't want her coming down the steps and seeing me topless, grunting, and possibly leaking tears as I struggle into my night shirt mutter-ing *sidestep*.

"Sure." Sarah pulls a T-shirt and some sweatpants from the shelf, then tucks her sketchbook between them. "Is ten minutes enough?"

"Perfect." It'll give me time to undress, dress, and stop crying if I need to. "Thank you."

"No problem." She picks up a pencil case and heads up the steps, leaving me alone in her musty, colorful room.

20
Sarah

Fri., May 3, 9:08 p.m. This is going better than I expected. I keep forgetting to be scared that her disease might be contagious, or that she'll die or move away.

But I also haven't asked her yet if she wants to work on a poster together. It's so nice to just . . . have fun.

Ruthie and Avery hit it off as much as James and Avery did in the car. I felt like a fifth wheel again. But it's my own fault for being silent. I'm just worried I'll say something dumb and Avery won't want to be my friend and I'll have that losing-someone terror again and be back where I started, only worse because I've failed to fix my own problem. All of it keeps going around my head in circles, like this:

I haven't panicked, though. It seems like the earlier I catch the fear, the better the chance three deep breaths will work.

And I'm getting better at catching it early.

When I don't catch it early, though, the other tactics fly right out of my head.

Probably I need to practice them when I'm <u>not</u> panicking. Maybe that'll help me remember them when I <u>do</u> panic.

While Ruthie and Avery and I played Jumanji, I kept thinking about when I was nine and James and I got lost in that huge corn maze at the pumpkin patch. "This is fun" turned into "this is scary" and I started to cry. He sat me down and gave me his water bottle and said if we started marking our path, we'd find our way out.

He held my hand after that, and broke some of the corn stalks as we passed them. It took a long time, and we were both exhausted by the end of it. But we made it out, and Dad gave me a hug and thanked James for staying calm and taking care of me, and everything was okay. James was even chill for the whole rest of the day after that.

Sometimes my thoughts feel like that corn maze. But when I panic, they're like when the pen jumps the Spirograph track and it all turns to chaos.

It's not <u>really</u> chaos, though. The line twists and bends and loops,

160

but if you picked it all up off the paper like a string, it would still be one long piece.

There's probably a lesson in that.

I think it's been ten minutes. I better give it a few more just in case.

I hope Avery is having a good time and that she'll want to come back. I hope she'll want to work on a poster with me, and maybe even go to Bible Study with me. Bible Study sucks because all the girls in it go to St. Joseph's Middle School and they know each other well and they go out of their way to exclude me. It would be good to have a friend there.

Unless Avery is interested in something more than friendship. But I don't think she is.

I still don't know what to feel about that.

It's definitely been ten minutes now.

Okay. Deep breaths. A few animashups, then I'll go back downstairs.

21

Avery

Once we're settled—Sarah in my sleeping bag on the cold floor, me in her bed with her pillows bracing my arm—and the light is off, we're quiet. I'm not remotely tired. It's too early.

"It's very very very extra dark down here," I whisper, mostly to check if she's asleep yet.

"It is." It sounds like the words came out through a smile.

"Is Ruthie's bedroom the one you'll have when it's your turn for upstairs?"

"Yes. But I'm going to tell Mom and Dad I'll keep the basement. Ruthie had it two years ago and she cried every night before bed."

"Oh. That's sad."

"Yeah."

"You don't like it down here either, do you?"

There's a pause. "I'm not terrified of it the way she is."

"Maybe she'll grow out of it?"

"That's what Mom wants to happen. She'll probably say no when I say I want the basement again. She says the best way to get past a fear is to go into it."

Sarah is such a mystery. A girl who can hide her fear. Who can make beautiful art with nothing but a pen and two plastic cogs. "Do you believe that?" I ask. "About going into your fear?"

"No." There's a rustling sound. It's too dark to see her, but I think she's pulling the sleeping bag tighter around her shoulders. "I run away from my fears. Because they're *scary*."

"What are your fears?"

Sarah laughs. "Um. You go first. Like that game. Truth or dare? Except I'll tell you a fear if you tell me a fear."

I stare up into the pitch black. There are so many answers I could give her. So many fears. Mason knows a few of them. The ones about what my future with hEDS looks like. And Tuney knows some, like that I'm afraid to ask anyone for help ever because . . . well, I don't want to think about that. And Mom knows I'm afraid of needles.

But would sharing those fears make Sarah think less of me?

"I'm afraid of getting shot at school," I finally tell her.

"Eh. Doesn't count. Everyone is, especially now."

"That doesn't make me less afraid of it."

Silence again, followed by another sleeping bag sound. "I'm afraid of . . . um. Of barf."

I laugh. "Yeah. Barf is *way* scary."

"I'm serious." She sounds a little hurt. "I can barely say the word. And I can't write it. I just . . . panic. If I do."

Shoot. Now I've made her feel bad. "I'm afraid of people," I offer.

"How so?"

"Today Logan Green bumped my shoulder. I was crying like a dope in the hallway when Mason—" I clear my throat. "People are unpredictable. You never know which direction they're going to move and now my body falls apart really easily and I'm scared if someone so much as steps on my foot it'll break and I'll—" Oof. I don't need to unburden all of *that*. "I hate this disease. I guess that's my biggest fear. That it's gonna eat my life."

"What . . . what is the disease?"

"Well, technically it's a syndrome. Ehlers-Danlos

syndrome, hypermobile type. hEDS. But my rheuma-tologist says the medical community hasn't caught up yet to how significant the hypermobile type is and gotten around to defining its biomarkers or whatever and calling it a disease."

"It's not contagious?"

"Nope. You can't catch being double-jointed."

Was that a sigh of relief?

Ugh. That makes me feel kinda gross. Like she'd have booted me out of this room if she thought she could catch hEDS from me.

She clears her throat. "Does everyone who's double-jointed have the disease?"

"No. That's just, like, one problem it causes. Among lots of others."

"Can it . . . um, kill you?"

I laugh, but I don't know why. It's not funny. "Not really exactly specifically." Ugh, that didn't come out right. "EDS has lots of types. The hypermobile type isn't the most dangerous one. You just get worse over time."

She sighs a little, again as if she's relieved. "What's it like?"

I don't really want to talk about this. But I feel bad for laughing at her barf fear.

So I tell her about how my connective tissue doesn't

connect the way it's supposed to, and how that means my joints are too loose and slip out of place sometimes. I tell her about how I think the word *sidestep* to get through the pain. I tell her how I used to flaunt my bendy-ness for fun. I'd put both feet behind my head and lick my own elbow at birthday parties, or twist my arms around 560 degrees to make a gross-you-out TikTok, or sit on a couch upside down and backward with my spine bent 90 degrees the wrong way. I tell her I used to fall asleep in bizarre positions, like someone dropped a pile of human parts and they landed every which way. I tell her my pediatrician said doing that stuff would cause problems, and that I didn't listen to her because I'm not exactly a Very Obedient Child Who Always Listens to Her Elders. I skip the part about my bathroom woes. I'm just going to hope I don't have terrible gas in my sleep tonight and that's the end of this friendship.

It feels weird but good to get some of my fears out of me. I keep them all stuffed down, because I don't want to seem weak. But I don't feel weak talking to Sarah. She listens to everything I say and comments with stuff like "That sounds really hard" and "I get what you're saying" and "That's awful" in all the right places.

It makes me feel listened to. And not judged.

When I come to a place where I can either stop talking or unload about how freaked out I am that the rest of my life will be all downhill, I pause.

Sarah's a great listener. I know she'd understand.

But I don't want to push this fragile new friendship too hard. And anyway . . . "It's your turn," I say. "What are you too scared to tell other people?"

There's a long silence. Long enough that I start to think she's not going to answer. Or that maybe she's fallen asleep because I bored her with my long list of laments.

"I'm terrified of death," she finally says, so softly I can barely hear her.

I wait for her to explain. But there's only silence.

"How do you mean?" I ask. "Isn't everyone scared of that?"

"Every time I think of it I just . . . overreact. I mean, it's maybe not an overreaction to be scared of death. But . . ." She sighs. "It's a constant worst-case scenario in my head. My mind keeps churning out the worst that could happen and then spinning around in it."

"What's the worst that could happen?"

She's quiet.

"Well. I guess that was a big question. You don't have to answer."

"I think . . . I think I could, if you tell me yours. You

167

told me a lot. But not the worst-case scenario, right?"

I clench my good fist. "Right."

"You're probably used to fun overnights. Instead of this."

"I like this better," I say quickly. "Fun is good, but . . . is it weird to say this feels like it means something?"

"Not weird. It feels like when Luci and I—" She sucks in her breath like she's scared.

"What?" I ask. "What's wrong?"

"I just—" Her voice is tight like she's going to start crying. "Told myself I—"

I wait, but it's completely quiet. I can't even hear her breathing. "Are you holding your breath?" I finally ask.

She exhales in a rush somewhere between a laugh and a cry. "Oops. Yeah."

"I have one functional arm and a janky knee, dude. I'm not scary."

She laughs for real. It's good to hear it. "I'm not afraid you're going to roll off the bed and deck me."

"What, then? What did you tell yourself?"

"It'll sound dumb."

"I'll tell you mine if you tell me yours."

"Ha. That sounds kinda weird."

I laugh. "But I will, though. We're this far in. It's like in *Stranger Things* when the elevator goes down a million stories to the secret Russian bunker. And Steve and Robin and Erica and Dustin are like, do we try to get back to the top, or do we see what's down here?"

"I haven't seen *Stranger Things*."

"It's so good! You totally need to watch it."

"I will. Someday." She clears her throat. "What's in your secret Russian bunker?"

"The future." This'll probably be easiest if I just push it all out.

So I do.

I tell her the worst-case scenario: how I'm afraid of internal decapitation and of losing control of my bladder and bowels and of what will happen to me after my moms die of old age and can't take care of me anymore. I talk about how frustrating it is to have an invisible illness, and how when I was a kid, I was always rolling my ankles and popping something weird in my elbow and dealing with pain that doctors couldn't figure out the reason for. A lot of them stopped believing me when I said it hurt to walk or reach up or turn my head. I talk about how in elementary school, Jolene Winfrey made fun of me for "faking" injuries when I wasn't, and since she was so popular, that spread to the other kids. I tell Sarah about the time in sixth grade when I was having a bad pain day because, who knows, a butterfly flapped its wings in China, and my back and neck hurt so bad I couldn't lift my backpack, so I asked Jolene to help me. Jolene laughed and said, "What, now you're faking a broken neck? Go ask hyperactive adopted boy to help you," and everyone laughed and started talking about the times I went to the nurse's office and got sent right back to class because the nurse was like, "Nothing is swollen or red, you're fine."

I tell Sarah how that made me never want to ask for help. How it made me hate being seen as weak or vulnerable. How it made me want to control everything I can, since so much is out of my hands now. I tell her how the drill brought all the stuff I bury up to the surface, and the fact that it happened while I couldn't use one of my arms made me feel so wildly out of control that I just started sobbing like a baby under Mr. Trevino's desk.

The words keep pouring out. I tell her I never realized that who I am is so wrapped up with physical movement until I couldn't be physical anymore, and how that's messed with me almost as much as the joint pain. I even tell her about the bathroom problem, how I'm either going all the time or I can't go at all, and it makes me feel sick and I get heinous gas problems and the only pants I can comfortably wear are leggings and I'm scared I'll never feel right in my body again.

Then I cry.

Sarah gets up and sits on the bed. She feels around until she finds my foot, and then puts her hand on my shin.

It takes a while to get myself back together. When I think I'm done, I sniffle heavily. "Thank you," I say. "That felt . . . weird. To talk about."

"You haven't told anyone that stuff?"

"A little of it, with Mason. But not . . . not all that."

"I'm glad you felt like you could tell me."

"It's easier in the dark."

"I know. That's how it used to be with me and . . ." She sucks in her breath again. "Luci."

I wipe my face with the back of my hand. Even though the scales are uneven, since I dumped out my emotional goop and she's still holding on to hers . . . I'm not going to push her to talk about stuff she doesn't want to talk about. "We don't have to play this game anymore if you don't want to," I say. "I think I kinda overshared."

"It's not really a game. I'm glad you told me all that." She slides back onto the floor, then scoots over until I can hear her breathing right next to my head. The bed shifts as she leans on it. I hear her take three long, deep breaths. "Luci and I used to talk down here about everything."

A flare of jealousy goes through me. "Sounds like you really miss her."

"I do."

"Why did she move?"

"Her mom, my aunt Camila, died. My uncle David moved them to Arizona."

"How'd she die?"

"She had a heart condition no one knew about until she got COVID. She got really, really sick. It took her a whole year to die."

"Oh. That's . . . awful."

"She was my other mom. I'm afraid—" Sarah makes a gulping sound. "Of so much. Loving someone and losing them like I lost Luci and Aunt Camila. And afraid of . . . the b-word. Because Aunt Camila did it so much before she died, and now every time I see it or hear about it I get freaked out that the person will die. And then I start being afraid that what happened to Aunt Camila will happen to me. Like what if I have a heart problem like that? And I die too?" Her voice is shaky. "What if that happens to other people I love? Like my family?"

"She's your aunt by blood? Not marriage?"

"She married my dad's brother. My uncle David."

"So . . . she's not genetically related to you then, right? If that heart condition runs in a family, you're safe."

"I know. It's just . . . hard to be logical during a panic attack. You know?"

I think she's crying. I want to roll toward her, but it'll hurt like the devil.

She clears her throat. "I'm scared I'll never find a friend like Luci again. Or if I do, they'll die and I'll lose them too. It was—" A choking sound comes out. "It was so hard for me to ask you over. I knew you had some kind of disease and I was scared I would start caring about you and you would die." She laughs, but it sounds more like crying. "That's silly, isn't it? That I'd be so scared of death I wouldn't even try to make a new friend."

My heart breaks a little. "It's not silly at all, Sarah." I've never lost anyone like she lost two people she loved so much. But the thought of it is terrifying. Something as comparatively minor as Mason going to a different high school next year jangles my nerves enough. "I'm sorry you went through all that. It must have been so hard."

"Yeah." She clears her throat like she's going to say more, but then she's quiet.

"I'm glad you asked me over," I say into the silence. "I want to be your friend." And maybe more. But only if she wants that too.

"I want to be your friend too," Sarah says quietly.

"Friends, then."

We're quiet for a while. I'm not tired enough to sleep. But talking any more feels overwhelming. I need to lie here and digest what we both said. "Oh, shoot," I say. "I forgot to take my melatonin." No wonder I'm not tired.

"Do you need the light?"

"Yeah. Like a tiny light, though. If you turn on the lamp you'll shock our eyeballs."

"I have a flashlight I use to draw after I'm supposed to be sleeping."

I laugh. "You rebel!"

I hear Sarah slide a nightstand drawer open and feel around inside it, then slide it shut. "Here you go," she says.

"Um—" I shift my center of gravity, rolling onto my side. "One sec." I make a grunting sound as I push myself to a seated position. "Okay."

Our hands find one another in the dark. As she passes me the flashlight, I grip her cold fingers for a moment. "Thanks," I say when the flashlight is in my hand. I click it on and both of us suck our breath in. "Tiny light, big oof!" I laugh.

Sarah kind of grimace-smiles. "Is it in your bag?"

"Yeah."

She reaches over to my bag on the floor and sets it

up on the bed. I find the melatonin and my water bottle. I swallow the pill and cap the bottle. "Do you ever take melatonin?"

"No. What does it do?" She leans the flashlight on the lamp base, shining the light up into the shade. It casts a diffused glow through the room.

"Helps me fall asleep. I get insomnia when my brain won't shut up."

She clears her throat. "Did the drill give you nightmares?"

"Yeah. The awake-problems are worse, though." I tell her about Mason leaving Maple Creek because of the drill. Or rather, because of the legit reasons his mom disliked the district, capped off by the drill.

"That's awful," Sarah says. "It's so hard to lose your best friend." She hugs her knees, still leaning on the bed. "I, um. I've been thinking about the drill a lot too. And what I could do to make sure it never happens again. To make sure Ruthie never has to go through it."

"We definitely share that goal," I say. "Did you hear some parents are gonna sue the school?" I haven't snooped on Tuney's laptop more, so it feels like stale news. For all I know that plan died in the water. Or maybe it didn't, and that lady who can't spell filed a lawsuit.

"No," Sarah says. "I didn't. I've been thinking of,

um, making a poster that has—"

"I'm going to get revenge on Ritter the Rat," I blurt. I shouldn't tell her this. It might jeopardize the closeness we're building. But we just shared so much. Maybe she'll understand. "I have a plan to make him see how bad he screwed up by scaring us like that."

"Oh." Sarah draws away from me in the dim light. "You sound like James. He's always talking about how much he hates Mr. Ritter."

My heart thumps harder. "Is that bad? To sound like James?"

"He's . . . hotheaded." She stretches her legs out in front of her. "He always has to have the last word. He's still fixated on Mr. Ritter because he *didn't* get the last word."

"I—uh." I should *not* tell Sarah I'm more like James than like her. Or anything about the revenge plan. *Bad* idea. I tug the hoops in my left ear. "I always say, uh, live and let live?" It comes out like a question.

Sarah turns and rests her head on the bed and looks at me. "Sometimes that's best."

"You're not—" Okay, well, no. Sarah is not angry at Ritter the Rat like I am. Obviously. "Well. It sounds like James has good reason to hate him."

She waggles her hand like she kind of agrees, kind of doesn't. "I don't want to talk about James, really. Or

Principal Ritter. Maybe we should go to sleep?"

"Okay," I say immediately, mostly to shut myself up. If I tell her anything else, the closeness might go right out the dusty basement window above our heads.

I'm not willing to sacrifice that. So I keep my mouth shut.

22
Sarah

Fri., May 3, 9:58 p.m. Avery fell asleep soon after she took the pill. Her nose is stuffed up from crying and she's snoring a little. I'm leaning against the bed and I feel it in my back. Just barely.

I almost asked her about the poster. I even got "poster" out before she said the thing about revenge.

I get why she said it, even though I don't agree with it. Talking with her like that was <u>intense</u>. I don't know what I feel right now. But I know what I don't feel.

I don't feel lonely.

That should scare me. Being not-alone means being at risk of losing the person I feel not-alone with. But . . . I'm not scared. It feels even better than not feeling lonely.

Not-alone is the exact feeling I want all the kids at school to have. The feeling I want to create by making a poster that unifies us and helps us all focus on the future.

I'll find a way to ask Avery to help. I think she'll want to. After that conversation, it feels like our vines are growing closer together. Reaching for one another.

A little basement beetle is crawling along the top edge of my journal. Aunt Camila said once that beetles are a reminder to look closer. That a thing's outside might look one way—hefty, earthbound, solid—but the inside could be hiding a secret superpower. In the case of beetles, a thin, folded-down wing strong enough for them to fly.

The way I feel about Avery is different now. Before it was hope and worry mixed up. Now I care about her in a new way. She was so brave to tell me all that about her disease, when it obviously scares the heck out of her.

I can't imagine facing so much fear and uncertainty and pain. But Avery doesn't have a choice. She <u>has</u> to. It makes my fears seem silly in comparison.

But I still feel them. There's so much to fear—hospice and STEM camp and the bus and downtown and

179

my summer being swallowed by homework. I'm not good yet at handling my panic. I'm getting better since I made that list, but I know I'll still have freak-outs.

Right now, though, after sharing so much with Avery, I'm calm. Like how Dad is calm.

It feels good.

I wonder if tomorrow morning will be awkward. If we'll be able to look at each other over our whole wheat pancakes, after all that stuff came out of both of us. Sometimes that happened with Luci.

It always passed by the time breakfast was over, though. Like we had to readjust in our heads the space the other person took up. Fit the new information in.

I'm going to pray that Avery forgets about her plan to get revenge on Principal Ritter. James did what he did because he wanted revenge on Mr. Ritter for suspending him for fighting. Even though James was just defending himself against a bunch of jerks who took advantage of how easy it is to make him fly off the handle. He had two good reasons to be furious at Principal Ritter: one, that Mr. Ritter didn't do anything about the bullying, and two, that he punished James instead of the bullies.

I understand why James wanted revenge. But there's a difference between <u>wanting</u> revenge and <u>getting</u> revenge.

James and Avery both have fire in their hearts. So maybe Avery, like James, might be likely to shift from

wanting revenge to getting revenge.

But it's dangerous. James isn't the only kid Mr. Ritter's kicked out. It's his go-to when kids take his punishments personally or try to get back at him like Avery wants to do.

I think Avery and I are <u>real</u> friends now, because we've shared so much. Which is scary by itself, because . . . well, what if she does something bad and gets kicked out of the district and I lose her like I lost Luci? What if all we're left with is texts? Brief messages that never tell the whole story of who we are and how we're changing?

I <u>really</u> don't want that to happen. I need to convince her the poster is a better way.

Okay. So I'll ask her tomorrow.

Under the colorful,
eye-catching shell
the shell that reflects the light
hides a wing as thin
as my voice when I sing
that lets the body take flight

23

Avery

Saturday when I get home from Sarah's, I carefully curl up on the couch with Tank and check my Amazon gift card balance. Tuney loaded it up for Christmas ages ago. I went on a shopping spree and then got distracted by the whole incurable-disease thing. There's still fifty bucks on there, so I order the biggest Spirograph kit I can find for Sarah, plus a thing called a Dream-o-graph that looks complicated to use but makes really cool designs. I use the last dregs on the gift card to pay for next-day shipping so the stuff will be here tomorrow and I can give it to Sarah Monday at school.

After breakfast, we went back down to Sarah's room to pack my stuff. She seemed freaked out about going to a hospice with her mom to read to someone who's dying.

Given how scared she is after seeing her aunt die, it makes sense. I'm not really freaked out by death (except, hello, if it's because dudes with guns are in our school, fake or not), and even I would be scared to read to a dying person. So maybe, if it kinda messes her up the way the drill messed me and Mason up, the Spiro-thingies will take her mind off that.

"Where are you going on your date tonight?" I ask Tuney while she's driving me to Mason's on her way to the grocery store. Usually, Mom and her do boring stuff, like dinner and a movie, but sometimes they do cool stuff. Like go to the eighties-style arcade and then hit up the amusement park. I always get mad when they do fun stuff without me.

"The sushi place, then bowling," Tuney says.

"Jealous. Bring me back some sushi." It's my favorite food. Especially California rolls.

"It won't keep in the car while we bowl. Sorry, kid."

I don't think she's sorry. I think she's glad she and Mom will have a kid-free night.

That stings a little, so I turn my thoughts to how I'm going to ask that Brad kid about getting some fireworks. Too late, I realize I could've traded him my Amazon gift card money for them.

I don't really have anything else to offer. I guess I should've thought this through more instead of letting my semi-obsession with Sarah fill up my whole brain.

When we get to Mason's, though, Brad isn't there. Mason's mom is at a soccer game with Xavier, and his dad is painting cabinet doors in the garage.

Mason is still quiet and tense. We sit in his rocker gaming chairs and play Minecraft for a while. I pelt him with terrible jokes until he finally loosens up and laughs.

"Wanna do something else?" I ask when I get bored of Minecraft.

"I want to finish this house." He's meticulously assembling a complicated mansion.

"Gimme a tour."

He spends the next five minutes explaining every feature, including the type and color of stones and wood he used, why he put bookshelves and paintings and light fixtures in certain places, the structure of the dungeon he's building under it, and what he's planning for the yard. My eyes glaze over during his detailed explanations. But he's still a little mad at me, so I say "uh-huh" and "cool" at what I hope are the right places.

When I finally manage to pry him away from the TV, we go back to his messy room. He picks up his velociraptor mask and puts it on. "Avery, I crave violence!" he says in a squeaky voice. The jaw of the mask moves as he talks.

"Hard same," I say. "Let's make a TikTok of you tearing something to shreds. Maybe this?" I pick up his flattened shark Squishmallow.

He takes off the mask. "That thing's old and gross. I'll ask Dad if we can shred it." He bounds out of his room and is back seconds later. "He doesn't care as long as we clean up."

"Sweet! Where are your scissors?"

It takes us a few minutes to figure out the best way to cut the thing open and then simulate a velociraptor eating fluffy shark guts. It's so fun to spend time goofing off—a reminder of all the *good* parts of our friendship, instead of the drama from the drill. Once Mason has flung fluff everywhere and sent us both into hysterics by calling it "beef," we realize we're going to have to stuff the beefy fluff back in, since there's nowhere else to put it.

"Put the mask on me," I tell Mason. "We can make a follow-up video: 'Velociraptor has regrets.'"

Mason straps it on my head. But I quickly realize it's very difficult to shove the fluff back in using the mask. I keep trying until a chunk of it gets in my mouth. "This does not taste like beef," I say. "It tastes like you've been using it for a pillow for five years and it's full of your bad dreams." I sputter and blow, trying to get the fluff out of my mouth. "Tighten the strap again. This thing's sliding all over the place."

"Why you gotta be so bossy all the time?" Mason asks.

"That's charm, not bossiness," I tell him.

"Charm, my butt. You bumbling dolt." He tightens the mask.

"Thanks, you ungainly meatloaf."

"Blundering dunce."

I throw fluff at him. "Nerf herder."

He starts to crack a smile, which means I'm winning, because whoever laughs first loses. "Klutzy chowderhead," he says.

I bite back the laugh trying to bubble up. "Awkward clod."

"Clodhopping blunderbuss."

"Plodding nut-bucket."

He covers his mouth, trying as hard as I am not to laugh. "Incompetent donkey!"

I dissolve into laughter. "Boneheaded galoot!"

He cracks up too. When we're done busting a gut, Mason holds the shark open while I use my functional hand to push the stuffing back in. "What do you want to do now?" I ask when we're finished.

"Minecraft. I didn't get to finish the house."

"Minecraft is boring. Let's edit the videos we just took."

"You can edit while I work on my house."

"I want to do it together."

Mason sighs. "Fine, we'll edit. Then Minecraft."

I sit on his floor with my legs in a W and start editing the video. Mason picks up his puzzle ball and rolls the marble along the track. I complain about Mom while I work, still grumpy that she made me finish half of my weekend homework before she brought me over here.

"How come you bad-mouth your mom when she asks you to do stuff you're supposed to do anyway?" Mason asks. "You get mad at her instead of, like, the school for giving homework."

"I don't bad-mouth her." I press my lips together. I think I was just bad-mouthing her.

"I'm gonna go work on my house." Mason leaves, giving me no choice but to follow.

I sit in the rocker chair next to his. "What should I name this movie file?"

"Beef explosion?" Mason suggests.

"Let's go with 'Velocibeef.'" I tap in the title, then twist my achy back that doesn't like this chair. It makes my shoulder hurt, but my back pops in a bunch of places, which feels good.

Mason shudders. "That sounds so gross. Like a centipede wearing flip-flops."

"Or that time we gave Tank Pop Rocks. Remember how confused he was?" I export the video, upload it to TikTok, and give him an evil grin. "Want me to tag Helen so she sees this?"

"No!" Mason says. Then he groans. "I can't freaking believe she saw me pee my pants."

"I doubt she thinks less of you for it. I saw her whack your butt with her trombone case at the bus stop yesterday. I think she likes you back."

"Pfft. Pretty sure a butt whack with a trombone case isn't a confession of love."

"You never know, dude." I glance toward the kitchen. I can hear Mason's dad in the garage, which means the kitchen door into it must be open. "So about the drill," I say under my breath. "And revenge."

Mason's shoulders pinch together. He tilts forward in his chair like he wishes he could climb into the mansion he's building. "I don't want to talk about it."

"Well, I do," I say, trying to mask my annoyance. "I met a guy who has a car. And guess what? He hates Principal Ritter as much as I do. 'Cause Ritter kicked him out of Maple Creek Middle a few years ago." I rock my chair with my foot.

"Good for him," Mason mutters. On the screen, he flies away from his house and throws a few blocks of

TNT onto a patch of sand. He starts building a brick room around them.

"So, he wants to help. We came up with a plan."

Mason stays silent. He seems mad, but intrigued. Like he wants to ask but doesn't want to admit he wants revenge too.

I rock my chair, hoping its squeak will prevent Mason's dad from hearing me. "Think Brad will come over to hang with Xavier later today?"

Mason shrugs. "Probably. Dude practically lives here."

"So, you know how Brad's always bragging about having those fireworks?"

Mason shoots me an angry look, then turns his attention to the screen.

"I want to get a couple big mortars off him."

"And do what, exactly?" Mason asks flatly.

"Set them off outside Ritter's house at midnight."

He gives me an incredulous look. "Are you out of your tree?"

I face the TV. "You sound like your mom when you say that."

"This is a terrible idea. No."

"It's a *great* idea," I insist. "All we need is like three shells. I have a getaway driver. We can pull it off in, like, thirty seconds. Tops."

Mason puts down his controller. "Avery. Don't be completely *daft*."

"But what if this makes Ritter the Rat apologize? And that makes your mom—" Oops, getting loud. "And that makes her change her mind?"

"She's not going to change her mind!" He rocks his chair harder. "Did you even realize that you trying to force me under Mr. Trevino's desk was the reason I got stuck in the middle of the room? If you'd just let me go where I was gonna go, none of that embarrassing crap would've happened! I wouldn't—"

"But *everyone* was freaking out—"

"—be getting made fun of constantly, like even worse than before. Jolene wouldn't be calling me a freaking crybaby and pee-pants and 'leaky boy'!"

"Everyone was crying!" I practically shout. "Even her. She can't make fun of you for that. It'd be totally hypocritical of her."

"Oh my god, Avery. Just because half the kids in our grade don't make fun of me around you because people are kinda scared of you, you think it's not happening. Open your eyes for once."

People are scared of me? "Well, they *shouldn't* make fun of you, because literally every person in that room except Sarah was crying."

"That doesn't even matter!" Mason rocks so hard

he tips over. His controller goes flying and he gets up to retrieve it. "Even if I hadn't peed, they'd still make fun of me for sloppy-sobbing. There's always a reason to make fun of the annoying pipsqueak Black ADHD kid. You've never understood that, and now you *really* don't get it, and I'm so sick of—"

"If it's really that bad, if we do this revenge plan, we'll be heroes. People won't make fun of you after that."

"*We?*" He flops back into his chair. "No. I'm not doing it. It's a bad idea and you'll get busted." He rocks the chair hard.

"It could be the only way to get you to be able to go to Maple Creek High with me. If your mom sees Principal Ritter publicly apologize for scaring the crap out of us—"

Mason barks out a laugh. "Apologize? *Ritter?* Get real."

"What, you don't think blasting him out of his freaking bed would make him understand how wrong that drill was?"

"I'm saying maybe I don't *want* to go to Maple Creek High."

I stop rocking and stare at his profile. "What?"

He keeps his eyes on the screen. "It's a fresh start without the crappy people who've been jerks to me since first grade. Plus I won't have to put up with you bossing me around."

I drop my phone. My stomach hurts. "I don't boss you around."

"You do. It's why my mom doesn't like you anymore. I didn't even bother asking her if you could come over today because I knew she'd say no. I asked Dad, because he hasn't noticed how stubborn you are when you don't get your way."

"But—it's not like I force you to go along with me!" My voice is shrill. "I'm not *making* you do anything."

"You're the most stubborn person I've ever met. You turn into a total crank if we don't do what *you* want to do every time we hang out—"

"I'm not stubborn!"

He laughs. "You can't even let me finish a sentence."

"Well—you're being just as stubborn as me right now!"

"No, I'm saying what I've wanted to say for a long time." He looks right at me. "It sucks that you have this disease. But since your surgery, you're all stuck in your head. Other people have crap to deal with too, you know. It's like your stuff is all that matters to you."

Tears sting my eyes. I blink them away. "You make it sound like I have no sympathy for anyone. Which is *so* not true."

He turns back to the TV. "I'm not saying that. But you steamroll me *constantly*. Remember when you were like 'Let's take the dirt bikes out without asking Tuney' and I was like 'That's a bad idea' and you were like 'We won't get caught'? Look how that turned out."

"I didn't force you to go with me!"

"Yet again," Mason says. "You were gonna be grumpy and cranky at me all day if I said no. Have you for real not noticed that your refusal to listen to literally *anyone* is stinking up your life?"

"I—no, actually, I haven't. Because I'm *not like that*." I set my jaw. "Just because a girl is assertive, that doesn't make her bossy or stubborn."

Mason explodes the TNT on the screen, sending bits of Minecraft brick flying everywhere. "Being a girl has nothing to do with this. You think girls can't be bossy and stubborn just because they're girls?"

"Well—girls are perceived as bossy and stubborn when they're assertive, because being assertive is supposed to be a guy trait!" I heard Tuney and Mom talking about it once. I didn't get the whole concept, but I picked up on that much. I think.

Mason makes an exasperated sound. "It's like talking to a brick wall."

"I'm not a brick—"

"Remember when I told you about my mom giving

me The Talk in fifth grade?"

I gulp back my retort. "The Talk," as Mason explained it, is not the one about the birds and the bees I got from Mom and Tuney. It's the one Black kids get from their parents about complying with police orders, no matter what, so they don't get shot. "Yeah, so?" I say.

"I've had *specific* fears for three years because of it. Fears about getting shot. Fears white kids don't walk around with all the time. Three years of being scared to death of guns, and then that drill—" He coughs like he's trying to cough away what he feels. "That's why I peed, all right? It was like The Talk coming to life. People with guns who wanted to kill me."

I open my mouth, then close it.

"All I'm saying is, for once, maybe you could think outside your own head for a minute. Okay? You think you can do that?"

Shame pushes words out my mouth. "Well—fine, then, I guess I'll call Tuney to pick me up. If hanging out with me sucks so much."

"Yeah, maybe you should," he says quietly without looking at me.

"Are you . . ." Ouch. "You're serious?"

He ignores me.

"You guys okay?" Mason's dad comes in, wiping paint off his hand with a rag. "I heard yelling. Not the usual friendly kind."

"We're fine." Mason's voice is cold. "Avery was just getting ready to go."

Tears prickle my eyes again, and there's no stopping them this time. I rock the chair forward and try to stand up, but I pitch onto the carpet. My knee pops and fire shoots through my leg and chest as I catch myself with my left arm on the floor.

"Do you need help?" Mason's dad steps toward me.

"No," I snap. "I mean." I clear my throat. "No, thank you." I stand up with a grunt. My knee hurts so bad I'm dizzy from it. Or maybe that's from Mason's words.

Mason's dad just stands there looking at me. Mason starts building another TNT house.

I limp to the bathroom, blinking hard so I can see enough to text Tuney: *Can you come get me?*

As soon as the door is closed, I sink onto the edge of the tub and cover my mouth to smother the sob. I'm not *bossy*. I don't force him to go along with my schemes. He's willing enough, and he enjoys whatever dumb things we do. He laughs and jokes and we have fun.

But. Maybe he's . . . I don't know. Maybe he's just super upset from the drill still. It affected me a lot, but . . .

But . . .

God. I never thought about how The Talk would've

made him experience the drill differently than I did. He really hasn't been the same since it happened.

Or since I bailed on him to hang with Sarah right when he needed a friend. That probably sucked for him too.

But . . . asking me to leave? Isn't our friendship stronger than this?

My phone buzzes in my pocket. *Finishing up at the grocery, can be there in 15 mins. Everything good?*

Fine. Mason has to do a thing he forgot about.

I hate how easily I lie to Mom and Tuney these days. But it seems impossible not to.

I wipe my face and look in the mirror. It's obvious I've been crying. One of the many benefits of fair skin and red hair.

I don't want to sit in here alone till Tuney gets here. I want that even less than I want to go back out and face Mason after he said those things.

I reach for the doorknob. But my hand is still shaky from my meltdown, and I guess I'm aiming wrong because I jam my knuckle into it. My index finger pops out of its socket and then back in with two painful snaps.

Which sets off a fresh round of tears, because what if he's *right*? What if I *am* stubborn? I mean, it's true, I'm stubborn about *some* things, but, like . . . not with him. Right? And I don't . . .

Well. I guess I do cut him off.

But I cut *everyone* off. It's how I communicate. And anyway, he cuts me off too. When we hang out, it's a tumbling ball of conversation, looping back on itself and jumping forward in leaps of logic and laughter.

But . . . now that I think about it . . . I guess it hasn't been that way for a while. Like since maybe before the dirt-bike incident.

I thought things had changed because of the surgery. Because suddenly my "invisible illness" became visible. The way everyone treats me changed, so I didn't notice that things with Mason changed too. I've been so focused on the pain and fear, trying to sidestep them like everything's the same as always and I'm not constantly freaked out that my life is over.

I sigh and rub my face. Maybe I could be a better friend. Less . . . I don't know. Not less of who I am, but more . . . open. To what Mason wants to do.

He really didn't have to say it like *that*.

"Avery?" Mason's dad calls. "Your . . . uh, Tuney's here."

I scowl. It's so annoying when people can't call Tuney my mom. Mason's dad is mostly cool, but seriously, how hard is it to accept that even if Tuney is six feet tall and has an Adam's apple, she's a woman because she *says* she's a woman?

It's zero percent hard. Z-e-r-o.

Ugh. I'm getting mad about this because I don't want to feel all this icky guilt about sucking as a friend. But I mean, he could be a better friend too.

Well. That's not true. He's been an amazingly good friend. Like . . . better than I deserve.

After a last swipe at my face, I go out to the living room. Seeing Tuney making polite conversation with Mason's dad makes me want to burst into tears all over again. Mason looks sick sitting in his rocker chair. You'd think he had a test on Minecraft in an hour the way he's staring at the screen with such intense focus.

"Hey, squirt," Tuney says when she sees me. Her expression changes just enough to let me know that she knows I've been crying. "Ready to go?"

I don't trust my voice, so I nod.

Mason doesn't say goodbye.

Outside, Tuney opens the truck door for me. I don't have the oomph to argue about not needing help, so I take her hand when she offers it. It's warm and strong and I want to curl up in her lap and cry all my tears out.

Tuney is quiet as we drive. At the second or third stoplight, she rubs the back of my head above Cthulhu's strap. "Whenever you want to talk about it, I'm here," she says.

"Thanks." My throat closes up.

I don't say anything else.

24
Sarah

Sat., May 4, 11:53 a.m. I was too scared about hospice to ask Avery about the poster this morning. Mom and I are there now. I mean here. At Loving Arms.

Mom keeps squeezing my knee like she knows I'm about to fly apart with fear. I just tried "Come back to your senses," but it's not the right tactic for here. This place is too much like the funeral home where we had Aunt Camila's funeral. Gray carpet. Quiet in a heavy, muffled way. Strong-smelling flowers on this table next to us in the lobby.

They're pretty. But I'm not going to take a picture of them to draw later. Flowers are supposed to make you feel hope. These remind me of death.

We're waiting in big squishy chairs for someone to "take us back." Wherever "back" is. What if my person dies while

I'm reading? What if they're young, like my age? What if they're an atheist and they don't want to hear the Bible? What if—

12:41 p.m. It's over. I made it through. I'm—

Ha. I'm so relieved I'm almost laughing. I don't know how I made it back to this lobby, my knees are so rubbery.

Even though I failed at Dad's focus-on-goals advice the first time, I tried it again while I followed the nurse to the dying person's room, because my life goal actually fit the situation. The point of reading to dying people at hospice is to help them.

I didn't think it could make me feel better. But it did, because I realized, hello, this is about the dying person, not about me—and then it was a little easier.

The lady I read to was very old. I don't know if she heard me. Her daughter said she could. The daughter was also very old, so I think the woman in bed with closed eyes and the oxygen mask was maybe ninety. She had wrinkled amber-brown skin and age spots along her forehead. Her daughter had darker skin, but the tone was the same as her mom. A rich, warm reddish brown. Their hair was also the same, a cool-toned gray.

I was relieved that the dying person—Charlene—was old. If I had to read to a young dying person . . . that might have been much harder.

The daughter said Charlene was in the end stages of Alzheimer's. I can't remember the daughter's name. I was too nervous for it to stick. I sat in the chair by the bed with my Bible and asked what to read. The daughter said I could read anything I liked.

I started reading the psalms I have marked. I read for a few minutes before the daughter asked me to slow down.

I blurted that I was nervous. Then I felt selfish. I wasn't the one whose mom was dying.

But the daughter smiled and told me there was no need to be nervous. She said her mom was fading in and out. That she had medicine to keep her from feeling pain, and that when her mom was present, hearing the words of the Bible was comforting to her. She said she was grateful I was there.

It calmed me, a lot, to think I was helping. Even if my voice was shaky and too fast . . . maybe I did a good thing.

I hope I did. I hope I helped Charlene.

I read for thirty-three minutes. I know because there was a bird clock across from the bed, the kind that chirps every half hour. The daughter said she'd brought it from her mom's room at the nursing home because it was a comfort to her.

I got the idea that hospice is all about making people comfortable as they die. Making them feel loved. I guess that's why it's called "Loving Arms."

Aunt Camila didn't get to go to a place like this. Her last days were the opposite of calm and quiet. In the hospital ICU. Fighting so hard to stay alive.

I need to draw and think for a while.

1:36 p.m. Driving home. Mom read to three people so it took a while. When she was done, we walked out to the car and had a long, silent hug in the May sunshine.

It was so good.

She's quiet now because her voice is tired. I keep turning over what Charlene's daughter said. She said the passages I picked made it seem like I'm afraid of death. I looked at Charlene, dying right there in the room with us, and said, "My favorite aunt died two months ago."

The daughter said that death is inevitable so it's pointless to fear it. She said something like, "The fact that our lives end is what gives them meaning. Spend your energy on what you can change, instead of wasting precious time worrying over what you can't change."

I just nodded. She smiled one of

those smiles adults give you when they've dropped something big in your lap that they know will take you time to process.

Now I'm processing "wasting precious time," but in a kind of different way than I think she meant it. Maybe the reason I didn't panic during the drill was because it happened so fast that I didn't have <u>time</u> to panic.

So maybe <u>time</u> is the problem. When I know ahead that something scary will happen—STEM camp, or going to hospice, or whatever—I wind myself up into a mess about it. But during the drill, the worst-case scenario happened with no warning.

It wouldn't have changed anything one bit if I'd had months before the drill to panic about how scary it would be. It would've made the whole thing worse. I would have wasted all that time and energy on a thing I couldn't change. Like I wasted time and energy worrying about Aunt Camila dying and Luci moving away. Those things happened anyway. My fear and worry didn't stop them.

I guess . . . since I can't change the fact that everyone I love will die someday, any more than I could change the situation when I thought I'd get shot at school . . . there's no point in "wasting precious time" fearing the inevitable.

That's what Charlene's daughter was telling me. And now that I'm thinking harder about it . . . maybe it's not death or illness I'm afraid of. Those could be <u>symptoms</u> of the problem, like my drawings are symbols of leaves and flowers. Symbols and symptoms are similar.

Which means my real fear, where the Spirograph goes off its track, might be: I'm afraid of my <u>response</u> to those things. Afraid my mind will come apart and I won't be able to put it back together and I'll be alone with the mess. That I'll feel, forever, the way I've felt since Aunt Camila died and Luci left.

I think that's the start of the string, when I pick it up off the paper: I'm afraid of my own fear.

Yes. That's it. And if I do what Charlene's daughter suggested, if I spend my energy on what I <u>can</u> change, I'll spend less time fearing my own fear.

Hmm.

I know it's not this easy to make panic go away. I still feel it moving around at the edges of my thoughts. My feelings. But something is . . . shifting. Like my brain is reordering itself.

I can't change the hard fact of death. But I <u>can</u> change how I respond to my fear. I've already started to change it, even if my technique is a little haphazard.

That . . . is actually very encouraging.

3:28 p.m. When we got home, Dad and I flew the dolphin kite. I asked him what I've wondered for a while: "Why do you like kites so much?"

He looked up at his nylon dolphin swimming through the blue sky and said, "Because it feels like my heart is up there too. Rejoicing." He didn't say "in God," but I knew that's what he meant. I guess for him, flying kites is a kind of praying, the way drawing is how I pray.

I felt brave-ish after that, so I looked up what to do with a Conté pencil. I don't know if this awkward drawing of my lamp has style or emotion or whatever Mrs. Gianno was talking about. But I sent a pic of it to Luci with the daily sunflower photo anyway, because I learned something about how to translate an object from three dimensions to two. It was a lot different from drawing plants and bugs and birds from photos. The tiniest shift in my position made the shape of the lamp appear different.

Probably it would be a more interesting picture if I'd drawn the lamp from an unusual angle, like from the floor or the ceiling. An unusual angle would raise a question in the viewer's mind. Maybe that's the "style" thing Mrs. Gianno was talking about.

While I was drawing, I thought about Avery plotting a revenge that could get her kicked out of school.

She might be getting stuck in her thoughts, like I've been getting stuck in thoughts about fear and death and Aunt Camila dying and Luci leaving. Avery might be having that kind of thinking about the drill. Like it's gotten hooked, in her mind, to her body not working right. This morning, when I was helping her with the strap she can't get to, she said, "Being stuck in this sling feels just like being stuck under Mr. Trevino's desk. I'm trapped and I can't do anything about it." She said the feeling makes it hard to breathe, and that she'd do anything to make that trapped, out-of-control feeling stop.

Maybe her disease makes her feel that way too, because it's so big and scary. So the disease and the drill could be linked in her mind, and that's why she wants to get revenge. Because all the trapped, helpless feelings about her disease could be tangled with her trapped, helpless feelings about the drill.

I'm going to ask Mom if I can FaceTime Avery. This time, I won't give up explaining the poster idea if she starts talking about revenge.

4:17 p.m. Mom said yes. Now I'm a mouse again, full of fear. So much fear that I'm going to—

Perfect love casts out all fear.
Perfect love casts out all fear.
Perfect love casts out all fear.
Perfect love casts out all fear.

4:31 p.m. Phew. Okay.

That was . . . different. I <u>did</u> remember that it's not death I'm afraid of. It's fear. For a few minutes at the start, that made it worse, because I got stuck in a feedback loop where I was scared of my fear and my fear was scary so I was scared of my fear. I knew I was wasting my time on fear, but I couldn't get out of it.

But then while I was breathing all wild, I flipped back through my journal and found the list of tips. I said the mantra aloud, slowly, as I wrote it.

Eventually, it kind of . . . took. My thoughts turned from death-sickness-terror and toward the perfect love God has for all of us, even when we aren't perfect. My writing was my speaking was my prayer. And then I was just a girl sitting in a basement alone talking aloud, and it wasn't scary. It was actually a little funny. I laughed. And that chased away the rest of the panic. Amazing.

Maybe I can do that again, next time.

Okay. I'm going to FaceTime Avery.

Even though I feel braver now, part of me is still hoping she won't answer.

25

Avery

"I can't play with you right now, Tank." I nudge away the drool-covered Kong he's dropped on my foot. "Scrubbing a toilet is way more fun." Having the use of only one arm did not get me out of cleaning my bathroom. It did get me out of sweeping the house, but Mom traded me that for loading the dishwasher and wiping down the kitchen after dinner. Chores galore, busted wing or no. Made extra fun today by the angry guilt in my guts after my disaster of an afternoon with Mason.

The FaceTime chime goes off super loud in my headphones, interrupting the "Rock Out for Revenge" playlist James made for us to listen to when we do the deed. I take my phone out of my pocket.

Sarah's calling.

My liver and spleen change places. I set the phone on the sink and smudge my palm on my cheeks to make them pink because Tuney said I look super cute with flushed cheeks. I hope I look more like I just came inside from a brisk walk than like I was scrubbing a toilet. I pick up the phone to answer, but it's stopped ringing.

Dang it.

I should get out of here so she doesn't assume I'm having a bathroom problem. I go to my room, disconnect my headphones, and call her. She answers right away. "Hi-hi!" I say too enthusiastically. "What's up?"

She's at the table where we ate pancakes this morning. "Hi," she says. "I've never FaceTimed before. Am I doing this right?"

"Really? Not with . . ." Shoot, I forgot the girl's name again. "Not with your cousin?"

"No. She has an Android so we just text."

"Ah. Yeah, you're doing fine."

I wait for her to tell me why she's calling, but she's just sitting there looking nervous and glancing back at the doorway. "So . . . how was hospice?" I ask.

"It was actually okay." She looks relieved. "It wound up not being that scary." She bites her lip. "It was at first. I was so jittery." She laughs. "Then it was okay."

"Glad to hear it."

I wait again. Tank sticks his cold, wet nose in my ear. "Tank, quit!" I try to push him away, but he's freaking huge and I have no leverage.

"Is that your dog?" Sarah asks.

"Oof, Tank—" I grunt as he flops next to me and puts his head in my lap. "Yeah." I show Sarah his big ol' head. "Dumb mutt."

"He's cute. How old is he?"

"Dunno. The vet thinks he's like six or seven."

"You don't know? Did you adopt him from a shelter?"

It seems like there's something she doesn't actually want to talk about. Or maybe she really is interested in my smelly, slobbery dog. "No," I tell her. "Tuney took him away from some dipwad who was abusing him."

"Oh. Really? That's—wow."

"Yeah, Tuney and Mom were at a park and this jerk was hitting Tank with a stick. Tuney straight-up cussed him out and took Tank away from him. It's part of the reason she's my hero."

Sarah smiles wide. "That's so brave. Why else is she?"

"Because being trans is hard as hell and she lost lots of friends and some family when she came out as herself. But it didn't stop her from being who she is." I was two when it happened, so I don't remember it, but sometimes she talks about it. Mom always gives her a big hug when she does, so I pile into it with her and we hug her tight, like we can squeeze out her sadness.

"Then she's my hero too," Sarah says.

It makes me like her even more. "She's great. She gave me dirt bikes for my birthday two years ago, one for me and one for Mason when he comes over. I don't think Mom was exactly on board with that decision."

"Dirt biking sounds . . . fun?"

"It totally is. We can go together when my shoulder heals." And my knee. And, as of this afternoon, whatever the heck is starting to grind in my left hip. Plus assuming nothing else falls apart between now and then.

"Okay," Sarah says.

There's another awkward pause.

"Wanna see my room?" I ask.

"Sure."

I show her my drum kit. "This is Galien. 'Cause of the gay alien, see?" I aim the camera at the rainbow sticker on the kick drum. "He's mad at me because he thinks I'm ignoring him." I show her my posters of dragons, my disaster of a closet, my bookshelf, my desk, the Christmas lights strung up around my bed, and a quick shot of the trampoline outside my window. "Can't jump on that anymore," I say mournfully. "So, um . . . that's it."

Sarah clears her throat. "It's nice. Um. I noticed . . ." She shakes her head. "I mean, I wondered if you wanted to, like, work with me on . . . I had this idea. To try to help everyone recover from the drill by focusing on the future." She sucks in her breath. "Do you want to help me make an anonymous poster and put it up by Principal Ritter's office?" she says in a rush.

"You mean like . . . telling him how much it sucked?"

"Yeah. With a blank paper next to it asking him to never do it again, and people could sign the paper. I could do the poster art. And maybe we could come up with the words together? Since you have strong feelings about it."

"Can we put cuss words on it?" Those are the words that reflect my strong feelings.

"No!" she says quickly. "I thought it should be like . . . logical. We could look up information and statistics. About how drills like that do more harm than good? I found some stuff already."

I scrunch up my face, hoping I look cute and not like I just ate something gross. "Hmm, I don't know. Sounds like work."

"Oh—I mean, you don't have to if you don't want to, I just thought . . ."

I giggle. "Duh, I totally want to." There goes my janky sense of humor again. "I have to finish my chores before Mom has a conniption. Maybe tomorrow afternoon?"

"Sunday's family day. I thought we could work on it on FaceTime tonight? After dinner?"

"Oh! Cool. Yes."

"Great." Sarah looks relieved. "So, um, I'll start sketching out ideas. When you're done with your chores, could you look up some info, maybe? And call me—I mean FaceTime me—after dinner and tell me what you found, and I'll write it on the poster and show you. Okay?"

"I love it. Yes." Research isn't my fave, but this will be good for two reasons: one, maybe it will make Sarah forget I blurted out that thing about revenge at her house last night and she won't think I'm a terrible person, and two, it'll get me some FaceTime with her—which I *so totally want*. "I'm going to my grandma's tonight while my moms go bowling. I'll tell her I have to do a school thing. She'll be cool with me disappearing into Mom's old bedroom for a while."

"Great. Maybe . . . seven thirty? Or so?"

I grin. "It's a date."

Sarah looks alarmed and glances behind her again.

"Not like that," I say hurriedly. Even though sort of yes, like that. "I just meant the date and time we should FaceTime is seven thirty this evening."

Sarah nods curtly. "Great. Okay, um, talk to you then." She hangs up abruptly.

I push my phone back into my pocket, a smile stretching across my face. This is the perfect distraction from mulling over what went down with Mason this afternoon.

By the time we leave for Grandma's at quarter after five, I've sifted through a bunch of websites and written down four points to put on the poster—including sources, if Sarah says we should include them. I think there should be five points. Five is a good solid number. But Grandma will want to do puzzles and board games and our usual stuff, so there won't be much time to search for another point.

The more I think about the poster, the more divided I feel. Sarah talked about focusing on the future. Which seems on the surface like a good idea. But for me, the future is scary. And not in a dirt-bike-thrill way. In an "I might be in pain for the rest of my life" way.

I think getting revenge is focusing on the past, and I got the idea she thinks that's . . . bad.

But I still 110 percent want to shoot fireworks outside Ritter's bedroom window. For *very good reasons*.

After Grandma and I eat fried chicken and French

fries and German chocolate cake, which is a delicious departure from the greens-grains-protein-sauce combo Mom usually cooks but is going to cause me some heinous indigestion later, we launch into an Uno game that lasts years. I finally duck out after Grandma lets me win by not-very-sneakily stacking the draw pile with draw-fours and skips.

I shut myself in Mom's old bedroom, which has pink walls that clash with my hair, and hurriedly dig up one last point for the poster. I finish writing, then FaceTime Sarah at 7:32.

She doesn't answer. I give it about twelve seconds, which is all the patience I have, then call again.

Still no answer.

I text her a picture of my messily written list of info and sources. Then I try to call again.

And again.

I collapse on the bed in despair. "I've been stood up," I tell Mom's old poster from college of Chloë Sevigny.

Chloë just smiles that enigmatic androgynous smile. The one that makes me get why Mom was fine with it when Dad hatched out of his egg and became Tuney.

I sigh and mentally prep to do the PT exercises I promised Mom I'd do while I was here.

I steel myself for disappointment and dial Sarah one last time.

She answers on the second ring and drops the phone. I giggle like a giddy little kid while she's picking it up.

"Hey, I'm so sorry," she says. "I had to help Ruthie wash and braid her hair and it took forever because my hands were—um, because she was so wiggly."

"It's fine," I say like I haven't been cursing myself for falling for a girl who doesn't like me back or even want to be my friend.

"Did you get some info?"

"I texted it to you."

"Oh—hold on, I'll look." She moves the phone away from her face, then hangs up on me.

She's really flustered. That probably shouldn't make me smile as much as I'm smiling.

I call her back and she answers right away. "Sorry-sorry," she says. "I've only had a phone for a few months. I don't know what I'm doing."

"Whoa, really?" I've had a phone since I was nine. So has Mason. Bree and Dariellis both had one when I met them in sixth grade. "I mean, uh. Did you get it for Christmas?"

"My mom gave it to me when Luci moved. She made me sign a contract with rules."

"Oh yeah, I signed one of those too." I barely remember it. I was so eager to get my hands on a phone that I would've signed my life away. All those rules have fallen by the wayside over time. Now I do whatever I want. Sometimes Mom tells me to get my face out of my screen after I've been mindlessly scrolling for hours, but that's it.

"I found your text," Sarah says. "This is perfect, Avery. Even better than I was hoping we'd be able to find. You did a fantastic job on this."

Every part of me glows with pleasure. "Really?"

"Yes. Here's what I thought might work for the art." She turns the phone to show me a bigger sketchbook than the one she carries all the time. It's open to a page with arrows around the edges, pointing in toward the center of the paper. The bottoms of the arrows are shaded with what looks like charcoal so they look three-dimensional. "Is it too obvious?" She sounds worried. "I wanted to draw attention to your words."

"It's great! Maybe once the words are on there, you could fill the rest of the white space with more arrows? Pointing at specific words?"

"Ooh, good idea. You should be an artist!"

"Ha! The only art I'm good at is the art of the fart." Oh lord, why did I say that?

"Pff!" Sarah covers her mouth and giggles. "James too. Especially on taco Tuesday."

One more thing he and I have in common. "You're so lucky to have such a cool brother."

"Eh, I guess. We're . . . different." She sniffles. "Which point should be first?"

We go through the list I sent and decide how to order it. I keep getting distracted by her pretty face. Everything about her pulls me in. Her confidence in drawing the arrows. Her voice that ebbs and flows in volume and steadiness depending on what we're talking about. The way she leans close to the phone and murmurs "I told my parents this was a social studies project" with a grin that would be devilish on anyone else but on her still looks angelic.

I keep forgetting what we're talking about and just watching her. I've had crushes before, but this . . . this feels bigger.

As she's drawing a curved arrow, the conversation reaches a lull. I ask if she's doing anything fun this summer.

Her face gets a pale, pinched look. "No. Are you?"

"We were gonna go to Key Largo to snorkel in the coral reefs before they're all bleached to death. But now Mom says we're not going because I won't be able to swim in the open ocean yet." She broke the news to me so gently I almost didn't realize what she was telling me. That one more piece of hope was breaking away.

"That sounds amazing," Sarah says. "I'd love to see

the reefs before they're gone."

"Where does your family usually go on vacation?"

"We don't go on vacation."

"Whoa. Like . . . ever?"

"We went to Gatlinburg to visit my uncle once. Does that count?"

"What's there?"

"Mountains. A lot of taffy shops. A place called Dollywood that has a roller coaster, but we didn't go to it."

"Sounds . . . fun?" Not even a little fun.

"My parents are making me go to a STEM camp this summer," she says with her face aimed down at her drawing.

"Ugh, jealous! Are you gonna do cool stuff like launch rockets and build robots?"

"I don't know." She shifts and I catch a glimpse of her lips pressed together.

"Wait, you don't want to go?" I would *love* to go to a STEM camp.

She just shakes her head.

"Why not?"

"I'm not . . ." She mumbles something I can't catch. "I'm not good at math and science," she says more clearly. "I'd rather go to an art camp." She glances over her shoulder again.

"So tell your parents that," I say.

She laughs nervously. "I couldn't."

"Why not?"

"They'd say no."

"So you won't even try?" Jeez. It's like Mason not standing up to his mom about changing schools.

Sarah ducks her head. "I need to go get Ruthie ready for bed."

I check the clock. "Oops, I didn't realize it was almost nine." I'm surprised Grandma hasn't hassled me.

"I'll finish this up and send the final to you tomorrow," Sarah says.

"We should print copies. I don't want to only put up one by Ritter's office and then have some jerkwad rip it down. Or Ritter might take it down."

"Oh. Um, good point," Sarah says. "What about the signatures on the paper next to it?"

"We could put that in the cafeteria. And then a note on the bottom of the other copies that people should sign the paper in the caf."

"Okay. But . . . if we put them all over school and Mrs. Gianno sees it, she'll recognize the Conté pencil shading. And like—do you have to get approval from the office to put up posters? What if we get in trouble?" Her voice trembles on the word *trouble*.

"You have Gianno too? I didn't know you had general arts this semester." I bet her stained-glass thing is perfect. Especially compared to the disaster I've been blundering through.

"Seventh period. When do you?"

"Second. We're not signing this, right? Mrs. Gianno could only *guess* who made it."

"But . . ." Sarah bites her bottom lip. "Can we not put any up near the art room?"

Why's she so afraid of getting in trouble? It's not like you die. You're just in trouble, and then eventually everyone forgets whatever you did. "Sure. We'll put your original version in the main hallway. Can you send me a picture of it? Or do you have a scanner?"

"No scanner. I'll send the best pic I can."

"Cool. Mom might be able to help if it comes out dark. She has some Photoshop skills since her nonprofit is small and everyone there has to be a little bit good at everything and a lot good at one thing."

Someone off-screen calls Sarah's name. "I need to go," she says. "Thanks so much for doing this with me. It was fun." She smiles.

"It was as fun as doing work could possibly have been." It made me forget that things with Mason are so bad. It made me mostly forget how much my body hurts. It made me hope that things with Sarah are headed in the right direction.

And who knows? Maybe our little poster full of research and Sarah's cool arrows will actually make a difference.

26
Sarah

Sun., May 5, 2:16 p.m. I'm still buzzing with excitement that Avery jumped on board with my idea. I think it got her mind off revenge. <u>And</u> I think it'll help everyone. Double win!

I had a hard time listening at church today because I felt excited about the poster. But I paid enough attention to know Father Moyer's sermon was on the Bible verse that says if you have faith the size of a mustard seed, you can tell mountains to move and they'll do it.

Mom and James argued about it when we got home after Sunday school. Father Moyer said a mustard seed can grow into a bush thirty feet high in just a few months. So of course James looked that up and told Mom Father Moyer was wrong, that it can only grow ten feet in a few months. He said that if Father Moyer couldn't get his facts right, how was James supposed to take on faith anything else he said?

Dad tried to explain that the exact facts weren't important, and that Father Moyer's point was that faith doesn't need to be large to be effective if you plant it and nurture it in your heart. James snapped at him that Catholics' bad relationship with facts has caused a lot of suffering over the centuries. Mom said something about how seventeen-year-old boys think they know everything. James told her it was a "crock of crap" how she and Dad always claim they're smarter because they've lived longer (which, they do not do that).

I came downstairs to my room after that and prayed for them. I could hear James and Mom yelling about chores and responsibilities and childish takes on important tenets of faith. Then a door slammed. Now it's quiet and I think family day might be canceled.

I don't know how I feel about faith anymore. My prayer drawings for James aren't doing any good.

But I'm still going to pray them. I don't know what else to do for him.

Please protect James from himself

Thank You for Ruthie's sense of humor

4:43 p.m. I redid the poster with ink and simpler arrows, just in case Mrs. Gianno might recognize the Conté and know I made it.

I'm proud of it. Even more than the bird poster. It's a good feeling.

I finally texted Luci last night that our school did a super-realistic shooter drill and everyone was stressed. She called me and we talked on the phone for ten minutes before Mom asked me to unload the dishwasher. We didn't talk much about the drill, though. Most of the conversation was her talking about fitting in at her new school where everyone else has known each other since kindergarten. Mateo and Diego already in trouble. Missing her mom.

She cried during that part. I did too, a little.

I'm glad we talked, even though it was brief and sad. She needed someone to listen. I've missed being that for her. It makes me feel like I matter. Like I'm doing some good.

I sent her a photo of the poster a minute ago. She wrote back right away that it's "amazing," and that she's sorry she did all the talking on the phone. I told her I was glad to hear about how she's doing. We're going to talk again in a few days.

I feel so much tingly excitement when my thoughts drift to Avery. Like . . . maybe too much. I keep telling

myself it's just the happiness
of having her on board with
the poster, and of making a
new friend. A close friend, a
good friend. Not to replace
Luci. No one can do that. But
I'm just . . . very happy about having
a new friend. It's nice to feel happy, so I've
been thinking about Avery. A lot.

There might be another piece to it, though.

When I was younger, I had a silly daydream that in
high school, I'd meet a quiet boy who likes art and has
a mischievous smile but never does anything bad. He'd
have dark wavy hair, and he'd be shy but he would warm
up to me when I complimented his art. He'd be Catholic.
We'd walk at the park holding hands, and draw together
without needing to talk.

That's as far as the fantasy went. Not very filled in. Just
an idle daydream.

Avery doesn't have dark wavy hair. She's not shy. She
doesn't draw, at least not that I know of. And she absolutely does things that get her in trouble.

She's also not a <u>he</u>. That might be the biggest difference. She's nothing at all like my imaginary boy.

But I get butterflies when I think about
walking at the park with her. Holding her hand.

Evidence this might be a crush:

I feel warm in my middle when I'm talking to Avery. All the way from my throat to my kneecaps. Mostly just to the left of my belly button, weirdly.

I keep imagining things we could do together. I want to show her the creek by our house. I know it's just a plain old neighborhood creek, with rocks and broken glass and trash and fossils and minnows. But I love it. I feel hope and adventure when I go there. I want to share that with Avery.

I've been having nonstop imaginary conversations with her in my mind. All day, I've imagined how she would react to the things that are normal to me that aren't normal to her. Singing at church. Kneeling during the consecration. Fake-smiling my way through Sunday school. Eating brunch with my family. Listening to Mom and James get into it again. Avery has been with me through all of it. Even though she's not with me. The image I've made of her in my mind has been here, at the top. At the front. Right with me.

Evidence this might not be a crush:

Um.

Well . . .

Sometimes, maybe, sort of, I don't feel . . .

Oh God. This is definitely a crush.

How I feel about Avery is a glowing ember inside me. Delicious, tingly. All mine. A spark of warmth and light and energy that makes me want to be the best version of myself.

Not just around her. All the time.

If I were to draw it, it might look like . . .

An Argument Against Shooter Drills

1. Active shooter drills in schools are associated with increases in depression (39%), stress and anxiety (42%), and physiological health problems (23%) overall, including children from as young as five years old up to high schoolers, their parents, and teachers.

Everytown for Gun Safety Support Fund

2. Students, staff, and families of students should not be led to believe that an exercise is a real event or misled about the injury to or death of others. Such a practice is harmful and unethical and is not justified by a theoretical benefit of evaluating people's response under extreme levels of stress.

The American Academy of Pediatrics

3. Participation in an armed assailant drill should never be required for students or staff. In advance of any drill, participants must be aware of props' purpose and potential presence, particularly when the purpose of the prop is not obvious.

National Association of School Psychologists and National Association of School Resource Officers, "Best Practice Considerations for Schools in Active Shooter and Other Armed Assailant Drills"

4. The odds of a student age 5-18 being a victim of a school shooting: 1 in 2.8 million. Odds of getting hit by lightning: 1 in 15,300. Odds of dying in a car crash: 1 in 103.

Science News for Students: "Do school-shooter drills hurt students more than they help?"

5. Many security measures were implemented with no consultation of studies done regarding their effectiveness. This failure has had financial and other unforeseen consequences that are only now being discovered.

Victims & Offenders: An International Journal of Evidence-based Research, Policy, and Practice. "Preventing School Shootings: The Effectiveness of Safety Measures"

Do you agree that Maple Creek Middle School should never have a drill like that again? Sign your name on the poster in the cafeteria!

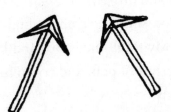

27

Avery

Before dinner on Sunday, I'm flopped on my bed with Tank watching TikToks with my headphones on when Mom startles me by suddenly appearing next to me. She's wearing the rainbow stretchy pants she wears to acroyoga.

I yank my headphones off. "Knock next time?"

"I did. Twice. Turn down your Click-Clock or whatever that's called." She sets a big Amazon box on my desk. "What'd you order?"

"A Spirograph set." I get up to find scissors to cut open the box. My right knee pops and I tip sideways. I bite back the grunt of pain and try to hide my limp as I cross the room.

"Avery . . . why are you limping?"

"My right butt cheek fell asleep."

"From all that strenuous screen time?" Mom shoots a disapproving look at my phone. "Did you do *any* homework or PT?"

"I did math and social studies yesterday. All I have left is science and language arts and the PT." Also a band worksheet. Ms. Everett is big on giving me worksheets since I can't play.

I cut the tape and flip open the box. The Dream-o-graph and the Spirograph set are nestled inside. I pop the air sacs with the scissors instead of stomping them like usual, then lift out the goodies. "Yowza. This is huge." The Spirograph box won't fit in a backpack. It might not even fit in our lockers. I set it on the desk and take the Dream-o-graph out. It's in a smaller box. "Now *this* looks cool. I could get into this." It has cogs and levers and looks totally STEM-y.

Mom sits on my bed and rubs Tank's ears. "Why the sudden interest in art?"

"They're for Sarah. She's super into Spirograph and uses it to make amazing art." I turn the Dream-o-graph box over. There are elaborate patterns on the back of the box. It looks kinda complicated to figure out how to use it.

Mom smiles. "You really like this girl, don't you?"

I shrug. "She's okay."

Mom's grin widens. "Just okay. Sure."

I stuff the tape and empty air sacs and receipt back into the Amazon box.

"Is her birthday coming up?" Mom asks.

"No. I just wanted to get these for her. All she has is a bag of old Spirograph pieces, plus a little kit from the dollar store. But she makes the most *amazing* art with them."

"Well . . . you might consider giving her just one of those to start," Mom says in the careful tone she uses when she's telling me something I don't want to hear. "I love how enthusiastic you are, honey. And how giving. But you might want to be cautious about coming on too strong."

"It's not 'coming on too strong' to give her this stuff. I had money sitting in my Amazon account. It's not like it was a huge sacrifice."

"Sarah might see it differently. Tuney mentioned her house is small and has five people living in it."

"So?"

"So, you might think about how she'll feel to get these. You don't want to make her feel like a charity case."

"You know what would be great? If you'd quit pooping on my parade."

"The expression is 'raining on my parade,' Miss Potty-

234

Mouthed Know-It-All. I'm just giving you a few pointers."

"I don't need pointers. And you better not be getting butt sweat on my bed with your grody workout clothes."

She holds up her hands, a gesture she stole from Tuney. "Okay. I hereby cease and desist giving you dating advice."

"Who said we're dating?" I ask. "I *just* started hanging out with this girl. You're acting like I'm gonna propose."

"Well, you did buy her two—oh, never mind." Mom sighs. "How's the shoulder today?"

"It's fine. I'll do my PT after dinner. Can we watch a *BBC Earth* tonight? The caves one where they show the mountain of guano?" A burning sensation hits the back of my sternum. It takes a second to realize it's guilty sadness. The "Caves" episode is Mason's favorite. He loves all those stunning shots of the crystal caverns.

"If your homework's done before dinner and you do your PT right after, we can watch whatever you want."

"Sweet. *Terror Trials* it is!"

"Anything rated TV-14 or younger," Mom says sternly.

"You're no fun," I grumble.

"Someone has to keep your sassy tush in check." She

ruffles my hair and kisses my forehead. "Finish your homework. Tuney's making haggis and cow brains."

"Ooh, sounds gourmet." I smear away the feeling of Mom-spit on my forehead, even though there's probably none there. "Now go away."

"Love you."

I stick my tongue out. "Love you more."

"Physiologically impossible. And pick up your laundry before dinner. Your room's a stinky dump." She throws a dirty sock at me and leaves.

I sit with my legs in a W and tilt the Spirograph box up to check it out. It has seventy-five pieces. You can make way more than just circles with it. There are squares and triangles and bars and oh man, Sunshine's going to *love* it.

During dinner, which I have a hard time eating because I still haven't gone number two and my guts are seriously unhappy, my phone pings. Sarah has sent the finished poster. It looks great. "Tuney, can we make copies of this?" I show her my screen.

"No phones at the table, Aves," Mom says.

"It's for a school thing." Not a lie, really.

"It can wait."

I finish shoveling in the garlicky kale and cranberry-orange couscous Tuney made. I have to use a spoon like a little kid, since I'm eating left-handed and I don't want to lose the load. It's so good, and normally I'd go back for seconds. But it's starting to feel like there's no more room in my body. "Now can we print it?" I ask when I swallow the last bite.

"Keep your priorities in line, kid," Tuney says. "Dessert first."

"Yeah, no schoolwork till you eat your ice cream," Mom jokes.

"Ha ha," I say. But also . . . heck yes ice cream. Whether there's room for it or not.

"I'm glad you've found a positive outlet for your frustration," Tuney says in her office. "You've seemed a little fixated on the drill." She rubs Tank's ears.

I pick up the ugly penguin paperweight on her desk that I made in third grade. "I'm not fixated." I'm so freaking fixated.

"It's understandable. Mom and I have been talking with other parents. We're going to the board meeting on Thursday to bring it up. More than a few people want your principal fired."

I already know this, because I snooped on Tuney's Facebook again when I got up to pee at two a.m. The lady who posted about "sueing" has a meeting with a lawyer this week. She got four other parents to agree to go with her. "Not gonna lie, Tuneykins, it'd be *wicked* sweet if Ritter got fired," I say. I bet *that* would change Mason's mom's mind.

"Turn it down there, kid. Mom and I don't think that's the best solution. We're planning to argue for a written commitment that the district will never run a drill like this again. We don't want any more kids traumatized—"

"Wait, that's *it*? You're just gonna tell Ritter 'That sucked, don't do it again'? So he gets off entirely?" I thump the penguin back onto her desk. Tank startles. "Sorry, dude," I tell him.

Tuney does the slow blink she does when I'm pushing her into irritation. "Revenge on one person isn't the answer. The problem is bigger."

"How so?" Revenge on Ritter the Rat is *totally* the answer.

"It turns out the district got a grant from the state to hire a company to run this drill." She wrinkles her nose, the sure sign she's about to go on a tear. "*Apparently*, since public education is chronically underfunded in this country and having shooter drills is mandated by most states now, schools can apply for federal grants to pay for drills. Because of course funding anything to do with the military-industrial *complex* gets the congressional stamp of *approval*, but funding social *services* gets *squat*. So, of course, there's an entire industry cropping up around taking advantage of these grants. The more elaborate the drill, the pricier." She looks disgusted. "You and I and the parents at your school might be mad at Mr. Ritter, but he didn't act alone."

I pluck a paper clip out of the bin on her desk. "Mr. Trevino didn't know a thing about it. And Ritter sounded awfully pleased with himself when he announced it was over and that he hoped we'd 'learned from the experience.'"

She sighs. "I get why you're mad, kiddo. I just want you to focus more on this"—she gestures at our poster coming out of the printer—"than on being angry at your principal." She plucks a poster off the stack and holds it up. "This is exactly what your mom and I want you to do when you're mad. Channel your feelings into making a positive change, instead of focusing on how mad you are. Reform measures are always a better approach than revenge."

I bend the paper clip into a straight line. "Easy for you to say." She's trying to turn this into a "teachable moment," as Mom says. "You weren't the one humiliating yourself in front of your crush by sobbing because you thought you were gonna die. You're not the one who might lose their best friend over this crap. You're not the one who had to hear Ritter say 'I told you so' after he freaking terrorized an entire school!"

Tuney half grins at me. "Your crush, huh?"

My anger derails. "That just slipped out." I stab the paper clip into the cushiony part of my sling.

Her half grin becomes a full one. "She is quite pretty. Seems a bit . . . I don't know, sweet and innocent for your tastes?"

"How do you know what my tastes are? I'm thirteen. I don't even know that yet."

"I just mean Sarah seems . . . lamblike. You're more of a firecracker."

My heart double thumps. There's no way she could know about the fireworks plan James and I are plotting. Mason might be mad at me, but he wouldn't rat me out. "She's not a lamb. It was her idea to make these posters."

Tuney takes them off the printer and I shift how I'm standing. The pain in my knee has gone from a dull throbbing to a constant ache that shoots heat up my thigh into my hip every time I put weight on it. W sitting no longer helps, and now it just hurts my hip too.

Tuney gives me the stack. "Ready to talk about you and Mason, squirt?"

"Uh, no. We're fine." Except I did just say I might

lose him over this. "I'm sure we'll work it out. We argue all the time, you know."

Tuney looks like she has something to say about that, but hesitates at my expression. She smiles and squeezes my good arm. "Well, if you need dating advice, you come straight to me. I'm an expert on wooing pretty girls. It landed me your mom."

"Okay, one, that's gross. Two, you and Mom are *old* and out of touch. And three, are you in cahoots with her? She was trying to warn me earlier not to 'come on too strong' or whatever."

"Your mom is beautiful," Tuney says like she means it. "And we're not in cahoots. Well, we are, but not about this. I didn't even know you were crushing until it 'slipped out.'"

"You're impossible."

"Feeling's mutual, squirt," she says with one of those Tuney smiles that make me feel 100 percent unconditionally loved. She plucks the paper-clip spear out of my sling and chucks it, then opens her closet and pulls out a fresh ream of printer paper.

I spin in a circle in her office chair, trying to spin away the sudden urge to tell her about my knee. If it keeps getting worse, I'm going to have to tell them anyway. I'd rather tell Tuney first and have her break it to Mom, because Mom is going to be up in my grill about how it started and how long it's been going on and what does it feel like and why haven't I said anything.

I'm not ready for that. Not ready to add more physical therapy to the stuff I already have to do every day. Not ready to face the possibility of another surgery. If something's gone way wrong in there, like I'm starting to fear it has, I could wind up in a wheelchair. It's not like I can use crutches with my arm in a sling.

All the kids on the Zebra Board who use wheelchairs say this sort of thing is exactly how it started. Something that seemed like a temporary situation wound up with them being in the chair for a lot longer than they ever thought they'd have to be in it. Even permanently. Two or three girls on there are obnoxiously positive. They talk about how they're grateful for their wheelchair because it lets them get around, and they try to encourage others not to lament being "stuck" in theirs.

I can't think about it that way right now. I can't even admit to myself how worried I am about my knee. That's like admitting this awful disease, or *syndrome* or whatever, is winning. And I'm losing.

I stand up from Tuney's desk chair. Losing is *not* what Avery Hart does. In fact, I'm gonna go win a battle with my bowels right now.

Monday morning, I get up feeling loads lighter and better, probably because of that epic (and horrible) bathroom trip last night. A text from James comes in during breakfast: *You get the goods yet?*

Not yet. I don't tell him it's because I've been distracted by his sister, plus I sort of got in a fight with the guy whose brother's friend could've been my source for "goods." *Is your mom gonna take your phone at night so we can't communicate to do the thing?* The worry has been in the back of my mind since their mom said kids in that house don't take phones to bed.

I know where she stashes it.

Of course he does.

I send the thumbs-up emoji. Now to figure out how I'm going to actually get fireworks, since my plan didn't exactly pan out. Maybe I can find Brad on social.

Well, but first . . . I really need to try to fix things with Mason. I watched our Velocibeef video last night and wound up crying myself to sleep like a dope.

A gift for him will help.

I go up to my room and tuck the off-brand Magic 8 Ball Tuney got for me into my backpack with the Dream-o-graph. It says stuff like *Consult a rabid cat* and *None of this is real* and *Your gut feeling is full of bacteria.* Mason's obsessed with asking it questions. I scrawl a note: *I asked it if you were still mad and it said "I'm busy, go play." So this magical orb is my peace offering to you.* I try to draw a hand making a peace sign, but I'm no Sarah, so I write *Badly drawn peace sign does not mean less peace* under it. I'll put the note and Magic 8 Ball into his locker for him to find.

It's not a real apology. But honestly . . . I'm not sorry for coming up with the fireworks plan with James. Yes, Mason and Sarah—and sort of my conscience, but to heck with that useless thing—are telling me it's a bad idea. But the worse this knee situation gets, the more I want to shoot off fireworks outside Ritter's window. Straight *into* his bedroom, honestly, but outside it is less likely to get me jailed.

Getting revenge won't fix my knee. Or my disease. I still think it might make him apologize, but even if he doesn't, it'll do wonders for my mindset to scare the absolute bajonkers out of that jerk.

By the end of second period, the knee pain is too loud to sidestep. When I first got to school, I saw Sarah's poster in the main hallway, and it looked great. I hobbled all over (except near the art room) sticking up our poster copies with sticky tack, careful to blend into crowds. Carrying the big Spirograph set, which wouldn't fit in my locker, had me just off balance enough with the shoulder-and-backpack situation that it made my knee worse. All morning, I've been straightening and bending my leg. It seems like a good knee pop will fix the problem. But it never pops. It just gets hotter and more painful.

I hustle to math despite the pain, hoping to get there before Sarah so I can put this chonky Spirograph box in her seat. By some miracle of physics, I make it there before her and Mason. I drop into my desk with a heavy whoosh of relief. I set the Spirograph box in Sarah's chair in front of me and dig the Dream-o-graph out of my bag.

Then I hesitate. Maybe it is "coming on too strong" to give her both. Maybe I should dial it back and just start with the Spirograph set.

I hear her in the hallway talking to Mason. I quickly drop the Dream-o-graph on top of the Spirograph, then dig in my bag for my folder. Trying not to look up because I feel all flustered. My hope and my fear that she's going to think I'm weird for buying her this stuff are all tangled around the pain frustration, making it hard to breathe. It's way too many feelings to have in my body at once.

Sarah reaches her seat. "What's—oh my gosh," she says. "Avery, did you . . . are these from you? For me?"

I risk a quick glance up. She looks sort of confused

and weirded out, like I was afraid she would be, but also . . . excited. Happy. "Yeah." I look down. "I had some money left on a gift card. It's not a big deal."

She puts the boxes on her desk. "These look . . . um, expensive."

I tug my earrings. "Not a big deal," I repeat. "Really."

"It's a big deal to me." She touches my forearm. "Thank you. These are . . ." She giggles like she was trying to hold it back and it's finally burst out. "I'm so excited! This is awesome!"

The sight of her grin reaches way down inside my frustration and fear and unwinds it. I smile too. "I'm glad you like it."

"What is this, give-people-stuff day?" Mason asks. "Are you trying to make everyone like you by handing out gifts?"

"Found the Magic 8 Ball, huh?" I smile at him despite the way he said that. "Did you ask it if we're friends again?"

"It told me to eat ants and ask later. But I'm your friend even if I'm mad at you, dingus."

I pout to hide my relief. "Aw. Don't be mad at me."

He shrugs. "Your plan's still a dumb idea."

My happiness evaporates. "Don't call me dumb." And why did he bring that up in front of Sarah? That's the opposite of what I want.

"I didn't. I said your plan is dumb."

I shift my knee again, trying to pop it. But it only hurts. "Why are you being mean?"

"How am I being mean? You told me you wanted to get fi—"

"Just stop!" I snap. The last thing I want is for Sarah to find out the specifics.

Mason frowns and starts to say something, but Mr. Trevino tells us to quit talking and pass our homework forward.

I grit my teeth as I take my homework out. This obnoxious pain has me on an emotional roller coaster. I do *not* want to squabble with Mason in front of Sarah. And this definitely isn't helping me get back on his good side.

Whatever. I'll figure something out. And then this will all go away once I blast the principal out of his cozy bed and feel the sweet relief of revenge and everyone is glad glad *glad*.

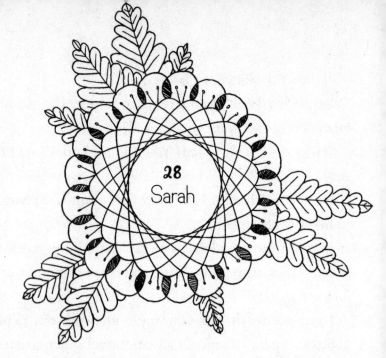

28
Sarah

Mon., May 6, 12:42 p.m. Lunch. Our posters are up all over school, and they look great. I've seen a bunch of kids slowing down during class changes to read them. I even saw a group of girls I don't know taking pictures of the original one. I hope they post photos on social.

The panic problem is continuing to improve! At breakfast, when there was a story on Mom's Fox News morning show about a kid with whooping cough, I prevented a panic attack about vaccine-resistant diseases by using "Come back to your senses." (The burnt-toast smell helped. I told myself it had germ-killing properties.) In science, before it was my turn to read aloud, I took three deep breaths, and my voice came out steady as I read. For a change.

In math, I was going to give Avery the St. Mary's youth

group brochure Mom picked up for me to pass along, but I got distracted by this giant Spirograph set, plus a thing called a Dream-o-graph. And now I have so many <u>feelings</u> that I need to list them so I can sort them out.

I looked up the prices on Amazon. She spent almost fifty dollars. That makes me feel . . . I don't know. Like I can never give her back a gift so expensive. And now I'm in her debt, but not really, because she just <u>gave</u> this stuff to me without me asking for it, so . . . I don't know. It feels awkward. I feel awkward.

She's rich, though, so maybe $50 to her is $5 to me.

I am SO EXCITED to use this stuff. Especially the Dream-o-graph. It looks like you set up the cogs and pen and paper and then turn the handle. So maybe you can't skip the track the way it's so easy to do with a Spirograph. (I wonder if that will make it less helpful during panic. Maybe it's easier to zone out while turning a handle than while focusing on both hands to make a complicated Spirograph pattern.)

The design guide that came with the Spirograph looks intimidating. Like there's a lot of math involved in making the images in the guide, which are, oh gosh, SO cool.

I don't want Avery to lose her friendship with Mason. Something more is going on than what I see in math class. Something big and not good, because of how angry Avery got.

I hoped the poster meant Avery had dropped the revenge idea. But it sounds like she hasn't. It sounds like she has a whole actual <u>plan</u>. Like she's going to do it even though Mason thinks it's a bad idea.

I hoped the poster would change her mind about that. But now I think it hasn't.

There <u>has</u> to be a way to stop her. To get in her head and find out what's going on, and whether I can help her.

Thinking about the shape and dimension and content of Avery's mind is like thinking about making new designs with this stuff she gave me. I get the same warm sense of hope about both, combined with twists of worry that I won't be good at either—that the Dream-o-graph will be too math-y and complicated. That Avery's mind is like a folded-shut lotus flower, too layered with privacy and fear for me to get into it and stop her from making a mistake.

But I have to try anyway. I care about her too much now to push away my concern for her.

29

Avery

At lunch, Bree asks me if I've signed the petition yet. "The one in the cafeteria?" I ask, trying to sound innocent.

"No, the legit one," Dariellis says. "Check your phone." She taps her screen and my phone buzzes.

I'm kind of offended she doesn't think our petition is "legit," but I tap the link. It opens to a Change.org page titled "End Active Shooter Drills at MCMS." Beneath that is a paragraph that starts *Realistic active shooter drills in schools do more harm than good, especially when students and staff don't know it's a drill.* There are a few sentences about the drill we went through, and a photo of the poster Sarah and I made over a red button that says *Sign this petition.*

"Wow," I say. I don't know what to think. I guess it *is* more legit than what Sarah and I did. Even if it kinda ripped us off by using the photo of our poster. I scroll to the bottom of the page, where it says *Justice for MCMS Students started this petition.* It also lists the number of supporters so far—112, but the number ticks up to 114 as I look at it. "Who made this?"

"It's a mystery." Dariellis cuts a glance at Mason, half a grin on her face. "Let's just say it's nice to have a study hall teacher who doesn't pay much attention to the kids."

Bree's jaw falls open. "*You* guys? No way! Can I tell everyone? I could sneak it into the morning announ—"

"No," Dariellis says. "And keep your voice down."

"We thought anonymous was best," Mason adds. "So it sounds like it comes from all the students. And if the posters get taken down, we still have this."

I bite my lip. Mason and Dariellis made this together. Without me. Using the poster Sarah and I made.

For half a hot-tempered second, I'm tempted to tell them they can't just go stealing our work. But I realize quickly that this would be dumb. Sarah wanted the poster to help, to create a common cause to rally around. And it's achieving that. In a bigger way than she planned, even.

She's going to be really happy about this.

I inwardly sigh as I forward the link to her. *Check this out!!!* I write. As soon as I hit send, a text from James comes in: *Asking around paid off. I'm picking up some super-spicy goods after school tomorrow. I'll be the getaway driver if you spark the magic. Still in?*

I suck my breath in at the quick thrill. But it's followed by a wave of doubt. I glance at Bree and Dariellis and Mason, all focused on their phones. *I'm in. When?*

Midnight's the prime hour for devious deeds. Tomorrow 11:50 p.m.?

Yikes. That's soon. *Let's make it Wednesday 11:50 p.m. My moms both have meetings Weds evenings and they're zonked by the time they get home. Will make it easier to sneak out.*

Weds works. Where should I pick you up? Not at your house. Don't want anyone to see you getting into a 17-year-old guy's car. That would not end well for me even if we're both gay and obvs not gonna get up to any hanky-panky.

I send a happy-puppy GIF. Then I bite my lip. *What if we get caught? Would be bad, I think.*

We won't. And even if someone sees us, you're a cute eighth-grade chick with a pixie cut and an arm in a sling. No one would believe an adorable little disabled girl would do something so criminal! He adds the baby emoji.

. . . Okay, that didn't feel good. I am *not* disabled. Not yet, anyway.

And now I'm about to cry. A-gain. "Yet" feels so inevitable. So out of my control.

I set my jaw. I'm not waiting for people to sue the school, or for the petition to create change. I'm going to control what I can while I can. Even if it gets me in trouble. If I'm gonna wind up in a wheelchair over this malfunctioning knee that got so much worse because of the drill, I'm not going down without a fight. I text James back: *I'm not a "little disabled girl." Don't make me feel like that.*

I'm sorry, he writes back right away. *You're right. I know how it feels when people discredit you for looking young. Won't happen again.*

My anger fades. I wish other people would listen to me like he does. I text him that I can meet him at the Shell station on Rosetta Pike at 11:50 p.m. Wednesday.

Awesome!!!! C U then, partner in crime!!

"Dude, what are you looking at?" Mason asks. "You've gone through twelve expressions in the last thirty seconds."

"Noneya, bruh." I turn my phone facedown on the table.

"Why are you so snappy today? Are you on your—"

"Don't you *dare*," Dariellis says. "Petition partner or not, I will smack you across this cafeteria."

"And I'll smack you back to your seat," Bree says.

I grin. "And I'll knee you in the—"

"Jeez, all right. See what happens when I eat with a bunch of girls," Mason says.

"Well, no one else wants to eat with you because you're so *annoying*," Dariellis sniffs.

Mason rubs his chest. "Ow. Mean."

"You deserve it after a comment like that." She goes back to her phone, her face stormy.

"I was only joking," Mason grumbles.

"Not really a joke-worthy topic," Bree says. "TBH."

"I picked up on that." Mason takes a bite of his sandwich, looking chagrined.

Bree smiles at him. "Don't beat yourself up. Just learn the lesson and move on."

He nods without looking at her. "For real, though," he says quietly to me. "What's up?"

I pull at the hoops in my left ear. "Nuh-*thing*. God." I suck at lying.

"You suck at lying," he says. "You tug your ear every time."

"I thought you didn't want to go to Maple Creek High. Why'd you bother making this petition?" My words come out bitter.

"Because I realized I don't want to just let it go," he says. "And this is a way better way to deal with it than what *you* want to do."

"Why do you even care what I want to do?"

"Uh, because last I heard, you wanted to get fireworks from Brad and—"

"Shh!" I hiss. "Keep your voice down."

"Tell me that's not still on."

"It never was on, because how am I gonna actually get them? It's impossible." Not that it matters now, since James came through.

"I know you," Mason says. "When you decide a thing's gonna happen, it's gonna happen. And you have that *look* on your face."

My excitement is gone, and now my eyes are stinging with tears. "The look that means I want to thunder-punch your questions?"

"That exact one. I hope it doesn't mean what I think it means."

I turn away from Mason and put my headphones on. I don't need to hear how dumb my idea is or how "disappointed" he'd be in me if I went through with it. Half the reason I'm doing this is so Ritter will apologize and Mason won't get yanked around by what his mom thinks is best for him. I can't stand the thought of us being torn apart. Despite all the mess since the drill, we're still best friends (right?). And best friends need each other, even if they don't get along 100 percent of the time. Best friends look out for each other.

I wish he'd try to see that I just want to keep us together.

30
Sarah

Mon., May 6, 2:51 p.m. English class. We're supposed to be working on our Charles Dickens essays, but I'm too distracted to focus. I've heard so many kids talking about the petition Avery sent me. I even overheard a hallway conversation about spreading the word by posting photos of the posters tagged #StopTheDrills.

Our posters are doing exactly what I hoped they would. More, even.

But Mason told me something during our group activity that's pushing the gladness right out of me. All the good feelings I had about Avery, all the excitement about the Spirograph and the Dream-o-graph and the way it seems like she and I have been building a bright light between

us . . . it suddenly feels up in the air.

Because apparently, Avery wants to get fireworks from Mason's brother's friend. And sneak out with someone—Mason didn't say who or when, I got the idea he doesn't know—to set the fireworks off outside Principal Ritter's window.

I don't even know what to think about that.

Mason said he's trying to convince her not to do it, but she's acting weird and he's worried she's going "off the rails." He said she was practically crying during lunch. He thinks she's hurt in some other way than her shoulder since she's limping. And that she probably doesn't want to admit it to anyone or even herself because she's so freaked out about her disease that she isn't thinking right anymore. He said he's more worried about her than mad at her, but that when he talks to her, the mad overrules the worry because she's so stubborn.

He wants me to talk to her. Since she won't listen to him. He said Avery <u>like</u>-likes me, and that he felt bad about outing her but it was necessary, because she might actually listen to me.

Avery <u>like</u>-likes me. Like I think (or thought? I don't know) I <u>like</u>-like her.

I'm so mixed up again. Like I was before Charlene's daughter helped me realize what I'm really afraid of.

Mason just slipped me a note.

Let's meet at her locker at the end of the day. If she hears it from both of us maybe she'll listen. My # is 555-2454 so we can text after if we need to regroup. —M

Mason is very organized about this. Which is weird because he's so disorganized in classes. Always forgetting stuff.

I feel the opposite of organized. What if this ends my friendship with Avery? And I'm alone again, with stray texts and calls from Luci not nearly enough to fill that void?

It felt so good to think that maybe I'm not alone. I didn't realize what a relief it was until just now. When it might go away.

Maybe I don't <u>have</u> to talk to Avery with Mason.

But then she might do this irrational thing and get in trouble. Or worse, get hurt. It seems dangerous. Some-thing only a person who's desperate would do.

Does she really feel that desperate about the drill? Or is it something else? Is it what Mason said, that maybe she's in more pain than she's letting on?

It seems like that could be the case. So maybe we just have to convince her to tell us what's wrong. What's hurting.

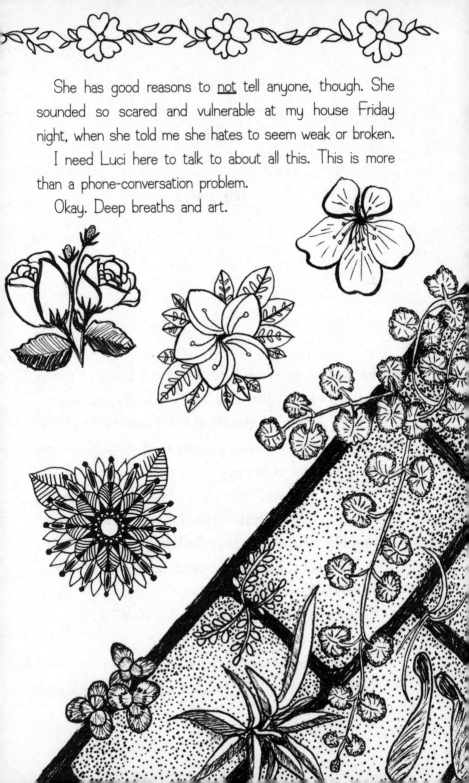

She has good reasons to <u>not</u> tell anyone, though. She sounded so scared and vulnerable at my house Friday night, when she told me she hates to seem weak or broken.

I need Luci here to talk to about all this. This is more than a phone-conversation problem.

Okay. Deep breaths and art.

31

Avery

In band class, my whole freaking body hurts so much that I can't stand listening to Carson playing wrong. When he derails for the third time and the band follows him into a crashing cacophony, I ask if he's even tried to practice at home.

"Of course I have," he says, his face red. "It's hard to change gears after I learned the bell-kit part first. And it's not like I have a drum set at home like you do."

"You could at least set up some cardboard boxes to work on the beat."

"Says the spoiled girl who has her own full set," he snaps.

"I'm not spoiled just because—"

"Can it, you two," Ms. Everett says. "Let's try again.

From the top. One, two—"

I grit my teeth.

When I limp into the 700 wing after last period, reciting *sidestep* in a futile effort to edge around the pain, I spot Mason and Sarah at my locker. Mason looks grimly determined. Sarah is hugging the Spirograph set and looks like she feels sick.

I could skip the locker. Go straight out to the bus.

But I kinda need my stuff.

I take a deep breath and head their way. I gotta practice my poker face. It's so hard to hide the pain grimace. "Hi," I say when I reach them. Like nothing is wrong. My armpits are sweating like mad from pain and stress.

"I told her about your fireworks plan," Mason says straight off.

I stare at him.

He and Sarah stare back at me. "Yell at me if you're gonna," he says. "So we can get it over with and talk about this."

I turn my back to him and spin my lock. "So you're ganging up on me now. Good for you two." My voice is tight.

"We're not trying to gang up—"

"That's exactly what you're doing." I yank my locker

open. All the crap I stuffed into it in a rush after lunch falls out. My social studies book lands on my foot.

I bite back a howl and shift my weight to my bad leg. But my janky knee gives out and whacks the locker underneath mine. I shift my weight back to my foot-pain leg, swallowing hard and blinking the pain-rage-frustration tears away.

Bodies are freaking *ridiculous*. I *hate* mine. And I especially hate Ritter for that terrible drill that messed up my knee in the first place.

"I'm worried," Mason says. "What's wrong besides your shoulder?"

"Other than you guys teaming up for whatever *this* is?" I shove the social studies book into my bag, then take it out. I'm too mad and hurt to remember if I have homework for that class. "Nothing. At all."

Sarah inches closer. "We just—we really don't want you to get hurt."

"So what if I do? What's one more stupid pain shoving its way into my life? Pile it on!" I'm choking up. I jerk my backpack's jammed zipper.

Sarah touches my good shoulder. "Please just think about—"

"No, *you* think!" I shrug her off. I'm so pain-mad I barely know what I'm saying. "Neither of you knows how it feels to be out of control of your life! To spend every freaking minute scared the future will be made of pain and your body falling apart and having to rely on people!"

Mason's face is stormy. "Actually, I think we *all* know how it feels to be out of con—"

"Don't 'actually' me!" I wipe away angry tears. "I'm not gonna live my life afraid to go after what I want. Like *you* both are." It's a low blow, but I can't stop my mouth. "I'm not just going to *accept it* when crappy stuff happens. I'm going to *do* something about it."

Sarah looks like she's about to cry too. "We're just worried. Mason—" She sniffles and glances at him. "Thinks something else is wrong. Than your shoulder. Is . . . is something else—"

"Yes! Two people I thought were my friends aren't even *trying* to understand why this matters to me." I can't get the zipper unjammed.

Sarah hugs the Spirograph set tighter. "But we do understand—"

"If you're trying to stop me, then no. You don't." I slam my locker. "Just leave me alone. *Both* of you."

"Aves. We're trying to help." Mason picks up my bag like he's going to carry it to my bus.

I pull it out of his hands. The weight throws me off balance. I catch myself with my left elbow against my locker and pain shoots down my arm into my hand.

I have no more capacity for pain or stress or trying to fend off people I know in my heart are trying to help me. I put on my headphones and limp away with my dumb weepy face turned down. At the entrance to the 700 wing, I rip down the poster copy I put up this morning. Drowning in oceans and oceans of regret.

They don't follow me.

32
Sarah

Mon., May 6, 3:21 p.m. In the car with James. Three deep breaths. Or four. Or twenty.

I'm shaking. Not just my hands. My everything. That went <u>so</u> bad. It hurt to see Avery cry. To see her lose the self-control I know she's determined to keep. And it stung when she tore down our poster.

I asked Mason if he's talked to Avery's parents. He said he's on the fence. He doesn't want to rat her out, but what she wants to do is dangerous and we obviously can't stop her. He said he's never seen Avery like this and that he's scared.

I told him I was scared too. We didn't have time to talk more. He had to go to the bus and I had to go wait for James. Mason's going to FaceTime Avery on his ride home.

I prayed so hard while I was waiting for James to pick me up. This feels way more awful than losing Avery as a friend. That was going to be scary and terrible. But now I've hurt her.

That's so much worse.

Even though she's so angry at me . . . I still want to stop her from whatever she's planning with fireworks. She could get really hurt. She barely seems to care if she <u>does</u> get hurt.

Actually . . . is that a clue?

Yes—and I missed it. She said, "What's one more stupid pain shoving its way into my life?"

I'll text Mason.

3:28 p.m. He wrote back right away. I guess he's not having luck calling her. His text said, "I realized that too. So it does mean something else hurts and she's hiding it."

I can't get lost in fear right now. I need to be logical.

I think there are only two options.

1. Apologize to Avery and tell her we won't say anything to her parents (assuming I can get Mason on board, which seems doubtful) and maybe save our friendship. But risk her getting hurt/in bad trouble if she does this awful plan.

2. Tell on Avery and lose our friendship. (Or whatever was happening between us. Which I guess is no longer happening.) And also save her from getting hurt/in bad trouble. Also I could stop worrying about crushing on a girl.

Maybe a third option is to pray. But it feels pointless. I've asked God to stop so many bad things from happening. Aunt Camila dying, Luci moving, James and Mom fighting. Avery's disease hurting her. Mason being stressed. My panic problem.

My mustard-seed faith is shrinking fast. And yet I can't seem to let go of it entirely.

Dear God, please uncoil James. And Mom. And Avery. Thank you. Amen.

7:03 p.m. In my room. Dad noticed me struggling with math at the table after dinner and patiently walked me through the problem set Mr. Trevino assigned. It was nice to get Dad to myself for a bit. To have his calm, steady presence next to me. It helped me stress less.

But then James and Mom got into an epic fight about mowing the lawn. Because when James doesn't have anything big to argue about, he argues about the yard.

I keep thinking of what Avery said about being afraid to

go after what you want. I didn't like the angry way she said it. It made me feel more mouse-like than ever.

But she's right. Whenever I have a want that goes against what my parents want, I push it down or try to ignore it. Because that's easier than talking to them. Like I want to ask why Mom never asks James to help us with babysitting the kids. Or why Dad gets us to church twenty minutes early every week when we can't even go inside until ten minutes before mass starts. Or why I have to go to STEM camp when I'm dreading it.

haha nope

7:41 p.m. Turns out drawing from my floor with a Conté pencil is very good for thinking. I guess a different perspective and tool can be helpful in more ways than one.

I think I fear being out of control of my mind in the same way Avery fears being out of control of her body because of her disease. And her disease is maybe getting worse, so she's lashing out. Instead of lashing in the way I do.

It's coming from the same place. A fear of ourselves.

I wish I could give her a hug. Tell her I really do think I understand.

9:18 p.m. In bed w/ flashlight. While I read Ruthie her "Bible Bedtime Stories" book, Mom and Dad were in James's room talking to him about whatever he did at school today that landed him in hot water. I kissed Ruthie good night and tiptoed out to the living room. I opened our computer and did a search for "affordable summer art camps near me."

There were a ton, mostly for kids Ruthie's age or younger. I tried "affordable summer art camps eighth grade." I found something called a STEAM camp and clicked on it.

It's a STEM camp, but the "A" stands for art. Art is "integrated" with science and math.

Which sounds perfect—the meeting place between what my parents want for me and what I want for me. The camp lasts three weeks. You go every day from eight to four.

It took forever to find the price while I was trying to eavesdrop on the voices coming from James's bedroom. When I finally found it, my heart sank.

It costs $1,000. Not my definition of "affordable." It won't be my parents' either, especially since they already paid the down payment on the STEM camp.

As soon as it sounded like Mom and Dad and James were wrapping it up, I clicked the weather website Mom has bookmarked. But just before it switched over, I saw a link that said, "Scholarships still available! Apply here."

I'll try to look it up at school tomorrow. And I have to remember to check the petition site again. I snuck a quick look on my phone while I was brushing my teeth. It's up to more than three hundred signatures, which feels . . . <u>amazing</u>.

Okay. I'm going to dig into this new Spiro kit to make a thank-you card for Avery while I pray for her.

33

Avery

Tuesday in homeroom, I'm hunched in my desk, failing to hug the pain out of my body, when my ears prick up at Bree's changed tone halfway through the morning announcements: "The student council wishes to thank those who made the poster of statistics and started the petition, and to express hope that both can create meaningful change."

Then she drops into a monotone recounting of the boys' tennis game yesterday.

I sink lower in my seat. Sounds like she wanted to say more, but whoever okays the announcements—Mr. Ritter, I bet—made her say that watered-down version.

I check the petition on my phone. There's now a big

string of comments from people saying stuff like *You can't just petition to end all drills, they have a purpose* and *lol what a crock of whiny crap*. It doesn't take much scrolling to realize the trolls have found it. *Weak AF,* one says. *Made by SJW snowflakes.* Other comments are uglier and full of slurs.

All that work Sarah and I did on the poster, the effort Mason and Dariellis put into starting this petition . . . What a waste of time.

It's a good thing, for everyone's sake, that I have a backup plan.

And mine *will* create meaningful change.

34
Sarah

Tues., May 7, 10:03 a.m. Math class. Behind me, Avery's pain and anger are coming off her in waves. She had her headphones on when I came in. She ignored my "hi," and Mason's when he got here.

I don't know what to say to her. I don't want to make anything worse.

My phone just lit up with a text from Mason. I peeked at it under my desk. He wants to text Tuney what Avery's up to instead of telling Avery's other mom, because he says Tuney will go easier on Avery. He's asked me to help him decide what to say, because "you're fire at writing." (I think he only thinks that because I won that writing contest last month where Mr. Carillo entered our stuff without telling us.)

Tonight, we'll try to work out what to tell Tuney.

9:31 p.m. Bible Study was . . . not great. I was crammed in the back with three girls who always talk a lot and get snapped at by Mrs. Marshall to pay attention. She lumped me in with them, and when she told them to stop talking, they all pointed at me and said I'd started it.

Which was ridiculous, because I'd said exactly zero words the entire time. But Mrs. Marshall still told us that if we're not serious about learning how to accept God's plan for our lives, we shouldn't come to Bible Study and disrupt the girls who <u>are</u> serious.

I didn't say I didn't want to be there in the first place. That Mom makes me go. That more socializing—especially with girls who don't seem to like me—after a full day at school, and an afternoon with small children crawling all over me, and then an hour of homework, then listening to James argue with Mom at dinner . . . it all makes my Tuesdays feel like they last ten years. I didn't say that her grumpy approach isn't convincing any of us to listen to what she says about God, and that it's not helping me ask about the question I really want the answer to: whether prayer is pointless when it doesn't ever change anything.

Maybe I'll be brave enough to ask her someday. But not while I'm twisted up about a million things. STEM camp. Avery. The petition that's now loaded with troll comments. It seems to have stalled out at a little over four hundred signatures. I guess most of the kids at school have signed it, which is good, but maybe four hundred signatures aren't enough to make a difference. Or maybe since they're from kids, they don't count. Or maybe the trolls have wrecked its credibility. The posters and petition made the announcements this morning, but . . . is that it? What happens next?

At least the text exchange I had with Mason after dinner went well. Here's what we came up with for him to send to Tuney:

"Hi, Tuney. I think Avery is planning something that could get her in trouble."

(Mason didn't want to say "get her hurt." He's planning to send this after Avery's bedtime but before Tuney goes to bed. So Tuney will have time to sleep on it before deciding how to handle it with Avery. And he thinks if he says "hurt," Tuney will wake Avery up and it'll maybe not go as well as it might otherwise.)

(Also, this is making me realize how much Mason cares about Avery. He's working such a careful balance.)

Next: "She's still fired up about the drill and has been talking about revenge. Something to do with fireworks. She thinks it will make Mr. Ritter apologize (which he totally won't). I also think she's injured in some way and isn't telling anyone. She doesn't like the idea of being vulnerable, so she's pretending she isn't."

(Mason clearly cares a lot about her, to be this aware of what she's doing in her mind. Even when Avery might not be aware about herself.)

(Mason seems like an amazing friend.)

And last: "I'm not sure what it is, but she's been limping, so I guess her knee or ankle. I have to go to bed now so I'm turning off my phone."

He wants to end it there because he doesn't want to have a conversation with Tuney. He just wants to send the messages and dart away. The text version of the ding-dong-dash game Luci's prank-loving brothers are so fond of.

I don't blame Mason. He's way braver than I am for doing this. If Luci had ever planned something that could've gotten her hurt (which she wouldn't, because she's Luci), and I felt like I had to tell Aunt Camila to make sure Luci stayed safe, knowing I could lose her friendship . . . I don't think I could've done it.

I asked Mason if he's going to send the messages tonight. He wrote back that he'll wait one more day, to give Avery a chance to change her mind. I suggested tonight might be better, since we don't know when Avery's planning to do whatever it is.

It took him a few minutes to answer. Then he said he really doesn't want to tell on her, because it will end their friendship, and even though he's mad at her, he cares. He wants to wait one more day just in case she might change her mind.

I still think he should do it tonight, but I get why he's hesitating. I sent him a blue heart. He sent back a GIF of dancing cats.

I wanted to call Luci and talk about all of this. It's just so <u>much</u>. But I had to give my phone to Mom and come downstairs for bed. I drew a few sketches of my lamp from other angles before Mom asked me to please turn the light off. It was just enough to start to feel my way into that "style" thing Mrs. Gianno was talking about.

I think it's in the weight of the lines. Or in the way I can emphasize or de-emphasize the lamp's curves by how hard I press with the Conté pencil—which is influenced by what I'm feeling as I draw. It almost seems like these lamp drawings show my emotions, in a way.

Maybe I should show Mrs. Gianno the animal hybrids I

draw for Ruthie. Maybe those have style. Or maybe they're just childish and silly.

I wonder if someone kind and caring and brave like Mason would ever consider being friends with a quiet mouse like me.

35

Avery

Last night's insomnia was one for the record books. All night, I mulled over my miserable after-school PT session, where I still didn't use the arm bike and Naila told me I've been doing the stretch-band exercise wrong and Mom got on my case for not listening to her. It feels like I'll *never* recover.

I finally fell asleep around five, then jolted out of a shooter-drill nightmare at ten till six with a stiff neck and a headache.

I don't even care. It's Wednesday now and I'm getting revenge on Ritter the Rat tonight. That's all the fuel I need to get out of bed.

At school, I feel so many feelings and their opposites at the same time. Numbly painful. Tired and wired all at once. My guts both locked up and bubbly. Excited and freaked out about the text James sent that said *This is gonna be EPIC.*

I'm barely able to pay attention in my classes. I play an imaginary video of tonight in my mind. It helps me focus less on how bad my stomach hurts right now. On the pain in my right knee. On the new ache lodged in my left hip that's radiating down my lower half, making even my skin hurt.

Sarah says hi in math class. Like yesterday, I half nod without looking at her and slump in my seat. I'm dying to put my arm on my desk and drop to sleep for a few minutes. But it's impossible with Cthulhu. Everything hurts too much for me to fall asleep anyway.

Mason tries giving me a meaningful look a couple of times during class. Like he wants to ask if I've changed my mind.

I absolutely have *not*. After tonight, James and I will be anonymous heroes. Ritter the Rat will understand *exactly* what he did to us all, and how much it sucked, and he'll apologize.

Mason will get to stay in Maple Creek. Sarah will realize that dramatic action gets better results than posters and petitions. My bold move will inspire her to tell her parents she doesn't want to go to STEM camp. (Even though she totally *should* want to go.)

They'll both understand once they see all the good that will come from this.

I spend lunch in the library, cracking my joints trying to release the pressure. My stomach's way weird and I don't feel like eating. Or like seeing Mason and Bree and Dariellis.

But the whole time I sit in the study carrel with my math book open and my headphones on, exchanging memes with James, I miss Mason. James is seventeen and has his own stuff going on that has nothing to do with me. Talking to him is nothing like talking to Mason. I miss having someone my age to talk to who understands me. Who's as much of a weirdo misfit as me, even if it's for different reasons. I miss how Mason can describe a situation I'm going through in such ridiculous terms that we both crack up and I feel a million times better. I miss feeling like I give that to him too. Like I make his life better.

Ever since the dirt bike incident, I've only made his life worse.

The hard truth of that sits in my guts with the last three days of food I've eaten.

It'd be so great to be four years old again. To do my bathroom business with no angst and then take a long nap and then get up and play silly games with Mom and Tuney. Free of pain and uncertainty and guilt.

Even though I barely slept last night, I'm wide awake at ten till eleven when Tuney and Mom turn in for the evening. At dinner, Tuney asked if anyone said anything about the posters. I told her it made it onto the announcements, but that the posters were all gone from the walls where I stuck them.

I didn't tell her about the online petition. She'd get all excited and it's a conversation I didn't want to have. I let her and Mom think that disappointment about the posters was why I didn't eat much.

Both of them looked tired when they got home from their meetings, as hoped, and they went right to bed. I wait through fifteen minutes of silence from their room. I need to leave by 11:30 to make it to the gas station to meet James.

At 11:19, I make my way as quietly as I can to the basement to grab my black jeans out of the laundry. I need to dress in all black so I can be a sneaky fireworks ninja. I'm glad Tank decided to sleep in Mom and Tuney's room tonight so I don't have to worry about the sound of his toenails on the hardwood as he follows me around.

In the basement, I squat to fish through the basket

on the floor by the washing machine. I find my jeans wrinkled and smelling musty. I stand up and head for the stairs.

My knee pops and I clip my good shoulder against the deep freezer. The sudden balance shift jolts pain through everything that hurts—my shoulder, knee, hip, guts. It's so loud I can't sidestep it. I can't even tell where it's all coming from. I lean on the fridge, slide down to the floor, and sit in a heap, trying to get my bearings and catch my breath and push down the tears. I pull my non-fiery knee up and wrap my good arm around it. Pretending I'm somewhere else. Some-one else. A person whose body isn't falling apart and whose friends aren't mad at her and who isn't burning with the need to get revenge on a jerk who terrorized the people she loves.

After a few tight breaths in my fetal-position emo ball, I slowly uncurl and sit up. I have to get moving if I'm going to meet James on time. I put my hand on the floor at the base of the fridge to stand up. My pinkie hits something with a hard edge and I look down.

There's a mousetrap tucked behind the deep freezer. All that's left of the creature it caught is a skeleton.

It must have been here for years. It's kinda cool how perfectly preserved it is.

"Hi, friend," I say to it.

Then I laugh. Talking to a dead mouse is no more outlandish than anything else I've done in the past few weeks. "I get you, bro," I tell the mouse. "I'm in a trap too. It's called hEDS and it sucks." I poke at what's left of the little curled-up tail. "But I'm not gonna wind up pinned down like you. I'm getting *revenge*."

The skeleton doesn't answer. Shockingly.

I pick up the trap and carefully pry it open. The bones fall onto my thigh in a soft dusty clatter. A few bits of clumped gray fur fall off.

The horror of how the mouse died suddenly hits me. The way the bar snapped over him, crushing his little lungs. Pinning him until the last breath and beat of life left his tiny body.

How long did it take? Did the poor thing struggle to escape for hours? Or even days? Fighting against a life-sucking force he couldn't control?

I feel his pain all the way to my bones. My control started slipping away the day Dr. Simmons said hEDS doesn't get better, only worse. Control has gotten farther from my grasp with every new pain, injury, symptom. Now I want it back so badly that I'm literally about to sneak out of my house to set off explosives.

That's . . . good lord. That's so stupid. It's a *terrible* idea.

A throbbing fear starts way down in my belly. I curl back up and cover my head with my good arm. My breathing speeds and my guts twist and my heart pounds. My hands and armpits sweat.

Is this a panic attack? Is this what happens to Sarah? This *sucks*.

I pull in a deep breath and snap my head up. I can't sit here panicking. I need to fight it.

I get to my feet using the fridge. I yank the black jeans from the basket and pick my way up the basement stairs, then up the steps to my bedroom. I check the time: 11:26.

Terrible idea or not—I don't care. I'm committed.

It's hard to change clothes quickly with one arm. I'm stuck in the blue shirt I wore to school since I can't get the sling off by myself, so I drape a big black hoodie over me. By the time I've struggled into my black jeans (which feel way too tight, thank you malfunctioning guts) and pulled on my black Converse and my black beanie hat, it's 11:33.

It's way colder outside than I thought it would be. I blow my warm breath on my cold left hand as I limp down the sidewalk. I have James's "Rock Out for Revenge" playlist pumping in my ears so I'll get hyped, but it's hard to focus on it when every footfall is pain. Lifting my left leg to take each step jabs a fire poker through my hip. Shifting my weight to my right leg makes the knee pain almost excruciating. My fear sits in my guts like a boulder.

I feel so gross and weird. So out of control of my body.

The old me might've bucked a few rules, even if I never would've done something *this* drastic. But I've got a few months of nonstop pain under my belt now, and everything's different. The pain has changed me. Made me harder. Meaner. It's taken all the Sarah out of me.

I don't realize the tears have started until I can no longer breathe through my stuffed-up nose. A quiet sob chokes out and I cover my mouth. "Stop it," I try to say, but my teeth are chattering from the cold and everything hurts so much I can barely move and I know, I know I'm going way too far.

I'm just like that mouse. It's not hEDS trapping me. It's my desperate scramble to regain control. Any kind of control. Because I feel so far away from it. So help-less.

That mouse reached into a trap for something he thought he needed. Instead, he was killed. The thing I think I need—control—is the bait in the trap I'm reaching into right now.

My need for control is controlling me.

I stumble off the sidewalk to a signpost in the grassy strip by the street, James's playlist grating against my ears. I pull my headphones off and grip the rusty metal. I slide down to the grass, dripping snot and tears. My reckless revenge idea is causing major harm, messing up my relationships with the people who matter most to me. Tuney's reform-not-revenge philosophy is right. Sarah's unite-everyone way is right. Mason and Dari-ellis are right.

And I'm wrong.

I choke and cry and shiver as I hug the sign. I have to tell James I can't do this. It was foolish to think this would make Mr. Ritter apologize. I'm going to lose Mason to private school, going to lose my hope that revenge will make me feel better about anything at all.

I have to tell James *right now*. Before I think my way right back into the trap.

I take my phone out. My hands are shaking from the cold, from too many feelings. It takes a zillion tries to tap out a message to James: *My knee and hip are all messed up. I can hardly walk. I can't do the plan. I'm sorry.*

I power my phone all the way off as soon as the message sends. I don't want to risk him talking me back into it. I'm scrambled and weepy and dizzy and cold and exhausted. I don't know if I'd be able to say no.

Especially if he showed up with a warm car.

I limp back toward our house, my fear tears changed to tears of relief. It's time to apologize to Mason. And Sarah. Tell them how sorry I am.

It's time to fix all of this.

PART III

Avery

Crimes + Contrition

Sarah

Compassion + Confidence

Thurs., May 9, 6:13 a.m. My sunflowers are dead.

6:49 a.m. On the bus. Heart so heavy.

Mom's morning Fox News was playing as I sat down to breakfast. I heard the tail end of a story about fireworks shot off at a principal's house late last night. Then it switched to a weather report about the record-breaking cold.

Mason and I were too late. And because of us, Avery's moms will know she's the one who did those fireworks.

She'll be in so much trouble. Maybe even legal trouble.

I couldn't eat. Dad asked if I was okay. I said I was sad that my flowers had died. Mom gave me a sympathetic look and said we can get new seeds.

What happened with my flowers is exactly what's happened with Avery. I got excited and ignored the obvious truth that I shouldn't rush into planting my hopes so early. Like I planted the seeds too early. Even though I knew a cold snap could kill them.

I didn't text Luci a flower update photo. Obviously.

I only saw James for a minute this morning before he left. He looked as tired as me. Maybe he didn't sleep either, after that fight he had with Mom and Dad last night at dinner.

I should have pressed Mason to tell Tuney sooner. I should have tried harder to understand why Avery wanted to do what she did. Instead of wrinkling my nose at her Friday night and telling her she sounded like James when she started talking about it.

If I'd handled that differently—better—none of this would have happened.

I'm dreading math class. I feel so guilty.

7:03 a.m. Homeroom. James just texted and asked why I looked so sad this morning. I could've shrugged him off, or told him about the dead sunflowers. But the panic was trying to come back and I didn't want to deal with it and I needed someone to know what I'm going through. Even if it's my hotheaded brother.

I told him Avery's the one who set off fireworks outside Principal Ritter's house. And that I'm disappointed because I liked her. <u>Liked</u> her-liked her. And now I'm not sure I do, because even though I thought I understood . . . knowing she did something so drastic to get revenge makes me think maybe I <u>didn't</u> understand. It makes me think we're too different from one another to be anything more than classmates.

I've turned my phone off. I don't want to think about it. I don't want to know James's reaction to me confessing I had a crush on Avery. I just want this to all be over.

Our vines have grown away from each other.

37

Avery

I can barely bend my knee when I wake up on Thursday with a clogged nose and salt from dried tears all over my face and my palms gritty from the rusty street sign.

But it's okay. Because now I can tell Sarah and Mason I'm sorry. That they were right, and I should have listened to them. I can tell Mom and Tuney about my knee. And my hip.

I can't control what's happening with my body. But I *can* control how I react. And it's time I get my mess in order and figure out how to live *with* this disease instead of in spite of it.

I laugh aloud. It's like a cheesy social post. A quote in a scripty font over a soft-focus picture of roses.

I put my feet on the floor. I'm still wearing my black clothes and black hat. I didn't even kick off my shoes last night. I just fell into bed and cried myself to sleep.

There's a rap at my door. "Come in," I say.

Tuney and Tank come in as I'm crossing the room to my dresser. It's impossible to hide how badly I'm limping. I make it to the dresser and turn to tell Tuney I've hurt my knee.

"We need to talk," she says.

I grip the dresser. "Um, okay?"

She sits in my desk chair and leans forward with her elbows on her knees, cracking her knuckles. "I woke up to find some texts Mason sent late last night. About a plan you were cooking up. Involving fireworks? And Mr. Ritter?"

Oh god.

Mason ratted me out.

Which . . . well. Which I deserved.

I'm so glad I came to my senses in time.

"I can't believe you," Tuney says. Anger creeps into her face. "I wish I would've woken up when he sent them last night. Now look what's happened."

A sinking feeling seeps through my guts. For once, it has nothing to do with my intestines. "What . . . do you mean?" I reach down to rub Tank's ears.

"Don't act innocent. There was a post this morning on the Parents of Maple Creek page. A link to a news story." She glares at me like she's expecting me to confess to something.

"Um," I say. "Okay?"

She runs a hand through her hair. "You're dressed in all black. You can barely walk. What's on your palms? Soot from the fireworks you set off?"

Oh my god.

James went through with it without me.

"Um," I say.

Tuney throws her hands in the air. "What on *earth* were you thinking? You *snuck out*? I don't even know what to do with you. Just—" She looks out at the frost on the leaves. "You're lucky Mom had an important meeting this morning, or you'd be getting it from both of us. How bad is it?"

"Is . . . what?"

"Your knee. Or whatever you've hurt." She looks disgusted. "How many times has Mom said you need to be careful? And what do you do, instead of listening? You sneak out, set off fireworks"—she grimaces like she's immeasurably enraged—"and get hurt. Who drove you?"

I swallow hard. Mason told her my plan. Every shred of evidence tells Tuney I did it.

I'm taking the fall for this. Whether I want to or not.

I hold my breath. I didn't expect I'd have to put my realization about giving up control into practice so soon.

Maybe James was right. Maybe they'll go easy on me because I'm a "little disabled girl."

I swallow the lump in my throat. I don't want to think of myself that way. But it's time to face that it's what I am. "I . . ." I tug my earrings. "I walked. That's why my knee is so bad." Hot tears well up.

"You walked six miles. Alone. In the dark. With a *significant* connective-tissue disorder that makes it *very difficult* to recover from strain." Tuney is angrier than I've ever seen her. "Which is it? Left knee? Right?"

"Right. My left hip too." I sniffle. "I'm really s—"

"Save it. You can explain to Mom and me at the same time later. Can you walk?"

I hobble back to my bed. "Yes." Not well, but I can.

"Come downstairs. I'll wrap the knee. You can take some ibuprofen and ice it while you eat breakfast to keep the swelling down till we can take you to get it looked at after school. Assuming I can get an appointment with Naila on such short notice."

"I'm . . . I'm sorry. Tuney." I wipe at my face. "I just wanted to—"

"I'm too mad to talk to you right now. I'll say things

I'll regret." She stands up, looking thoroughly disgusted with me. "Come downstairs and eat. I'll drop you off at your bus stop so you don't have to walk on the bad knee. Even though dropping you off will make me late."

Tank follows her out.

The air outside feels strange and thick, like winter and summer are battling for control. It smells like right before it rains.

It feels weird to not have my headphones around my neck. But I couldn't bring myself to put them on this morning. It feels like I don't deserve to have something comforting that I love.

I couldn't eat either. Not with Tuney slamming around the kitchen, putting our lunches together. Ignoring her eggs and toast.

I'm sorry, I text Mason and Sarah while I wait for the bus. *You were right.*

Neither of them answer. I search for a GIF to express how I feel. But nothing is right. GIFs are for silly situations. Not serious ones.

This one's very, very serious.

When I get to school, Mr. Ritter isn't outside the front office greeting kids like usual. Maybe he's talking to the police.

That's more than I want to think about while I'm still adjusting to this accept-my-disease-and-my-flaws business.

I keep my head down in homeroom. The ibuprofen Tuney gave me is helping me sidestep the pain, a little. I have just enough brain space left over to register that the kids around me are talking about fireworks. And Mr. Ritter.

They're . . . oh. They're really happy. Tyler says that whoever did it is his hero. Three other kids agree. One says this is way better than "that petition the stupid trolls ruined."

I don't look at anyone. James wouldn't have done it if I hadn't suggested it in the first place. If I hadn't been so enthusiastic.

There's no way Tuney or Mom will believe me if I say I didn't do it. Not with all that evidence staring Tuney in the face. They'll think I'm lying. Which will make everything worse.

I can't help but feel a small thrill, buried under all the stress, that James pulled it off. Even though it's wrong to feel that way. The dead mouse showed me that sticking my hand out for the reward of "feeling in control" was a deadly trap. That if I don't get it together and face my reality, I'll wind up pinned beneath my need to control what I can't control.

Like the fact that James did the fireworks. And my knee and hip and guts are a mess. And I'm probably going to wind up in a wheelchair for a while, with everyone angry at me for a crime I dreamed up but didn't commit.

Well. I guess confessing to the fireworks will at least keep James out of hot water. He's been in enough of that already to last a lifetime. And he had his own very good reasons for wanting to get back at Mr. Ritter, so it probably felt good to do what he did.

But confessing also means admitting how bad my knee is, and that what messed it up initially was me trying to pull Mason under Mr. Trevino's desk against his will—which was the reason he got stuck in the middle of the room and peed. Because I was trying to control him, instead of trusting him to decide where to go. Confessing means admitting it's my own fault that my knee has gotten so bad, because I didn't tell Tuney and Mom right away. I didn't tell Naila, who probably could've kept it from getting worse.

I hug my ribs with my good arm. I can't go back and change the past.

But I can take responsibility for the mess I set in motion. I can learn from what I've screwed up. I can become a better person.

* * *

Mason and Sarah are already in math class when I get there. I limp to my desk with both of them watching, their faces a mix of apprehension and disappointment.

I get settled in my seat, feeling self-conscious. I clear my throat. "It was me," I tell them.

Jolene turns to look at me. "What was you?"

I bite my lip. It's probably best if this doesn't get out.

Well. It's going to anyway, with all that evidence. "The fireworks," I say.

She laughs. Not in a nice way. "Yeah, right. You and hyperactive adopted pee-pants."

"Don't call him that," I snap, all my old defenses springing up. "And why is it such a stretch to think I did it?"

"Uh, because you're a total attention-seeker who wants to be the one everyone's calling a hero? Like you didn't get enough attention pretending to be crippled, so now you're pretending you did the fireworks?"

"She's not pretending," Sarah says. "She had surgery. And Mason's not adopted."

"Well." My good shoulder slumps. "It's my own fault about the surgery." I don't need to be defensive about hEDS anymore. It's actual facts. Time to face it.

"Whatever," Jolene says. "Just don't take credit for crap there's no way you did."

Mason folds his arms on his desk and rests his head

on them. He seems so disappointed. Like he's losing his best friend because she did something incredibly dumb he told her not to do. Sarah says nothing. She just keeps her eyes quietly on me. It's impossible to tell what she's thinking.

She turns away when Mr. Trevino starts class.

38
Sarah

Thurs., May 9, 12:41 p.m. It was weird to see Avery in math without her headphones around her neck. It looked like something important was missing from her.

It's pouring outside the cafeteria windows now. If all this water had fallen out of the sky overnight when the air was cold enough to kill baby sunflowers, it would've been snow. But it's warmer now. So it's just rain.

I had a panic attack in French class. Even though I know so many ways to prevent and even stop them now. I didn't have the energy to put up a fight, and it just sort of . . . happened.

It didn't last that long. Like the fear didn't have much energy either.

I guess I should turn my phone back on. See what

James has to say about me confessing my crush on Avery.

12:53 p.m. Everything has changed. Because of THIS BANANAS CONVERSATION.

James: You're gay too????? SARAH FOR REAL????

Me: I don't know. Doesn't matter. I can't like Avery that way anymore after what she did.

James: Sarah. SISTER. Keep liking her!!! It was ME!!!

Me: ?? It was you what??

James: I did the fireworks! It was me! Her idea, but she backed out and I had the stuff so I did it without her lol lol lol

Me: You are KIDDING ME

Me: You have to confess! Avery told her parents she did it! She's going to be in SO MUCH TROUBLE!

James: She will not, she's a cute little 8th grade girl with her arm in a sling. She'll get a slap on the wrist at worst. I'd probably go to freaking jail after all the delinquent crap I've done.

I can't even process this. And now lunch is over and I have to go to art.

2:02 p.m. I needed a distraction from stressing about Avery, so I showed Mrs. Gianno the Conté pencil drawing of the lamp from my floor. Her face lit up and she said I'm on the right track. That this drawing has both style, because of the way I used curving, fluid lines to draw it, and emotion, because of the angle.

So. That was a nice few minutes of distraction from this bonkers afternoon.

2:28 p.m. Hiding in the bathroom. My knees are rubbery. This is turning out to be A DAY, as James says.

Mason barfed.

Look at that. I wrote it.

I guess he was feeling really guilty. Like I was until I found out it was my FREAKING BROTHER. Twenty minutes ago Mason ran to the front of the room and chucked in the trash can, right in front of everyone.

It was like when the drill happened, when my mind skipped over panic and shifted directly into "You can't control this, so just get through it." I care so much about Mason now, and I saw that he needed help. And it was like I just grabbed my fear by the shoulders and said, "Don't go there right now." (Still not entirely sure how I did that, but I hope I can do it again.) I calmly picked up my sketchbook and told Mr. Carillo I'd walk Mason to the nurse.

Isn't that something. Even knowing he might throw up again. On my feet, even.

I was scared. But I did what needed doing.

I told Mason on the way that it was my brother. That Avery didn't do it.

He started cry-laughing. "You mean I just barfed in front of everyone, after peeing myself last week, and she didn't even <u>do</u> it?" he said.

"Yeah," I said. "That's what I mean."

"Oh my God," he said.

I left him in the nurse's office. Now I'm in the bathroom. I needed a place to cry-laugh too. From relief that I pulverized the panic when Mason threw up. From relief that Avery didn't shoot off the fireworks. From stress over how in the world I'm going to convince James to

confess (and <u>I am going to</u>).
From worrying about what's
going to happen to him when
he does, because he's right. He could go to jail.
I hate thinking I might have a part in that by making
him confess, but also, what the FLAMING HECK
was he THINKING? The drill didn't even CONCERN
him. He <u>WASN'T THERE</u>.

I should have realized when Mason told me what
Avery was planning that James would be the driver.
I'm the one who introduced them. And they bonded
over their hatred of Mr. Ritter.

The rain on the roof is louder here in the bathroom
than it is in the English room. It's echoing on the tiles
and metal walls. It's calming, falling hard and steady—

Oh no. I forgot to turn on the sump pump this morning
like Mom asked me to right before I left. I was too upset
about the sunflowers and the fireworks.

My room's going to be flooded.

Well. I've got more important things to worry about at
the moment.

Weirdly . . . that seems fine. After all my training
with panic, "worry" is a walk in the park.

39

Avery

I skip the lunchroom and head to the library again. I can't eat with my guts hurting this bad. Plus I don't think Mason wants to see me. I can't sit with Bree and Dariellis pretending everything is fine when it's so *not* fine, and I don't want to hear any more of my classmates arguing over whether Ritter deserved what he got. Over whether what happened last night will make him understand. A guy in my social studies class said he hopes someone does it again tonight, and tomorrow night, and for enough nights that Ritter gets the freaking point. But then a girl said the poster and petition were a better approach and that violence solves nothing.

I don't know what I think anymore in the reform-versus-revenge debate. I'm still mad as a hornet at Mr. Ritter. But the fireworks have well and truly caused more problems than they ever could've solved.

Tuney messages me during band to tell me the news story has been updated. Mr. Ritter has a five-year-old daughter. The fireworks went off outside her bedroom, not his. The little girl freaked and ran full tilt toward her open bedroom door in the dark. She hit the edge of it so hard she had to go to the hospital. Tuney said she didn't have a concussion, just three stitches and a black eye.

I thought I felt bad before. Now I'm turned inside out with it.

Mr. Ritter is at school now. I passed the office when I was limping from the library to band. He looked . . . not great. I guess because he was awake at the hospital all night with his child. He gave me only a tired glance, so I don't think he suspects me.

I'm starting to think I should tell him it was me. Even though I didn't actually do it, it was my idea. It's my fault his little girl got hurt that bad.

My brain is already a churning mess with too much in it. But more messages come in from Tuney. *This brings a lot more gravity to this situation. Mom and I have set up a meeting after school with Mr. Ritter. We expect you to tell him what you did and accept the conse-*

quences. Mom and I will tell him we'll cover the hospital bill and the cost of any follow-up care the girl requires, including any therapy she may need.

Creative + Strategic Problem-Solving FAIL. Now it's *really* time to find out if I can let go of my need for control.

I deserve whatever I'm gonna get for this. I got a little girl hurt. I upset my parents and stressed out my friends. I know Mason didn't tell on me to get me in trouble, or because he was mad. He did it because he was scared for me.

Which means he cares.

It must have been hard for him to reach out to Tuney. But he did it anyway.

I text him: *I'm so sorry for everything. I'm meeting with my moms and Mr. Ritter after school to tell them it was me.*

It's minor torture to wait for seventh period to be over so Mason can answer when he's done with his social studies class.

But he doesn't answer.

By the end of Spanish class last period, my heart is racing, my mouth is dry, and my palms are sweating. The conversation between my parents and me and Mr. Ritter is minutes away from starting.

My phone pings with a message from Mason while

I'm limping to the office. *Aves, my dude. Interesting new info has come to light. We need to talk.*

Oh god. What on earth could that mean? *What info?* I write.

But I'm at the office, and there's no time to wait for his answer.

I gulp down my fear, pocket my phone, and push the door open.

40
Sarah

Thurs., May 9, 3:22 p.m. I did it. I've convinced James.

I'm almost laughing, I'm so relieved.

I was <u>furious</u> at him when he got to school to pick me up. He started driving us home and I said all the things I've been afraid to say to him for <u>ages</u>. That he acts irresponsibly. That it's hard on Ruthie and me to hear him fighting with our parents all the time over silly things that don't matter. That he didn't help me with babysitting the kids when Mom had to take Ruthie to urgent care for stitches, that he <u>never</u> helps, just does whatever he wants and leaves all the work to us. That he always assumes

Dad is on Mom's side when it's not even about sides. That he got kicked out of Maple Creek for good reason. That he doesn't need to try to protect me with some harebrained revenge scheme that wound up getting an eighth-grade girl in huge trouble. I told him that right at that moment, Avery was telling Mr. Ritter that it was her, because she looks up to James and doesn't want him to get in trouble.

Who knew righteous anger could be so effective at combating fear? I'll have to add it to my list of tactics.

To use sparingly, of course.

James tried to give me nonsense about how it was Avery's idea, so she should take the blame. I told him that intent is one thing and action is another, and that he's older and should've been the one to make the responsible choice. He said Avery would get off easy, and if he admitted to it, he'd go to jail.

I could see that he knew, as he was saying it, that he'd gone too far. That he was way out of line and that the "chickens are coming home to roost," as Mom says.

So I told him if he didn't turn the car around right now I'd send Mom and Dad screenshots of his texts saying he set off the fireworks.

He said, "Then they'll see our other texts, and know you're gay too."

I said, "I don't care." (It's not true. I care. I just have bigger concerns right now.)

That did the trick. James turned the car around, and now we're driving back to school.

This is <u>exhilarating</u>. I'm no longer a mouse. Now I'm the cat.

It doesn't mean this isn't scary. It's <u>so</u> scary. But I've got some practice handling fear, and I won't let it hold me back.

Now I just need to figure out how I can support all these people I care so much about who have gotten themselves into this bananas situation.

And I think I owe Avery a big apology.

41

Avery

The secretary points me wordlessly to Mr. Ritter's open door.

Mom and Tuney are inside, along with Mr. Ritter, Officer Clark, and a policewoman.

Fear pulses in my chest. It has less to do with the cop and more to do with my parents. Mom and Tuney were already angry with me. But I guess having to cut their workdays short and getting soaked by cold rain while walking into the building has tipped them over the edge. They both look quietly furious.

I sit meekly in the only unoccupied chair. Mom and Tuney are next to me. Mr. Ritter's sitting at his desk. Officer Clark and the policewoman stand by the window.

"Why?" Mr. Ritter asks. He doesn't even look angry. Only exhausted. "Just . . . why would you do something like this?"

My stomach makes a weird nose. "I, um." I clear my throat. He's giving me a chance to explain. But after finding out about his daughter, I don't feel I deserve it. "I don't know. I'm sorry."

"No." Anger creeps into his tone. "I don't want 'I don't know.' I want honesty."

"Uh. Okay." I clear my throat again and glance at Tuney. Her face is pinched, but she gives me a slight nod.

"Okay," I say again. "Um, I was diagnosed with hypermobile Ehlers-Danlos syndrome." I twist my fingers together, even though I have to hold my left arm at a weird angle. I speak to my lap. "And, um. My body has felt—it's sort of falling apart while I try to live in it. I'm in pain all the time. It's really scary—" My throat starts to close up. "It's really scary to think it's downhill for the rest of my life. Since EDS doesn't get better. Only worse." Tears spring up, but I blink them away. This isn't the time for a pity party. "When the drill happened, I, um. I felt out of control in the same way I feel out of control about EDS. Like . . . a gut-level fear about how I can't control what happens to me. Whether that's getting shot at school, or, um, losing control of my—of my body. It felt the same. Like I'm just . . . totally helpless."

I risk a glance at the grown-ups staring at me. Mom and Tuney have marginally thawed. Mr. Ritter, not so much. Officer Clark and the policewoman still have no expression.

"Um, so, after the drill, I needed to do something to feel in control again," I say. "For me, but also for my friends. Because it affected them so badly too. I, um, I helped make that poster—I don't know if you saw it—with the statistics on it?"

Mr. Ritter is still scowling. "That was you?"

I nod.

"And you were behind that petition too?" He shakes his head. "What was that, a front to distract us from your real plans?"

"No!" I almost shout. Undermining Sarah and Mason and Dariellis is the last thing I wanted to do. "No," I say more calmly. "The—um, the person I did the poster with, and the people who started the petition . . . they wanted a peaceful way to make sure a bad drill never happens again. I was—" I clear my throat. "I was the one who thought revenge would be better."

He just sighs. "Go on."

"So, um. Mason's—" My throat closes again. He's been such a good friend, and I've . . . well. "After the

319

drill, Mason's mom told him she's taking him out of the district. So I thought if—if I scared you the same way you scared us"—I'm crying now—"that you would understand how bad it was. And maybe you'd apologize. And then maybe Mason's mom would decide he could stay." I hug my bad arm with my good one. It sounds so convoluted now. So desperate. It seemed to make so much sense before I came to my senses. "I just wanted to feel like we had some control of our lives."

"Setting off fireworks at my house is not how you control this situation," Mr. Ritter says.

Tuney shifts in her chair. "Faking killing children with guns is not how you control children."

I glance at her in surprise.

"I'm not in any way defending what Avery did," she says to Mr. Ritter. "It's inexcusable, and she's absolutely going to be disciplined. But you've got to understand what this drill did to these kids."

Mr. Ritter looks like he's coming down with the bubbleguts. "The assumption you're all making is that I *wanted* to do the drill. For the record, I did not. I voted against it when the school board proposed it. I was overruled."

My jaw drops. "Then why were you like 'I told you so' after it was over?"

"Avery," Mom says. "Watch your tone."

"Because I never want to deal with this again," Mr. Ritter says bitterly. "I knew exactly what was going to come down on my head. Do you know how many enraged phone calls I've fielded? How many times I've been sent the link to your petition? I'm being sued. Parents are demanding I be fired. And you"—he points at me—"you were so steamed you set off fireworks at my house at midnight. Which caused *significant* pain and trauma to my child." He's about to blow a gasket, and for once, I can't blame him.

"I—I know," I choke out around a fresh bout of tears. "I'm so sorry." Outside the closed door, I hear arguing, like someone's having it out with the secretary.

"We need to talk about consequences," Mr. Ritter says. "Legally, it seems our options are to charge you with—"

There's a knock at the door. Everyone's head swivels to it. "Who is it?" Mr. Ritter says sharply.

"It's Sarah and James Bell," Sarah says clearly. "We need to speak with you, please."

**42
Sarah**

Thurs., May 9, 6:10 p.m. Riley and Grayson and Layla have finally been picked up. I made spaghetti for me and Ruthie, plus some for the rest of my family when they get home. My room is a soggy disaster, but I've been waiting all afternoon to write down what happened because I don't want to forget any of it. So I'm doing this before I deal with my room.

To say everyone in Mr. Ritter's office was surprised to see us is an understatement. I looked at the shocked faces, then fixed my eyes on Avery's. "We're here to clear this up," I said.

I still can't believe how confident I sounded. I felt it, some, but mostly I was bluffing.

It worked, though. (I'll have to add it to my tactics list.)

Everyone seemed to take me seriously.

"James has something to tell you all," I said.

For a minute, I thought he wasn't going to confess. He looked the way he does right before he blows up at Mom. Defiant. Anger driving him.

But then he noticed Tuney looking at him like she cared about him, despite only having met him for like two seconds when she dropped Avery off for the overnight. It seemed to melt him. "I did it," he said. "I did the fireworks." He looked at me. "And I was going to let Avery take the fall since it was her id—"

I kicked his foot. Just enough to jolt him.

He cleared his throat. "Because I thought she'd get in less trouble than I would. 'Cause of all the stuff I've done." He looked defiant again. But also ashamed.

That was when I realized that all his bluster and anger and rebelliousness are covering up fear. That he's just as scared as I am. Maybe because he's growing up gay in a Catholic house with parents who don't get him. And all he wants is for them to tell him they love him no matter what.

It broke my heart a little. He started to say more, but his voice was all squeaked up into that register it reaches right before he starts crying, and I knew he'd hate himself if he cried in front of everyone and that would make him mad and everything would go wrong. Plus I could see Mr. Ritter's anger shifting off Avery and onto James, and, well, it's kind of scary when grown men get mad at someone you love. Even if the person you love did something super foolish and needs to be put back in line.

So I interrupted. I told Mr. Ritter that part of the reason James did it was because he wanted to protect me. I said, "Some of us laughed at the earlier drills to make it less scary. That doesn't mean we didn't understand the danger." I wanted to look at Avery, because even though I wasn't with her during the drill before the big one, I'd bet my whole entire sketchbook she was one of the kids who got in trouble for laughing during it. I said something like, "We don't need you to force fear on us. We're growing up in an incredibly scary world. But we're just kids, and we can't live in fear all the time. Sometimes we have to laugh at it to defuse it."

Tuney told Mr. Ritter I was right. That she and the other parents had been discussing a way to ensure their kids aren't terrorized again.

Mr. Ritter sounded <u>very</u> bitter when he said they'd have to take it up with the school board. Tuney said they were

already planning to, and that she and Avery's mom would pay for his daughter's medical expenses and therapy if she needs it. I don't know what that was about. I forgot to ask Avery after all the stuff that happened next.

James interrupted and demanded to know what his punishment will be. He kept looking at the police officer and then at me like I'd dragged him into a trap.

The policewoman started to tell him he'd be charged with things like illegal use of fireworks, trespassing, criminal mischief—and then James exploded and started yelling at Mr. Ritter that if he'd stopped the bullies when James was a student here, none of this would've happened. Mr. Ritter told James not to play the innocent victim when he wasn't. He said James had brought some of what happened on himself.

I went so tense when James started yelling. I knew something awful was about to happen.

And it did: James threw the car keys at Mr. Ritter.

He missed (thank you, God) and everything derailed into shouting and chaos. James wound up in handcuffs, crying. The rest of us were escorted out by Officer Clark. I was so shaky my knees barely worked to walk. Mr. Ritter called my parents to tell them James was headed for the police station in the back of a cop car.

I still can't believe James threw the keys. And got <u>arrested</u>. I've been praying all afternoon that they don't make him stay in jail for weeks and weeks.

Avery's moms offered to take me to Avery's house while my parents dealt with the James situation. I called Mom to see what she wanted me to do. She was super stressed and told me I needed to get home immediately to watch Riley and Grayson and Layla so she could go to the police station. Then she said, "Oh hell, where's my car? Is my car at the middle school?"

I said it was.

She said a word I've never heard her say.

Tuney must have heard her. She asked for my phone. I'm not sure how she did it, but she calmed Mom down and told her we had the keys now. She offered to drive Mom's car to our house so Mom could drive it to the police station. She said she could drop me off there so I could watch the kids.

It surprised me that Mom said okay. I guess she didn't have much choice.

So that's what happened. Avery's mom and Avery and me followed Tuney driving Mom's car to my house in the rain. Avery sat in the front seat, and her mom was right there, so we didn't really talk. Neither did she and her mom. I think we were all trying to process.

At home, they dropped me off and gave Mom the car keys. Mom kept saying "Thank you so much"

and "I can't believe my son got arrested" and "What am I going to do with him?" and dropping her phone and umbrella and purse until Tuney told her it would be fine, that she'd been a firecracker like James as a kid and that even though she'd seen him on what was probably not the best day of his life, she could tell he was a good kid with a good heart who likely felt his feelings a little too hard and just needed to know other people understood him.

Mom started crying. She said that was James to a T. She told me to take care of the kids and left.

Avery's moms asked if I needed anything. I said I didn't. Avery looked like she wanted to say something. Tuney and Avery's other mom said they'd wait in the car for a minute.

Time seemed to slow down. I glanced at the kids, who were absorbed in "Elmo's World," then back at Avery. She did this adorable thing where she stepped on one black Converse shoe with the other and bit her lip. When she looked up at me, her eyes were reddish, like she was trying not to cry again. "I'm sorry I made you feel like you had to tell an adult what I was planning," she said.

I wanted to hug her. But I was worried about hurting her shoulder. So I just sort of cleared my throat and said, "I'm sorry I encouraged Mason to tell on you."

"You were right to," she said.

She stepped really close to me then. She lifted her good

arm like she wanted to hug me.

My heart was beating almost as hard as it does during a panic attack. But this time it was in a really good way.

I put my arms around her. Very carefully.

It surprised me how hard she hugged me.

It went on for a long time. Like a really . . . nice . . . long time. I didn't want it to end. It felt like our two vines had finally reached one another, and were trying to grow together.

Avery's mom eventually rolled down the car window and said, "Come on, kiddo, it's been a long day and we're ready to go home."

So we let go of each other, and I went inside to take care of the kids and Avery left.

It feels like part of me went with her.

43

Avery

Mom drives the three of us back to school to get Tuney's SUV. We're quiet most of the ride. I guess we're all trying to process this berserk day.

"Why in blazes did you say you did it?" Tuney finally asks when we're nearly there.

"You wouldn't have believed me if I said I didn't. You had too much evidence."

Mom laughs, but not like she's amused. "So instead of telling the truth to get out of trouble, you lied to get *in* trouble. I'm not sure I follow."

"Well, I *almost* did it. And it was my idea, so I feel responsible for that little girl getting hurt. I got as far as dressing in all black and sneaking out of the house. I made it to Hamlin Street before I realized how bad an idea it was."

"And the soot on your hands?" Tuney asks.

"Not soot. Rust from a street sign I was hanging on to while I had a meltdown."

"Child . . . I don't even know what to think or feel," Tuney says. "I'm just so glad you're okay. And glad you didn't do it."

Mom pulls into the parking spot next to Tuney's SUV. "What made you come to your senses?"

"A dead mouse in our basement."

Tuney barks a sharp laugh. "Explain."

I tell them how I was in the laundry room looking for my jeans and saw the trap behind the deep freezer. How I realized right away that I was in my own sort of trap. That at first I thought it was hEDS and later I realized it's my need to control what happens. "I confessed because I might as well have been the one to do it, since I thought it up," I tell them. "I set a dumb plan in motion and it got away from me. Like a million other things lately." I choke up thinking of all those million things.

Mom and Tuney give each other that look that means *maybe we need to reassess our approach*. The same look they exchanged the day I was officially diagnosed with hEDS.

"How about we grab some takeout, stuff our faces, and sit in the den and talk?" Tuney says. "We'll feel better with full stomachs. And we can figure out some new strategies for helping each other."

I'm pretty sure *helping each other* means *making sure Avery doesn't come up with more ridonkulous ideas and almost execute them*, but also . . . "Takeout sounds great," I say. "Can we get California rolls?" They're easy on my guts. Which are still not even remotely happy with me.

"I'm in the mood for Mexican," Mom says at the same time Tuney says, "Pizza."

We argue until we realize we don't have to agree since we have both cars here. Tuney says she'll grab pizza for her and sushi for me, and that Mom can pick up Mexican. She kisses my head and gets out of Mom's car. "See you at home," she says.

"Hey," I say as she's closing the car door.

She opens it back up. "What?"

"I'm glad you two are my moms."

"And we're glad you're our little demon spawn," Tuney says. "Love you, squirt."

"Noooo!" I howl. "I hate that nickname!"

"Okay, squirt." She closes the car door before I can yell at her some more.

"Want to DJ?" Mom taps the touch screen to switch the stereo from her Bluetooth to mine.

I put on "It's Raining Tacos."

Mom tells me I'm lucky I'm cute.

44
Sarah

Thurs., May 9, 8:10 p.m. Mom and Dad and James got home twenty minutes ago. James looked like he'd cried years of tears and was ready to sleep for a week. Dad squeezed James's shoulder in the kitchen, and James actually gave him a tired half smile in return. Then he went to his room and closed the door quietly instead of slamming it.

Before I go to bed, I'll check on him. He probably needs someone to listen to him.

Mom and Dad looked worn out too. Mom thanked me for taking care of the kids and helping Ruthie with her homework. She and Dad ate the rest of the spaghetti. It wasn't very good—it didn't have the seasoning Mom puts in, and I was so flustered earlier that I forgot it's

Thursday and maybe we'll have spaghetti again tomorrow—but I don't think they cared. I came downstairs to start working on my disaster of a room.

The standing water's gone now, though the floor is still soaked. Mom said she turned on the sump pump around lunchtime when she came down to check the dryer and found the mess. But she was too busy with the kids to clean anything up. So I've been doing it, between bouts of staring at the wall and writing. Trying to put myself back into some sort of order.

My new Spirograph set was half-stuck under the bed with a drenched shirt that's been on the floor since I wore it three days ago. The box and the design guide were ruined. I nearly started crying till I realized that duh, all the pieces are plastic and I can download the design guide on the Spirograph website.

So it's fine. I'll put the pieces in a bag. A quart-sized one instead of a sandwich-sized, since there are so many.

The thank-you card I was making for Avery is a mess in a sort of pretty way, with how the ink bled out from the patterns. But the paper's warped and damp and I'd be embarrassed to hand her something that looks fished out of a bathtub. I was disappointed, because the card was really cool. But after I sat there holding the soggy design and the Spirograph pieces for a while, I realized I still have everything I need to make art.

I have my head. My heart. My hands.

And an amazing Spirograph set. Plus the Dream-o-graph, which is not waterlogged or busted because I left it on my desk instead of the floor.

As soon as I'm finished cleaning, I'll open the box.

9:42 p.m. "What a day" turned itself into "What an evening."

I finally texted Luci about the sunflowers. I was afraid she'd be disappointed, but she said, "That's okay. You can start over and the new ones will be healthier and stronger because it's later in May now!"

I miss her so, so much. I wrote back "You're the best xoxoxox" and she sent the happy-cowboy emoji.

James came downstairs while I was cleaning. His face was blotchy and his nose was red. He told me he was sorry he never helped with babysitting. And that he was sorry he'd argued with me when I told him he needed to confess. He said he shouldn't have done it in the first place, and that he shouldn't have tried to let Avery take the fall. He said the stuff I yelled at him in the car was sinking in. That it was all stuff Mom's been telling him for a long time, but that coming from me, it was different.

Because he cares what I think of him. Because he wants

to be a big brother I can look up to, instead of one who always gets in trouble or dodges responsibilities.

That felt really good. I never forgot why I love him so much, but it was a great reminder when he said that.

My big brother is a good person. Giant emotions included. He just needs to do some work on his anger, like I did some work on my panic.

Maybe I could help him with that.

He asked if I thought Avery would forgive him. I said that she's pretty feisty, but I think she will. And then I gave him a hug and told him I love him.

We both cried a little. He said he feels like the worst person in the world because of Mr. Ritter's daughter. He had to explain because I hadn't heard about that part of it, which is . . . awful. But I told him that he feels so bad because he has a conscience, which proves he's not the actual <u>worst</u> person in the world. "Do you still hate Mr. Ritter?" I asked.

"I don't know," James said. "He seems more human now that I know he has a kid."

"He didn't seem human before?"

James sighed. "I think I just wanted somewhere to put all the bad stuff I feel. And he was a convenient place because he kinda sucks."

"I wonder if he picked the wrong job. I don't think he's a very happy person."

James laughed and tugged my braid. "You're the only person I know who would think about stuff from his perspective, you weirdo."

I didn't know what to say to that. It doesn't seem weird to think about other people's perspectives. It seems weird that most people <u>don't</u> do it.

James said he knew I was looking at a STEAM camp website. Apparently, he always erases the browser history on the family laptop after he uses it (I did not ask why, I do not want to know) and saw it in there. He said it looks right up my alley, and that the scholarships are need-based and he thinks we'd qualify since Mom's babysitting income is under the table, whatever that means. He offered to help me talk to Mom and Dad about it. He said I was right about him assuming Dad is always on Mom's side, and that when he pulled his head out of his (ahem) long enough to think about it, it seemed like Dad was usually trying to calm the situation. He and Dad are going to fly kites this weekend. James even said he's looking forward to it.

That made me glow with happiness. I decided to take him up on the offer to talk to our parents right then. I didn't give the panic a chance to get going. I cut it off at the source with the magic of <u>action</u>. (Another tactic to add to my list!)

So that's what we did. I felt nervous as we walked up the steps, and I took three deep breaths and it helped. As soon as Mom was done tucking Ruthie in, the four of us sat at the dining room table. I started with something like, "I know I need to get caught up in math and science, but I'm very stressed out at the thought of the STEM camp. I found a STEAM camp that does STEM stuff with art integrated. Could we talk about me doing that instead?"

I felt a buzz of pride for saying "integrated," and for how calm I sounded.

Mom was shaking her head by the time I finished, but Dad asked where the camp was.

"It's in Glenwood," I said. "And they offer scholarships. Maybe we could apply?"

"We've already put the down payment on the STEM camp," Mom said. "And the bus can get you there. It can't get you to Glenwood."

My heart sank to my feet.

James said Glenwood isn't far from Dad's job, and asked if the STEM camp might refund the tuition. Mom said she doubted it.

"I suppose we could find out," Dad said, and my heart came flying back up.

It turns out they offer a 90 percent refund if you withdraw by next Friday. Dad looked up the STEAM camp too, and he and Mom looked over the website until Mom abruptly said it was late and we all needed to get to bed.

"Is that a no on the STEAM camp?" James asked. I think he knew from looking at my face that I was too worried to ask.

"It's a 'We'll think about it,'" Dad said.

James gave me a big smile. "I bet that means yes."

Mom told us not to count our chickens before they hatched. (Why does she have so many sayings about chickens?) Then she sent us to bed.

I don't know how I'll sleep tonight with this warm, tingly bubble of hope pushing on the inside of my skin.

I think it's time to open the Dream-o-graph.

45

Avery

Tuney was right; we do feel better once we've stuffed our faces with our takeout of choice. She picked up four California rolls for me. I ate two—all that would fit in my roiling belly—and put the other two in the freezer to give to Mason at lunch. His family is weirded out by eating raw fish, but he's as much of a sushi hound as I am since he's gone out for it with us a bunch of times. Frozen-then-thawed isn't as good as fresh, but it's still heckin' tasty and I know it'll make him happy.

Well. I hope it will. Maybe it'll work better than my Magic 8 Ball gift did.

Mom notices me rubbing my belly after dinner. "You okay?"

I nod. "I think I need to go to the bathroom."

She gives me a sympathetic look. "Go ahead. Tuney and I will clean up here."

"Thanks." I limp off to the bathroom under the stairs.

Twenty minutes later, I feel like a new person. I wash my hands—I can finally move my right forearm just enough to scrub both of them, which is *great*—and then wander out to find Mom and Tuney piled onto the big puffy couch in the den with Tank.

"Feel better?" Mom asks.

"Much."

"Your bathroom habits have changed the last few months. I was hoping it would resolve, but it doesn't seem to be. I'll make an appointment with Dr. Simmons. Hopefully we can get you feeling better."

I make a noncommittal sound as I sit on the couch. Talking to Dr. Simmons about bathroom problems is not a party I'm looking forward to. But it would be nice to sort this out, if it can be sorted out.

"So," Mom says, and my stomach dips. "When did the knee problem start?"

I breathe a quiet sigh of relief. It's not the hardest question she could've started with. "The drill. It was sore before, but then during it . . . I was trying to pull Mason under Mr. Trevino's desk and it, like, popped. In a really bad way."

"Why didn't you tell me that day?" Mom asks.

"I didn't want to admit I was responsible for Mason being stuck in the middle of the room during the drill. He wanted to hide behind the projector stand and I'm the reason he didn't make it there." They don't need to know he peed, or how guilty I feel for being a stubborn jerk and trying to control him. I need to give him a real apology. The honest one he deserves, where I tell him I've realized how bad I screwed up. "I just wanted the whole problem to go away."

"How are you feeling about the drill now?" Tuney asks. "We knew from how closed up you were afterward that it was bothering you. But everything that happened today makes me think it affected you way more than you let on."

Tears fill my eyes. "It was . . . a lot. It's like I said in Mr. Ritter's office. It made me feel out of control the same way hEDS does."

"I didn't realize you were struggling so much, honey," Mom says. "Why didn't you tell us?" She looks like she's going to cry too. "We could have helped you."

"I don't know. I thought I was so frustrated and mad because I can't do the stuff I love anymore. But . . . it's bigger than that."

"You're going through so much all at once," Tuney says. "Puberty, this diagnosis, shoulder surgery, the drill. Stuff with your friends. New injuries. Speaking of which, Mom's taking you to see Naila first thing tomorrow morning about the knee. Then you'll do PT right after, so you'll be there for a while."

"It's so hard feeling like I'll be dependent on you for the whole rest of my life," I blurt in a choked-up rush. "I don't want to be a burden. I hate feeling like I'm not in control of my body anymore. Like—I've figured out—" I wipe my eyes. "I'm ready to stop making excuses that I'm only acting like a jerk because I'm stressed out about hEDS. I'm just really struggling with . . . with accepting—" Ugh, why is it so hard to say this stuff? "With accepting all these limitations."

"Oh, sweet pea," Mom says. "You've always had such big plans and hopes and dreams. And you're used to barreling through anything that stands in your way."

I smile through my tears. "I wonder where I learned that from."

"What you're going through lately is too much to barrel through on your own," she says. "You're at an age where you naturally want more independence. hEDS has made it especially hard because you're physically dependent on us right when your developmental stage has you wanting to spend more time with friends than parents."

I sniffle. Sometimes it's annoying when Mom tells

me what I feel and why. But right now . . . feeling seen feels really good. "It's like my mind overreacted to the problem of my physical flexibility," I say. "By getting stuck in inflexible thinking."

Tuney gives me a sad smile. "That's very insightful," she says. "It sounds like that's exactly what happened."

I smile too, even though I'm a snotty mess. "I'll try to be more honest. About what's going on with my joints and my guts and stuff."

"Glad to hear it," Mom says. "And we'll try to make you feel more supported. Honesty all around."

"Agreed," I say. "Can you support me with a cuddle puddle now?"

"Sure, baby." Mom and Tuney pull all the cushions off the couch and put them on the floor with a blanket over them.

"You take the middle," Tuney tells me.

I get situated first, and then Mom and Tuney pile carefully around me. I wind up with my head on Mom's stomach and my right knee propped up over Tuney's legs. Tuney fends Tank off until he gives up trying to be in the middle with me and lies down next to her.

"I feel like the peanut butter at the center of a Reese's Cup," I say.

Tuney licks my forehead. "Funny, you taste like a salt-and-vinegar chip."

"Gross!" I wipe her spit off.

"Stop moving," Mom tells us. "I'm tired."

"We could just sleep like this tonight," I suggest.

"I'm too old to sleep on the floor," Tuney groans.

"I'm not. Acro keeps me limber." Mom settles deeper into the cushions. "Night, all." She fake-snores.

"You guys are the worst," I say.

"We love you too, squirt." Tuney kisses my cheek and gives my arm a squeeze.

Friday morning, I'm still feeling all raw and emotional. I listen to lo-fi and try to put up my usual walls while Mom drives me to PT, since Naila's brusque manner might send me back into tears. But it's hard to seal off all my feels when I know a bunch of them are happening because I needed to grow.

Why does growing have to be so dang *messy*?

At the PT office, Mom opens the heavy door. For once, I'm not mad that she's doing things for me. I'm just grateful, because with the way my hip and knee are feeling, I don't think I could get that dumb door open if I tried.

Naila greets us and Mom explains what's going on. Naila starts to get that grim look when I go backward instead of forward in therapy, but then Mom explains that things have been rough for me since an active-shooter drill at school got too real and that what I really need right now is support.

It just about makes me cry again.

Naila's expression changes to sympathy. "I heard about that drill on the news," she says. "I didn't realize that was your school."

"It was worse for some of my friends than for me."

"I'm sorry you kids had to go through that."

"Thank you."

"Let's start with the hip," she says.

I hand my headphones over to Mom. For once, I'm grateful to pay attention to my body.

Naila leads me through a bunch of moves that show me exactly where the edges of the pain are, especially when I have to lift my right knee and when I take extra-long steps to extend my left hip joint. She tells me to lie on my back and lift each leg, then she carefully removes Cthulhu and has me lie on my stomach.

I feel all the floppy vulnerability I've become familiar with since the surgery. But this time, instead of wanting to curl into a protective shell . . . I lean into it. I remind myself that Mom brought me here to get help. That what Naila's doing, figuring out what's wrong, is to help me.

hEDS affects so many parts of my life in a negative way. But I have people who love and support me.

And even though this is difficult and painful, what I'm doing right now will make things better.

"Okay," Naila finally says. "The hip problem is clear. Your SI joint is out of whack."

"Is 'out of whack' an official medical term?" I ask.

"Very official," Naila says. "Your sacroiliac joint links your pelvis and lower spine. Yours isn't sitting in its socket properly, probably because your tendons are too flexible to hold it in place."

"So . . ." Mom says. "What I'm hearing is that her butt is out of joint."

Naila laughs. "Accurate. In most cases, physical therapy can improve it quite a lot, so we'll hope for that. Now let's get a look at the knee."

That's a relief, at least—hip surgery sounds even worse than shoulder surgery. We go through a second assessment, and at the end, she says it's highly likely I have a torn meniscus. "You'll need to get both the SI joint issue and the knee diagnosis officially confirmed by Dr. Chen. He'll order some imaging to see the extent of the damage and decide whether you need to stay off your feet for a while."

"But . . ." I don't want to say it. To make it real. "Does that mean a wheelchair? Since I can't use crutches?"

"It could. But a torn meniscus can also sometimes be helped by therapy, so keep your fingers crossed."

I nod. There's not really anything else I can do. I have to accept this reality. To work *with* my body instead of fighting against it.

"The next few months are going to be a challenge," Naila says. "But with some hard but *careful* work this summer, plus a little luck, you'll walk through the doors on the first day of high school with no sling, no crutches, and a smile on your face."

My heart beats quicker. "You think that's possible?"

"Depends what you bring to therapy. And your commitment to doing your exercises at home every day. The *right* way."

I smile at her. "I guess it's time I brought my A game to this therapy thing."

"Oh! *Well*, I was wondering when that would happen."

I swallow my pride. "You mentioned a preventive program the first day I came here. Like a whole-body strength-training something or other. To get my muscles to do some of the work my tendons and ligaments can't do."

"I did," Naila says.

I wait for her to say something else. But she's totally gonna make me ask.

"So, um, could I start some of that? If it's possible with the stuff I have going on now?"

"A spectacular idea," she says. "Truly. Glad you suggested it!"

"Okay, I get it," I grumble. "You don't have to rub it in."

Naila points at the poster over her table. "Rule number six," she says.

"Never argue, because I will always win," I read.

She just smirks. "Now you're getting the picture."

"You know," I say. "I think I am."

PART IV

Avery + Sarah

Fight + Flight

Healing + Happiness

46
Sarah

Tues., May 15, 9:41 p.m. In bed w/ flashlight. I don't
know if I'll ever consider myself a brave person. But I've
done a few brave things lately.

Like I went to hospice with Mom over the weekend again.
I was nervous, but not panicky. I did three-deep-breaths
and mentally repeated "Perfect love casts out all fear" on the
way there, and it helped a lot. Charlene was still hanging on,
just barely, so I got another chance to read to her.

I read hopeful passages this time. Her daughter's name
is Angela, which I love because it has the word "angel" in
it. When I finished reading, I thanked Angela for what she
said last time.

She gave me a hug. It was a very good hug.

On the way home, Mom and I stopped at the garden store and bought sunflower seeds. I mailed a packet to Luci yesterday with a Conté drawing of flowers around her favorite Bible verse, about hope filling you to overflowing with joy and peace. The seeds won't grow in the desert, but maybe she can plant them in a pot.

Another brave thing I did: I gave Avery the thank-you card I spent all weekend making. It took me forever to figure out how to make a Spirograph "A" using the set she gave me, and then to create the art without the pieces jumping the tracks I set up. But I finally got it on the sixth try. The brave part is that I put a little heart inside the "A" and wrote "Love, Sarah" at the bottom. I had too many butterflies to give it to her in person, so I stuck it through the slot in her locker at the end of the day. I hope she likes it.

And I did one more brave thing, at Bible Study this evening. It was warm in the room, which at first I was glad for—after that cold snap, I want weather that's hot hot hot, for months and months so all the green things can grow—but the warmth got to be too much too quickly.

Mrs. Marshall started by reminding us of Father Moyer's Sunday sermon about the part of the Bible where Paul says we should rejoice in the Lord no matter our circumstances. She said that if Paul could celebrate God

while locked in a jail cell awaiting death, us girls, with our cushy middle-class lives, should find it easy to identify many reasons to be thankful to God.

What she said was true. I've figured out that focusing on what I'm grateful for is a good way to focus less on what I'm afraid of—which is, mostly, losing the things I'm grateful for. (I've added "Focus on gratitude" to my tactics list.) So instead of being afraid of the pain of losing Aunt Camila and Luci, which sits lodged inside me all the time and pokes its head up now and then to remind me how much it still hurts, I can feel gratitude that I got to spend the time with them that I did. Even though I wanted that to go on for longer—for my whole life—nothing lasts forever. Like Dad says, "Change is the only unchangeable constant."

When I came out of thinking about how it hurts to lose what you're attached to and how a better approach is to focus on what you have while you have it, I tuned back in to what Mrs. Marshall was saying. She was talking about prayer.

Which I've had a lot of trouble with lately. I hear people say "the power of prayer" at church. I haven't stopped praying, but my faith in its effectiveness sure has taken a ding.

I raised my hand. That was the brave thing. I asked: "Why should we bother praying if it doesn't change anything?"

Mrs. Marshall blinked at me like she'd never seen me

before. In a sense, she hasn't-seen this side of me, at least. The side that's decided to ask hard questions even though I might be afraid of the answers. Because not knowing equals not growing. And I want to grow.

She asked how I prayed. I told her I draw prayers asking God to help others.

Mariah Welch made a sound like she was stifling a laugh at the idea of drawing prayers. But I didn't care.

"So your prayers are petitions," Mrs. Marshall said. "And you feel that your petition prayers aren't working?"

I nodded.

She thought about it for a minute. I liked that she did that, instead of how grown-ups sometimes answer kids' questions. Offhand, like they're barely giving it consideration. Then she said, "When someone needs help-whether they say 'I need help' with their voice or they show with their actions that they're in trouble-then consider how you can help them directly. The way God works is through humans."

I suddenly felt guilty for the prayers I've drawn or said for James, and Avery and Mason, and Luci and Ruthie and Aunt Camila and everyone I've ever prayed for. When I could have tried to help them instead. It felt like I was failing to do God's work. I asked, "So should we stop praying for people and <u>only</u> help them? Like that's how I should pray, by helping instead of drawing or speaking?"

"You're full of questions tonight." She smiled again, and I

realized I've been misreading her. I thought she was grumpy from dealing with a bunch of sarcastic middle-school girls. But she wants to connect with us. To answer the <u>real</u> questions we have, instead of fending off eye rolls and stifled laughs and snippy statements about biblical contradictions.

It made me see her in a new way.

She said, "You should do both." She told us that any time we do something for others, whether that's small like helping at home with the dishes or big like devoting our full lives to service, that's a prayer. Even when it's not obvious how to help someone, or when it's impossible to solve their problem—like if they're sick or dying—we can always ease one another's burdens with kindness and compassion. Always.

She said it a second time like that. With space around it.

❧ ❀ *Always.* ❀ ☙

I realized then that I <u>haven't</u> failed—and neither have my prayers. I've been doing God's work and praying all along, in my own small way. My actions are a prayer for Mom when I help her with the babysitting kids, and for Ruthie when I make stories with her and tuck her in at night. I prayed for Mason by giving him a pencil. I prayed for Charlene when I read to her at hospice and I prayed for Luci when I listened to her when she needed to talk. I even prayed for Avery by working with Mason to figure out the best way to stop her from her revenge plan, and I prayed for James by

convincing him to take responsibility for his actions.

It felt like the sun rising inside me, pushing out darkness and fear. It still feels like that now, in bed with my flashlight. I'm smiling as I write this.

I thought Mrs. Marshall's "Always" had gotten to all the girls in the room the same way it got to me. Since everybody went quiet for a minute.

Then Jenna Lutz belched and they all exploded into laughter.

Mrs. Marshall looked so disappointed. Before, I would've closed my eyes and wished I was somewhere else. But I wanted to do something kind for her.

I spoke loudly so my voice would carry over the laughter. "Mrs. Marshall, you made a big difference for me tonight. Thank you."

It didn't stop the laughter. It might've made it worse.

But Mrs. Marshall smiled a sad, beautiful smile and said, "I'm so glad, Sarah."

It felt like Aunt Camila had come back, just for a moment, and given me a hug with those words.

47

Avery

I'm not sure if this is a date, since Mason and Mom and Tuney are here with Sarah and me, and I'm not exactly going to go jaunting into the sunset with my one true love when the evening is over. (The one true love being Sarah, obviously.)

But it's Friday night, and it feels like a date. I'm even wearing a nice pair of jeans instead of leggings for a change. With my cool new zebra-striped Chucks from Mom, of course, and two small zebra earrings I let Tuney put in to replace the boring hoops that have been there for weeks.

We're at the mall, which I didn't know was a thing people still did. I've been here like twice in my life, dragged on a shopping trip for some randomly specific item Mom saw in an ad.

But it's . . . nice. In a creepy abandoned way, since at least three-quarters of the stores are empty and have dark paper taped on the insides of their huge windows.

The nice part is the floor. Tuney said it was installed back in the heyday of malls in the 1980s, like the one in *Stranger Things*, and that it's real marble. And yowza, you can *really* get going on a marble floor in a wheelchair. Mason and Sarah have been taking turns run-pushing me past the big central fountain in their socks, then laughing and shrieking as our momentum pulls them across the floor. Mason says it feels like that time we took him waterskiing.

I won't be able to run for a long time. So feeling the wind on my face—even stale mall wind—is glorious.

We take a break to stuff our faces with Auntie Anne's pretzels, then we do the run-laugh-shriek thing again until a security guy on a Segway shows up and tells us to knock it off.

He clearly doesn't know what fun is.

My meniscus, unfortunately, is torn bad enough that I can't walk on it and I need surgery. I don't know when it'll be yet. I'll have to use crutches afterward and my shoulder won't be up to that for a while. Naila said maybe another two months, which gave me a big *oof* because so much for that pretty picture of starting high school on my own two feet with no crutches.

But I finally did the arm bike today.

It felt *great*.

It's not like I went anywhere. It's literally just a stationary bike for your arms. But I moved my shoulder and arm in a way I haven't been able to for a long time—and it didn't hurt that bad. My left arm did most of the work. But Naila said to try to use my right arm as much as I could.

I used it more than I thought I'd be able to. Once I was warmed up, I tried a few rotations using only my right arm.

And I *did* them.

It shot a big dose of potent hope right into my heart. I hadn't realized I was scared that my shoulder would never heal, after going backward instead of forward so many times in therapy. I'm still far behind where I should be—or at least far behind where someone without hEDS would be in their surgery recovery.

But I'm making progress. Maybe because I'm finally taking this seriously. Accepting my limitations. I'm working with what I *can* do now, instead of pounding my fists against all the stuff I can't do.

I'll get to play drums again. Maybe I'll even get to run and ride my dirt bike and climb trees again. I feel a new sense of hope that those are possible.

But I also appreciate that even though my right arm is out of commission for a while, my left arm still works. I can get myself out of bed and butt bump down the steps to my wheelchair, even if I need Tuney or Mom to help me after that. I have a little time left with Mason at Maple Creek Middle, and he and Sarah volunteered to push me to my classes. Mason said he's just doing it because it gets him out of a few minutes of each of his classes. But I think that's only partly true.

When Tuney dropped me off at school this morning, Mr. Ritter was standing outside, telling kids hello. Mason came over to me to push me to class. "Can you wheel me to Mr. Ritter?" I asked him.

He gave me a look like *Don't do anything stupid*.

"It's cool," I say. "Promise."

He pushed me over to Ritter. "Hey," I said. "Good morning."

Mr. Ritter looked down at me with no expression.

"I just wanted to say thanks for voting against the drill when the school board proposed it," I said. "I appreciate that you did that."

His eyebrows shot way up. Then he cleared his face and nodded.

"Is your daughter doing okay?" I asked. "I've been thinking about her."

"She's better," he said stiffly. "Thank you for asking."

Then he told me and Mason to get to class.

Ritter and I are never gonna be friends. But I guess we don't have to hate each other.

I got over myself on Wednesday and patiently walked Carson through the drum measures he was having so much trouble with. It finally clicked for him and he rode the beat like a champ. Then he laughed and told me he was so intimidated by my mad drum skills that he always screwed up whenever I was watching. I apologized for being a crabby pants. He said he'd be all in knots too if he had to give up drumming. So who knows, maybe I'll wind up being friends with Carson. Stranger things have happened.

After school yesterday, Mom brought me over to Mason's house to hang out. We played Minecraft for ten minutes—me sitting quietly in my wheelchair and constructing a fence, Mason adding to his mansion while he rocked in the gamer chair—before I got up the guts to blurt, "I'm sorry I was the reason you got stuck in the middle of the room during the drill."

He didn't answer right away. I kept stealing glances at him, trying to get a read on what he was about to say. He finally sighed and said, "There's just like . . . more to all of that than you thought about."

I swallowed. "How do you mean?"

"You keep acting like you know what's best for me

better than I do. Better than my mom does. It's offensive. Black people don't need to be saved by white people, Aves."

"I—" I quickly closed my mouth. I'd thought I had reached the bottom of the bucket full of mistakes I've made, but whoops: a trapdoor covering a whole other reservoir of selfishness. My face burned with shame. "Um. I didn't think of it that way. I'm sorry."

He shrugged, but not like it was okay. "There's a lot of parts of being Black that people who aren't Black don't always think about. And it's not super fun to have to explain it." He cleared his throat. "I mean, I'm not saying I'm perfect. I made that period joke and you guys—I mean girls—shut me down."

I forced a laugh. I appreciated that he was trying to make me feel better, even if I didn't deserve any slack. "It must have made you feel awful when I did that during the drill," I said. "And when I acted like that after. I'm . . . I'm sorry. I'm working on sucking less."

"We all screw up. Like Bree said, learn the lesson and move on."

I chased some pixilated piggies into my shoddy fence. I wanted to say something like *Sorry I'm an incompetent donkey* or *I'm such a clodhopping blunderbuss*, but being goofy in response to the weight of what he'd said would be insulting. So while Mason added details to his rooftop swimming pool, I saddled a piggy, put a carrot on the end of a fishing rod, and absently rode the little oinker through the forest, thinking about all the ways I need to be a better person.

There are a lot of ways. I had a lot to think about.

I knew I owed Mason's mom an apology too, for steamrolling her concern about Mason getting in more trouble than me when we do the dumb stuff I dream up. So when she got home from work, even though it was hard to say "I was wrong" so many times in one day, I apologized to her for how inconsiderate I'd been.

I think I'm still on probation with her. But she seemed to soften toward me, a little, when I said I was working on seeing things from others' perspectives, instead of childishly focusing on my own. I told her I was trying to be more aware that my place in the world gives me a lot of advantages that others don't have.

She got an *Oh, you think?* look when I said that. But Mason touched her arm and said, "Better late than never," and that he still wants to be my friend because even though I'm a hot-mess pain in the rear, I'm the least boring person he's ever met.

I laughed at that. The kind of laugh that has a little bit of crying in it. Mason knows one of my life goals is to never be boring. So when he said that, I knew he really did still want to be my friend. Showing me that even though he hasn't said it, we're headed toward something that looks like "back on track."

I won't steer us off again. I care about him too much.

After our fun with the wheelchair on the marble floor, Mom leads us to the movie complex at the far end. I ask if we can see the R-rated horror movie, but Tuney just laughs and buys tickets for the latest Disney flick, even though we're too old for that stuff.

But really . . . sometimes it's nice to pretend we're ten again. That life is a playground we can fill with our harebrained hooligan games and laughter and silly ideas.

The theater is mostly empty when we go in. The view from the wheelchair seating on the floor level is neck-cramp-inducing, so Mom helps me out of my chair and carefully braces me as we hobble up a few flights of steps to sit right in the middle. On the third step, I put too much weight on my bum knee and lean into her.

She immediately shifts to support me better. "Okay, sweet pea?" she asks.

It takes a minute to say "Yeah" around the choked-up feeling.

I can't believe I was mad at her for trying to take care of me. She's so attuned to what I need. She and Tuney are so ready to either support me when it's necessary or to let me fall on my face when it's clear I need to learn some life lesson I haven't picked up on yet.

I have such good moms.

We sit in the big cushy seats: Sarah on my left, then me, then Mason, then Tuney and Mom. Tuney distributes popcorn and we all mess with getting our footrests open to exactly the right position while the ads with the terrible music play. Tuney and Mason get into an involved conversation about Minecraft, so I turn and ask Sarah if she's having a good time.

"Yes," she says. "Very much so."

"I'm so glad you could come."

"It made a big difference that your moms helped us the day James got arrested," she says. "My mom was so grateful for that."

I grin. "That worked out like a dream, then. Well, except for James getting arrested."

"That was kind of a good thing too. Not that day. But later." Sarah clears her throat. "So . . . remember how I was telling you about the STEM camp? And how you said you weren't going to live your life afraid to go after what you want?"

I duck my chin. I feel bad about how I said that. As if she and Mason were doing things wrong by not tackling their problems the bullheaded way I was trying to tackle mine.

"What you said helped me get up the nerve to ask them about the STEAM camp. And . . . they said yes."

"Really?" I smile at her smiling face. "I'm so happy for you!"

"Me too. I think parts of it will be hard. But at least there's art to make it better."

"I can help you with the math and science if you want."

"That would be amazing." She grins wide, showing her adorable, slightly crooked teeth.

"Maybe you can help me with this." I take out my phone and show her the text of the updated petition Mason, Dariellis, Bree, and I have been drafting. I got the idea for it when Mom and Tuney came home from the school board meeting last week and told me there was so much public outcry against the drill, and that our petition had gotten enough student and staff signatures, that the board had already drafted a resolution to only run standard drills from now on. To always let everyone know ahead of time that any drill is a drill and not pretend it's real. They voted on the resolution that night, and it passed.

It felt *amazing* to hear that. Like Mason and Dariellis and our poster had made a difference after all. I started a group text with the lunch group and asked if they wanted to make a bigger, broader, better petition.

All three of them immediately said yes.

So we've been working on the new one for a few days. It's focused on ending realistic active-shooter drills nationwide, instead of just at our school, and it's loaded to the gills with statistics and info—found by Dariellis, who was so mad at the trolls on the first petition that she'd already been gathering stats to shove back at them in the comments section. If anyone trolls this one, they'll have to actually answer to all the info Dariellis added. Mason has been logging some hyper-focused hours researching hashtags and how to most effectively spread the word about grassroots social justice campaigns.

"I've been thinking," I say to Sarah. "It would be amazing to have a first-person account of what the drill was like to add to this petition. And you have that journal, so I thought, maybe, you wrote down how it felt? And you'd consider sharing your words, since facts and stats are kinda dry and this could add a human-interest angle?"

Her eyes widen and she swallows. "Oh. Um . . ."

I want to jump in and roll over her hesitation with all the reasons this is a good idea. But I've finally realized that steamrolling is a crummy tactic that hurts people. This is Sarah's decision, not mine. It's a personal thing I've asked her to share. I'll respect whatever she decides.

She blinks like she's shaking something off. And then she looks at me and smiles. "Yes," she says. "I would love to work on this with all of you."

I pump my fist. "Yesssss!"

"Maybe I could . . . I don't know, do some art for it too?"

"Duh!" I giggle. "Why do you like art so much, anyway? Like what does it do for you?"

Sarah laughs. "Jeez, ask a harder question, will you?"

"Does a one-legged duck swim in a circle?"

She wrinkles her nose, and it's the cutest thing I've ever seen. "I don't know exactly why I do. Maybe because . . . it's like experience turned into . . . or, I don't know, *condensed* into symbols that hold meaning. Like more meaning than it seems like symbols should hold." She pauses. "Does that even make sense?"

"I think so. I read once that for artists, art is another dimension of the senses. Beyond the standard five."

Her face brightens. "Yeah. I think art takes all of what our senses tell us and like . . . bakes it in the furnace of our heart. Art is what we make with the ingredients that go into it." She nods like she's agreeing with herself. "Like when you mix eggs and sugar and flour and butter and things that have an individual taste, and then you put it in the heat of you—your heart and your mind—so that when it comes out, it's something new. And if you do it right, it makes you happy to be alive while you're making it. Or consuming it, I guess, if you're the viewer instead of the creator. Or baker or whatever. Okay, this is starting to fall apart."

"So you like art because art is cookies," I say. "Got it."

She laughs. "You're so literal."

"You're so cute when you talk about art." I grin at her blush. "And every other time, if I'm honest." I bet she'd taste like cookies if I kissed her.

That thought makes *me* blush.

"You're, um, you're cute too," Sarah says.

Mason makes a gagging sound. "Dudes. Too much."

"Oh, stop." Tuney swats at his arm. "They're adorable and you know it."

"You think snakes and lizards and pit bulls are adorable," Mason says.

Mom laughs. "He's not wrong, hon," she says to Tuney. "You even liked the cicadas."

The lights dim and the previews start. Sarah and I face the screen. Maybe she's pretending the last part of our conversation didn't happen.

Or maybe she's turning it over in her mind, like I am. Like I've turned over and over the heart she put on that beautiful card she made for me. With *Love*,

Sarah at the bottom of it.

Ten minutes into the movie, right when the hijinks are winding up, she reaches for my hand and holds it.

My heart swells with joy.

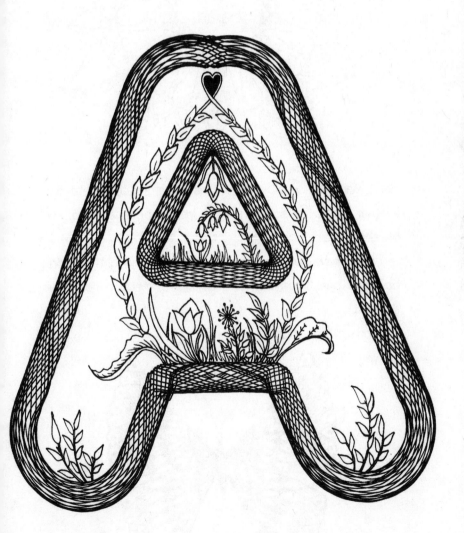

48
Sarah

Sat., May 19, 9:30 p.m. I was so afraid to try to find another friend. So scared I would lose whoever I found, and be alone again.

Now I have two new friends: one kind, thoughtful, funny boy, and one firecracker of a girl who's, maybe, more than a friend.

And I'm not afraid.

My mind made storms inside the calm.

Then I felt calm inside a storm.

Now I can calm my storms.

10 Tactics to Handle Panic and Fear

1. Take three slow, deep breaths (or as many as you need).

2. Say aloud: "This fear is temporary. It will pass."

3. Focus on each of your five senses, one at a time.

4. Repeat a mantra. Try: "Perfect love casts out all fear."

5. Pick a goal (immediate or long-term) and take one action toward meeting it.

6. Remember a positive event, and use that to get back to a logical mind.

7. Make a list: pros and cons, things that comfort you, people you love, etc.

8. Harness your righteous anger. (Carefully!)

9. Don't stop what you're doing to worry—fake confidence and soon you'll feel it.

10. Be grateful for all the good in your life!

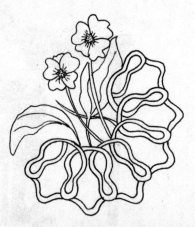

I can't stop my panic
I can't stop
I can't sto
I can't st
I can't s
I can't
I can
I can s
I can st
I can sto
I can stop
I can stop my panic!

acknowledgments

It's impossible to express the extent of my gratitude to all who helped make this book happen, but let's give it a whirl!

Thanks to super-agent John for having faith in this story from the get-go and for all the encouragement over the years. I'm wildly grateful to have you in my corner.

To the hardworking team at HarperCollins: Thank you to my incredible editor, Alyssa Miele, for popping open the hood of this thing and digging into its machinations, for asking excellent questions that helped me grease the gears, and for loving Avery and Sarah in all their messy humanity. Your brilliant insights made this book so much stronger, and I am deeply grateful for the care, compassion, and good humor with which you approach the editing process.

To David DeWitt, thanks for the InDesign crash course via Zoom, the patient re-explanations when I goofed up, and the reassurances. You made a big gnarly project very enjoyable! Sherry Li, thank you for a gorgeous cover that brings Avery and Sarah so vividly to life.

Several authenticity readers gave extremely valuable input; thank you for your time, your emotional labor, and your wisdom. It is greatly appreciated. Thanks to Nicole Moreno, Gweneth Morton, Sonja West, Rye White, and Jessica White for your copyediting eyes, and to Jessica Skrocki Gould for your proofreading expertise.

A big shout-out to Anika Hussein at the Young Editors Project and to the student readers who so generously shared their time and insights. Your help was vital. In the US, thank you to Isabella from Missoula, Montana; Montserrat from El Paso, Texas; Corinne from New York City; Teddy and Will from New York; and Shivali from North New Jersey. In the UK, thank you to Cara from Doncaster and to Isabelle and Charlotte from Sheffield. In New Zealand, thank you to Elena from Dunedin. In Italy, thank you to Ilaria from Trieste.

Thank you to the booksellers, bloggers, librarians, teachers, and bookstagrammers who do so much to get books into the hands of young readers. You truly change lives with your work, and I am grateful.

For writerly advice, commiseration, and celebration: Thank you to Sara Bennett Wealer, who helped me launch my first book; to my debut buddy and enthusiastic supporter, Jean Meltzer; and to Amy Bearce, Georgine Getty, and Sarah Archer.

For friendship and love across the miles and years: Thanks to Cara Olexa, Karen Anderson, Larissa Howell, Renee Jacobs, Jen Decker-Strainic, Katie Kovach, Michele Thomas-Dixon, Sid Birkett, Allison Haden, Shannon Ursrey, and Maria Southman. Maddie Jacobs, thank you for explaining pit bulls and teenagers to me.

Thanks to Megan Zien, my mega-boss physical therapist, for putting my shoulder and elbow and jaw and neck and hip and knee back together, and for sharing your endless fascination with how the human body works and fails to work. You manage to make me laugh even when I'm in stupid amounts of pain. Thanks also to my local EDS community, and particularly those in the Cincy Zebras Facebook group, many of whom have shared their time, energy, and experiences in the hopes of moving us all toward a future with better medical recognition and treatments.

Thanks to the Insight Timer app and all the teachers who use the platform to offer guidance to those of us who get lost in the thickets of our messy minds.

Thanks to Mom for hugging my books, to Pops for saying "I'm proud of you, kid," and to both for the constant reminders that I am loved. I love you so much!

Thanks to Matt for co-parenting, dog husbandry, and house care so I could write and draw all this, for gifting me with art books, fancy pens, and lots of erasers, for constantly cracking me up, and for listening when I whine about writing and health insurance and my falling-apart flesh prison. You're a heckin' fine partner and I am lucky to have you. I love you.

Thanks to Max for teaching me how to ride a Minecraft pig, for making me want to be the best and most transparent trans parent I can be, for picking stellar friends, spreading irreverence, and mock-twerking, and for being the dirt-biking drumming sass-master memelord you are. Sorry I coded your genes with Ehlers-Danlos syndrome and a busticated brain. I didn't do it on purpose. I'm wildly proud of you and love the bajonkers out of you.

And, of course, thank you to my dogs for giving me farts to smell and borks to yell over and bodily fluids to clean up and a thorough covering of every color of fur for my clothes and furniture, and for the snuggles and love and unconditional companionship.

A final note: hypermobile Ehlers-Danlos syndrome

is a spectrum disorder, and Avery's experience with it (a sped-up version of my own) will not match everyone's experience with it. Some folks have milder cases, and some have worse ones. But nearly everyone who has hEDS experiences pain and functional limitations, along with a lack of understanding from medical practitioners who expect horses instead of zebras or who haven't yet been educated about EDS. Researchers are making new discoveries every day, and more and more folks with hEDS and hypermobility spectrum disorders are sharing their experiences and advocating for increased understanding and more medical studies.

There's a lot of reason to hope. So hang in there, friends—with braces and mobility aids if you need them!